T0009295

ALSO BY ETHAN JOELLA

A Little Hope

A Quiet Life

THE SAME BRIGHT STARS

A Novel

ETHAN JOELLA

SCRIBNER

New York London Toronto Sydney New Delhi

Scribner
An Imprint of Simon & Schuster, LLC
1230 Avenue of the Americas
New York, NY 10020

First Scribner trade paperback edition July 2024

Interior design by Hope Herr-Cardillo

Manufactured in the United States of America

1 3 5 7 9 10 8 6 4 2

Library of Congress Cataloging-in-Publication Data has been applied for

ISBN 978-1-6680-2460-7
ISBN 978-1-6680-2459-1 (pbk)
ISBN 978-1-6680-2461-4 (ebook)

To June Peruso, who gave me a love for books and travel and beautiful things.

Also, to Rehoboth Beach, the storybook town that saved us.

He wished he had inhabited more of his life, used it better, filled it fuller.

—Anne Tyler, *The Amateur Marriage*

THE SAME BRIGHT STARS

PART ONE

—

You enter Rehoboth Beach over a drawbridge and instantly feel as if you have been transported. There is a welcome sign and a lighthouse in the middle of a traffic circle, and as you drive the main street, you see boutiques and restaurants and a local bookstore with a wide green awning.

In the summer, the shops have geraniums and impatiens spilling out of window boxes, and people leave their rescue dogs waiting for them by the parking meter as they buy croissants or coffee in the morning.

The beach is wide and generous with striped metal sheds that rent umbrellas and chairs in the summer, and there is a mile-long boardwalk with ice cream places and souvenir shops. The rides at Playland Pier have been around since your parents and grandparents were young (a carousel, antique boats that go in a circle with bells on a string). And there are games like Skee-Ball and Whac-A-Mole and Frog Bog.

Rehoboth Beach is a mix of yesterday and today, at once a small town and a city. Planes creep by in the sky trailing banners, and you will look up and read their messages and feel as though the words were written just for you.

—*That's Rehoboth Beach: A Guidebook*

ONE

When Jack pulls up to Schmidt's on the day before Thanksgiving it occurs to him that he might just take the offer from DelDine.

Finally give in. They may keep it the same, as they've done with some places in town, or renovate it into a bistro with an eco-friendly kitchen and QR code menu or an Italian-fusion restaurant with zebra-print place mats.

Jack doesn't usually have epiphanies like this early in the morning, especially right before a major holiday, when there are mountains of potatoes to peel, and the stress of all those turkeys defrosting and the phone ringing with pie orders and last-minute reservations. He puts the car in park, and the wind blows sand against his door. He steps out, feet hurting, his old Jeep the only car on the whole beachfront block, the boardwalk looking battered.

He squints at the Atlantic Ocean in the distance, and the restaurant's blue awning trembles above him.

He looks at his family name written in cursive on the sign, *Est. 1954* underneath, and he thinks, *It's time.* It's time to figure out his life.

—

Their offer is pretty appealing. A no-brainer, his dad would have said.

Jack can keep slogging through hot summers, his feet quitting by ten in the morning and him forcing them to keep going anyway. All summer, him in a damp T-shirt, face pale, working, working, morning until night, married to the place, as Kitty said before she moved west, like some long-ago prospector hoping to find a better life.

Jack is fifty-two, but an old fifty-two. A fifty-two that feels like assisted living is right around the corner. His best friend from high school, Deacon, just had a baby and ran a half marathon.

Jack never wanted to sell, especially not to DelDine, enemy number one to Rehoboth Beach family businesses, all their corporate lingo and management team members smiling and buying everything they can, as though quality and originality mean nothing. They already own ten restaurants up and down the Delaware coast, and it seems they won't stop until every place has that same menu with a custom font, the same servers repeating the lackluster script, the same overpriced beach-themed cocktails and lobster appetizers.

But this business landed in his lap like Prince Charles's right to the throne, and he has never *really* had to struggle. He knows how lucky he is. The money has never not come in regularly. Sometimes he looks out at the Mother's Day brunch crowd or on Fourth of July weekend, and it's a sea of people waiting for tables as far as his vision goes. Tell them it'll be two hours, and they don't even bristle. The money comes in, he does payroll and handles the utilities and upkeep, and there's always a nice amount left.

He is blessed, he could say if he used a word like that, to mostly have been free of financial worry. He never had to struggle or prove himself the way so many restaurant people do. He more or less inherited the life.

But it's a lot.

It's a whole lot almost all the time because you blink and the shingles outside need painting or the roof needs replacing, or one of the ovens isn't keeping up to temperature. Property insurance, health insurance, life insurance—the numbers are strangling. Hurricane season comes, and you never know when a storm might rip apart the boardwalk, pulverize the dunes, and dismantle everything you've worked for. You find yourself a cook or a server who does a bang-up job, and you think you're set, and the next day they don't show.

This morning, Thanksgiving eve, is the first day where he thinks the choice is pretty simple: count his dollars or count his days. He's scared he'll die while running the restaurant, like his grandmother Hazel did, like his dad did, like his own kid would, if he had a kid. If he hadn't wasted all this time.

The thing is, he feels shipwrecked. Left behind. Has he gotten grouchier lately? He used to feel like an older brother to his employees: caring, generous, mostly fun. But lately he feels like Squidward or Snape when the employees are laughing—irritated, distracted, sometimes scowling. He misses the way he used to feel in his twenties, thinking something good was up ahead, like there was a door he could walk through, and inside would be the life he dreamed about: people smiling, as if they were all waiting for him.

He looks down at the keys to the place. How many thousands of days has Jack wiggled that one key, dull and tarnished, into the same lock, pushing his hip against the door and letting it squeak open? He stands before the restaurant, the sun barely up, a woman walking by with a dog in a sweater, the air so bitter it cuts right through Jack's coat.

I could be done with this.

This could all be over.

He sees the choppy ocean, and he feels a hint of guilt, thinking about his grandmother Hazel, standing at the hostess stand with her hair pinned back, her lipsticked smile, greeting the customers who came back year after year.

"Of *course* I remember you." She'd hold the menus and lead the eager patrons past the glass case of pies, past the framed photos of opening day and the rubble from the big storm of 1962, past the counter with the barstools, and she'd show them to a seat by the window. "Best seat in the house," she'd say.

The door opens easily for him now, as if it knows what he's thinking, as if the restaurant is on its best behavior. And he sees it all, a landscape of chairs and tables and windows and dusty marine decor he knows too well, and his heart sags for a second.

TWO

Deacon comes by, his baby in one of those chest slings, sucking on a pacifier and studying everything in the room. "Look alive, Jackpot," Deacon calls, like he always does, and Jack steps out from the back kitchen, the refrigerator humming its familiar sound as he passes by. The baby kicks her feet when she sees him.

"You again," Jack says to Deacon. Then: "It's Evie!" His tone naturally softens to something kind, even though he's preoccupied, already worried that Vivian, one of his servers, will call in sick, as she tends to do every few weeks, and he needs her here to help set up. Or that the host Sam's anxiety will be too bad and he'll be in the coatroom doing his breathing exercises, Genevieve helping him through it, while customers pile up at the door.

Deacon stands in the middle of the dining room, the sunlight glowing on his face, his jogging pants and hoodie immaculate, his sneakers brand-new. Deacon could probably still fit into his high school soccer uniform, and Jack, well, could not.

"Look at you," he says to Evie, and even though she's well past the point of doing that finger grip thing new babies do, she clutches Jack's finger anyway almost like she's humoring him, and he stands there for a second and feels the warmth of her small hand. "Tell Daddy you need a tiny Porsche," he says in that same higher voice, and she looks up at Jack with her small eyebrows that look like a sketch, a first draft of a portrait.

"Okay, enough baby time," Deacon says with his usual wry smile, and looks around. "Why's it so damn cold in here, man?"

Jack rolls his eyes. "Heat's coming on. I can't leave it at seventy all night. This place is insulated with gauze and horse hair, I swear."

Deacon looks Jack up and down and sucks his teeth. "Are you even trying anymore?"

Jack wears a baseball hat because his hair is messy. He's unshaven, sporting basketball shorts with ankle socks and an old pair of comfortable Crocs. His zip-up hoodie with holes in the sleeves hangs off him. He shrugs. "Forgive me for not having a fucking stylist."

"As if," Deacon says. He takes Evie out of the carrier and hands her absently to Jack. Jack's headache seems to go away when he takes her, and her weight feels just right in his hands. She grips the shoulder of his sweatshirt.

"Well hello." She is rigid at first, but then he feels her settle against him. "Want to look at the fishies?" Jack says like he often does, and he leads her over to the big aquarium that his dad installed in the 1980s. He watches her eyes widen as the zebra fish and clownfish zigzag by. If he sold the place, would he sell the fish with it, or would he put this giant aquarium in his living room?

Deacon stands behind him. "So how many reservations tomorrow?"

"Too many to count."

"As in . . ."

"Three fifty or so."

"Fuck."

"Language!" Jack says, nodding toward Evie. He knows he just cursed a minute ago, but holding her now, he feels a strange duty to protect what she hears. He points at the small frog he got a couple of weeks ago, its legs butterflying in a rhythm, and Evie seems to follow its path. "Good problem, though, right?"

"Hell of a good problem."

Jack clears his throat. "So I've been thinking about DelDine. I think I'm going to say yes."

Deacon walks over to the beverage station, dips the scoop into the big ice machine, and fills his cup with water. He shakes his head in slow motion. "No, you aren't."

"Pretty sure I am." Evie reaches up and tugs on Jack's ear. He looks past the tables by the window, and the sun is bouncing off the ocean and lighting up the salt and pepper shakers. His head spins with all the preparation he needs to do for the day: the pots of water that should be on the stove to boil already, the bread cubes he needs to soak for the stuffing, the walnuts and gelatin he needs to pick up for the cranberry salad, Genevieve finishing the pies—her pained face as the arthritis grips her every so often—and the phone ringing nonstop.

His mind gallops, but Evie in his arms makes him pause, makes him say screw all that work, it can wait. "Look," he says, pointing to the small diver in the aquarium that bobs up and down in the bubbles, chained to the treasure chest below.

"You're so full of shit." Deacon stands next to Jack now, slurping his water in the way that drives his wife, Andie, crazy. "What the hell else would you even do? Set up a booth at the farmer's market?" Evie reaches for Deacon, so Jack lets him take her, and Deacon bounces her and pats the space between her shoulders. "You're just going through your annual restaurant crisis. It's like the Macy's Thanksgiving Day parade."

Jack stretches and groans. He may complain about the workload here, but he's never seriously considered selling the place until today. He takes in the vast dining room filled with tables and one wall with nets and starfish, a seagull-and-dune-grass mural painted by Kitty years ago. He's stopped thinking about her when he sees it. The wide, half-open kitchen behind it. His office and storage and the walk-in freezer in the back. "You'll see. You're going to show up here one day, and it'll be empty."

Deacon kisses Evie's head. "Sure, buddy." He looks at Evie and then back at Jack. "More like I'm going to have to stage an intervention when you're ninety, and drag you away."

"You'll be ninety, too."

"Yeah, but a better ninety." Deacon side-eyes Jack to make sure he's laughing. He takes a squeaky giraffe out of his pocket for Evie. "Well, time to hit the boards."

"Gotta keep that trim figure."

He grins, but then his expression shifts. "Oh, have you run into *her* yet?"

He follows Jack into the galley between the hostess area and the kitchen. Jack takes out a giant filter and dumps the coffee grounds in. He presses start and listens to the bubbling inside. "Who?"

"Who." Deacon sighs. Evie puts the whole giraffe head into her mouth. "Kitty." He says her name quietly for some reason.

Jack's stomach tenses, and he feels his face lose some color. "Kitty?"

"I told you."

"What?"

"Didn't I?" Deacon twists his mouth. "Didn't I say the other day that she's in town again? Her mom's bad. Won't be long."

"Shit." Jack can see Kitty's mom, Janet, years ago, sitting by the pool at her house, drinking a wine cooler and reading a paperback mystery or romance. She was always so nice to him. "I didn't hear about that."

"I'm positive I told you, man. You just have your head up your ass."

"See, it's the damn restaurant."

"Then sell it, and we'll see if you get any better." He waves goodbye, his empty baby sling still hanging from his chest like a husk, Evie in one arm, his water in the other. He will put her in a jogging stroller the way he does every day. "But Andie saw her last night, and said she asked about *you*, my friend."

"Kitty did?"

He nods. "Apparently."

"She's married."

"Apparently not," Deacon says, and shrugs, and then Jack feels the blast of cold wind as he watches them leave.

THREE

Genevieve comes in at ten, a pleasant smile on her face, but with something guarded and worried about her that Jack can't put his finger on. "Morning, Jack." She wears a Schmidt's shirt, fresh looking, from many years ago. She sets out her tools on the back table in the big kitchen: giant mixing bowls, two big whisks, rubber spatulas.

Jack always likes working with Genevieve because she's a calming presence. She doesn't have a title here—he doesn't know if she ever did. He pays her a manager's salary, and she sets her own hours. She's the most capable person he knows; she's in her early sixties with grown kids and grandkids, some of whom live with her.

Genevieve will reassure Jack that the soup isn't burned or tell him if she thinks the dining room is too warm. His dad called Genevieve the angel of the restaurant, and maybe he's ready to sell because he knows she will want to retire soon. Some days he hears her taking deep breaths when the pain in her hands and fingers gets to be too much. And how would he run this place without her? She does prep work, she can serve, she can run the hostess stand. She knows where everything goes. She can clean better than a professional janitorial service, and she knows if they're out of something before they're even out of it.

Once, about five years ago, Kitty wanted to take the ferry to Cape May for the weekend, and Jack kept saying he couldn't, but he finally gave in when he could tell she was getting seriously pissed about it. He asked Genevieve if she could hold down the fort, and she didn't even blink. "Of course," she said.

Jack wasn't the best company that weekend because he ended up calling the restaurant six or seven times, and then he called to confirm the two deliveries they were expecting. When he wasn't calling the restaurant, he was worrying about the restaurant. Kitty found him sitting on the hotel room balcony, and he saw the disappointment on her face. "Can't you just be away?" she asked.

"It's hard," he said. He didn't tell her what else he was thinking about—stuff that had nothing to do with the restaurant. The worry that always seemed to catch him off guard, the guilt he felt whenever he was approaching something like happiness.

But when he returned to the restaurant early Sunday evening, Kitty getting into her car that she left in his parking spot, not saying a word to him and speeding away, he looked up at Schmidt's. The sun was low. Genevieve was pressing the letters into the marquee board outside, and it stunned him that he couldn't identify any sort of crisis. "I'm back," Jack said.

"Yes." Genevieve smiled, her eyes reassuring. *Don't you know I can run this place in my sleep?*

But Jack went back to his office and stayed there until after midnight, catching up on bookkeeping and payroll and inventory. He rested his chin on his hand and looked around the quiet room and wondered if he should take more time off and be with Kitty.

But he only wondered about it and didn't have a chance to do much else.

In three weeks, Kitty gave up her apartment, took her stuff from

Jack's place, broke off their half engagement or whatever their deal was at the time, and moved across the country to Oregon.

He can't say he was surprised. It was like he had been waiting for it.

—

Jack's dad, Johnny, used to sit in this same office and painstakingly go over every single facet of this place with him. He described health inspection guidelines and workers' comp and food preparation and noncapital expenditures. He showed Jack the grids on the schedule and how to post them and how to handle employee requests for time off.

Jack always felt a little smothered by the restaurant. He sensed its pull, and he didn't want to get buried in it the way his dad was. He liked it well enough, had been fully involved since he was twelve and his mom went away, but he didn't want it to be his future. He tried to make that clear to his dad.

"What if I find something else to do with my life?" Jack, just out of college, said to his dad one night.

They each had a glass of beer, and the leaves were wet outside the window, the wind sticking them to the siding and street. It was dark, and even in the office, Jack could feel the presence of the ocean, like some forgotten emotion thrashing around. He looked at his dad's blue eyes to see what he'd say, expecting him to say Jack had no other choice. That it was the Schmidts' duty to keep this restaurant going.

But his dad shrugged. He reached out and put a calloused hand on Jack's cheek. "Well, then it'll be someone else's turn to have it."

Jack can't help but think of his dad when he sees Evie. What would he have said if Jack had a kid? Would he have been enamored the way Deacon's dad is? Jack thinks of how you pass your life and your family's legacy on to a child in small and big ways. But he missed that boat, and even if he did have the opportunity now, he wouldn't want to be an old dad. He's sure as hell not like Deacon.

The closest he's ever come to having a kid was way before Kitty. His girlfriend's name was Alexis, and Jack's not sure he ever loved someone as truly as her. Kitty used to ask questions about her, and he found himself going quiet. "It was a long time ago," he'd say.

FOUR

1989

He met her in the summer. He was nineteen, home from college, and she was staying in her aunt's house in North Shores that looked like something out of *Architectural Digest*.

It was warm on the boardwalk, one of Jack's only nights off, and Deacon had gotten them a pack of cigarettes from the machine next to Tony's Eats, the smell in the air of cheesesteaks and onions and oil from french fries.

They were walking aimlessly as they did every time they hung out, Deacon never afraid to strike up conversation with anyone who passed by. They were working their asses off that summer, Deacon at Wave Break in Dewey, which rented out Jet Skis and gave paddle-board lessons; and Jack at the restaurant, of course, nodding politely as his grandmother barked something at him, his dad gripping his shoulder every so often, saying, "Don't let her wilt you." She was his grandmother and she loved Jack, and Jack thought the world of her, but man could she be prickly. He was everything that summer: waiter, busboy, dishwasher, host. It helped him learn the restaurant like a complicated language he would someday need to be fluent in.

But that evening, late June, a perfect breeze, he and Deacon wore their new Ocean Pacific T-shirts like jackasses, savoring the early summer evening and all its possibilities. He was just about to light his Camel when a girl his age with hair-sprayed bangs and startling brown eyes stopped him by the pavilion and said, "Those will kill you."

He looked down at his pack of cigarettes, and Deacon, Mr. Future Health Nut, shook his head and blew smoke rings at her, his mouth open and defiant. Jack thought of his grandmother's raspy voice, the way she'd sit in the back office and twist one cigarette after another into the ashtray, always a mint in her mouth, always something vaguely sickly looking about her, and thought this woman might be right. "I'm just a social smoker," he told her.

She was carrying a bag from Candy Palace, and Jack wondered what was inside and who she'd share it with. "Still," she said.

"Do you always lecture strangers?" Deacon asked, that devilish look in his eyes. Jack could hear the music starting from the bandstand, a brass band that tourists were wild about.

She shrugged. She was wearing jean shorts that fit her perfectly, and her toenails were painted bright green. "I lost my grandpa to lung cancer," she said. "It's not pretty."

Deacon looked at his lit cigarette, and dropped it from his hand. He stomped his Nike over it. "Sorry to hear that."

"Anyway," she said. "None of my business." She looked at Jack longer and then down at her candy bag. "Sorry, my aunt's waiting."

She started to walk away, and Jack glanced at his pack of Camels, watched her perfect shoulders in a pink tank top. Deacon looked at him, gritted his teeth. "Aren't you going to get her fucking number?" he whispered, and Jack handed him the Camels and galloped after her.

"That's my boy," Jack heard him say.

"Um, hey," he said, slightly out of breath.

She turned around, not seeming surprised. As if guys chased her all the time. "Yes?"

"If you ever want to hang out or whatever . . ." She looked him up and down, and he wondered if his new shirt was already wrinkled. He wondered if any sweat was showing. He had just gotten a haircut and didn't feel too bad, but she was so beautiful that she made everyone else seem meager.

"How long are you here for?" she asked.

People passed them with stuffed animals from Playland, bags of cotton candy, and giant waffle cones with towers of ice cream scoops that would soon melt all over their hands. The sky was pale and hazy, and Jack saw one lone surfer out in the water. "I live here," he said.

"Perfect," she said. "Then we'll find each other."

She walked away. "Want to make it easier?" he called. He imagined memorizing her number, repeating the digits over and over until Deacon, back by the pavilion, knew them, too.

She turned around. "No," she said, and winked at him, and it was a wink that burrowed into his guts and turned him inside out.

He watched her disappear into the boardwalk crowd, the backs of her flip-flops slapping down in rhythm, a family with two kids in strollers almost bumping into her as she slowly faded into the crowd.

Jack stood there, knowing Deacon would make fun of him, knowing he'd probably never see her again. His heart quickened. He heard the familiar jingle from the mini golf place above the arcade that meant someone got a hole in one on the last round. He looked up at their windmill and wooden clock and mermaid, and he felt happy.

He turned back, and Deacon was walking toward him.

"Didn't even get her name, I bet," Deacon said, shaking his head, handing Jack a new cigarette.

FIVE

A week ago, Jack discovered something. And maybe that's part of what's making him want to sell.

He was counting the totals and looking at the reports, and noticed multiple promotions keyed in that the restaurant wasn't offering. A Tuesday five-dollar cheeseburger they haven't done in years on one register, a buy-one-get-one wine special they used to do in fall. Police and firefighter discounts every so often. A ladies' night appetizer special. He didn't even know some of these were still available in the computer.

All the totals were okay, but he started to find these odd discounts everywhere. If a person did them right, they could manage to make a couple hundred dollars here or there. One of his employees was stealing from him.

That night, he felt the glow of the computer on his face in the dark office, and a familiar sentiment returned like words to a song: a sinking feeling, a hint that someone was letting him down, the way people always did sooner or later, as regular to Jack as the lampposts that line the boardwalk switching to life each evening.

—

Now he watches Genevieve work. Three years ago, she brought in a pie for Tammy's retirement, a beautiful coconut cream pie with a perfect crust and a smooth whipped topping with toasted coconut. Jack said, "You can bake?"

"Of course," she said.

So he canceled the bakery order, and started having Genevieve make pecan pies, chocolate silk pies, strawberry pies. And different cakes, too, depending on the season: carrot, cheesecake, red velvet.

She holds a block of butter in her hand now and glances at Jack as he moves some of the reservations around to different tables. He notices she is hesitating. He notices her polite smile is gone. He was thinking of telling her about the missing money because he doesn't trust any of the others quite enough, but he stops.

"What's up?" Jack says.

She takes a breath, and her eyes are troubled, jeweled with worry. "Not much."

He looks over at her, and she's wringing her hands. "What's going on, Gen?"

"*Him* again," she says quietly, and rolls her eyes. "Who else, right?"

"Ziggy?" he whispers. Her son. He's had trouble after trouble since high school, and Genevieve worries about him nonstop. It must be the grip of some kind of addiction, Jack figures, but he always thought Ziggy had a good heart and would one day turn things around. Jack often thinks back on a Schmidt's holiday party when Ziggy was a little boy; Genevieve's husband, Mort, was still alive then, and someone had brought in their Saint Bernard puppy to show the crew. He remembers how Ziggy got on the floor and pet the puppy and hugged it, his smile wide and springlike, his eyes joyful. He rolled around with the dog and asked the owner if he could come play with it sometime. "I want one. Just like this. It's at the top of my Christmas list," Ziggy told Genevieve, and she laughed and said, "Not on your life." When Jack thinks of Ziggy, he always thinks of that wide-eyed boy in Converse sneakers and a flannel shirt who wanted a puppy more than anything else.

Now she nods. "He owes someone, and his moods are the worst I've ever seen." She shakes her head and inhales. "I don't know what to do. I'm worried about what's next." She exhales and crosses herself and looks up at the ceiling.

And that's when the phone starts ringing.

Jack puts his hand on Genevieve's shoulder.

"I'm scared he'll end up dead," she says, "or hurting someone." She grits her teeth, and the sound of the phone continues, echoing through the whole place. "Two guys showed up at my door last night, looking for him. They were like *bad* news. I'm so worried, Jack. I told him months ago to find his own place, but he doesn't have anywhere to go. I hide my purse when I'm home." She stands still. "I keep praying," she says quietly. "It's all I can think to do."

Jack had been thinking of Kitty back in town, nervous about what he would say to her, thinking about all those people showing up tomorrow wanting a memorable Thanksgiving. Now he's thinking what he can do to help Genevieve and solve Ziggy's problems. He watches Genevieve and tries to find the right words, but his mouth feels dry, so he lamely pats her shoulder and goes to answer the phone.

SIX

He's processing Genevieve's report when Vivian shows up in the back kitchen, a big scratch on her face, sipping her Dunkin' Donuts, and he can smell the caramel from the drink. "What the hell happened?" he says, looking at the cut on her cheek.

Vivian reaches up and traces the scratch. "Some bitch last night," she says, and laughs. When she smiles, Jack sees the gap in her front teeth that reminds him of Madonna.

"What? Did someone just come up and scratch you?" He feels like he should focus on Genevieve, but he can tell she is relieved for the distraction of Vivian. The phone keeps ringing, but luckily Sam is in now. Jack hears him say the only time he can accommodate them tomorrow is 11 a.m., which Jack knows will not be anyone's first choice.

"Pretty much," Vivian says, looking at Jack. She sips her coffee with a triumphant grin. This will be her performance of the day, and everyone will gather around her dramatization of the events. "At the football game. I was minding my own business, and this girl started talking shit about my face paint—I had the school colors on there. So I told her to mind her own freakin' business—I did *not* say *freakin'*—and she pushed me." Vivian shakes her head. A delighted smile forms on her lips. "So I tore the hell into her. Of course, the security guys pulled me off, and I had to leave, my face bleeding, and I said, *What about her*? So they dragged her out, too, and Kirk was like pissed at me because he was into the game, so I give him the finger as I'm leaving." She winks at them.

Genevieve sighs. She is dusting flour onto the stainless steel counter. She flours the rolling pin, too, and shakes her head. "You're thirty, angel."

Vivian laughs. "And?"

Jack keeps quiet, still trying to sort Genevieve's news, to think of some way to reach Ziggy, or help him find a place where he could get help, have a fresh start. He's worrying about her, and also about the missing money, and about selling the restaurant, and at least 350 people showing up tomorrow. And now Kitty's in town. Shit.

"It's probably time to leave this high school business behind," Genevieve says, a wise assessment. Vivian still goes out drinking until two in the morning most nights; she still lives with her parents and has her mom put gas in her car. Vivian will spend a good portion of a shift plotting revenge against a customer who looks at her sideways.

Vivian walks up to Genevieve and kisses her cheek. Only Genevieve could say the kind of thing she just said. "I love you, Ma," she says, the nickname cemented years ago whenever Genevieve cautioned her against something. "Besides, turns out the girl was pretty cool. We started talking after we got kicked out, and she said we should go to the Lucky Toad one night for trivia." She sets her drink down and looks at the pie ingredients and then at Genevieve. "You okay?"

Genevieve glances at Jack and then wipes her floury hands on a towel. "Just lots to do," she says, and Jack looks at her and hopes she knows what he's thinking. *We'll figure this out. I'll help you.* "Time to get these pies finished," she says, and turns away.

—

Back in his office, Jack sees a notification on his phone, but he's stuck for a second, thinking about how his dad told him years ago that this place can swallow you like a big wave, so you have to keep swimming sideways against the current.

"What does that mean?" he asked his dad.

"You'll see," Johnny said.

His dad was only seventy when he died twelve years ago. Never went to a doctor. Hardly ever ate a vegetable or piece of fruit, even though good food was all around. But when he got the diagnosis, he shrugged. "Had to happen eventually."

Jack looked at him back then and tried to prepare himself to lose him, though he couldn't imagine it. Johnny had a mischievous grin and kind blue eyes. He smelled like black licorice cough drops and called him Jackie. Jack probably stayed here all these years because of Johnny. When Johnny was sick, Jack felt like he was standing on an island, watching the only boat drift away. Jack wanted to ask him so many questions, mostly about his mom, but they hardly ever talked about her.

In the kitchen now, Jack hears the sizzling of food, the pleasing clatter of pots and pans from the head cook, Saul, and the music on the speaker. It was Christmas music before, Perry Como singing "Home for the Holidays," but Vivian screeched at Sam to turn it the hell off until at least Friday. "I'm not ready for that shit yet," she said.

The text on his phone makes him dizzy. Kitty. It's been so long he wasn't sure her name was still in his contacts.

Did you hear I'm in town?

He holds the phone in front of him and wonders what he should say. *Just a bit ago*, he finally replies, hitting send and quickly sliding the phone back into his pocket, hoping the conversation will stall for a while.

The restaurant phone rings again and he thinks of Genevieve's face. How her expression crumbled. How he realized in that second that he loved her like family. He wants to sell, but maybe she needs this place to be stable for her since her home life isn't. It's not easy to make a change when your employees are rooted to you and, even though you have tried to stay unattached, you care about each root.

—

On the wall in the office is a picture of Jack's grandmother Hazel holding him as a baby on the boardwalk, sitting on one of the white benches, the wind blowing her hair, her face relaxed and happy, back in the days before the beach was replenished, when you could jump down onto the sand and walk under the boardwalk.

Jack thinks of his dad behind the camera, and wonders where his mom was that day. After his mom went away, he and Hazel and Johnny were a trinity, Hazel used to say, and now he's like the only candle on a candelabra that isn't snuffed out.

He scribbles down his list for tomorrow. He doesn't know why he writes lists because they only make him more nervous, but here he notes anyway: *print Thanksgiving coloring sheets, light candles by ten, tell Sam only instrumental music* (keeps the crowd calmer, he's found)*, check with Vincent—can his niece bus? Check linen service, unclog carpet sweeper, wash bar towels.* He pauses. *Cut extra lemons + limes + oranges.*

The list is getting so sloppy he can barely read it when Vivian sticks her head in the door. "Your lover's here, Schmidt," she says in a high voice, and smirks, and immediately Jack expects Kitty to walk in. Would she show up without telling him first? He feels unkempt and unprepared and not in the right headspace to see her.

But then he realizes Vivian's referring to Nicole Pratt from DelDine, who Vivian has taken to calling his girlfriend. Also his wife, his lover, his soul mate. Ugh.

"Oh," he says. "Okay. I'll be out in a sec."

"I'm right here," Nicole says behind Vivian, and Vivian's face looks glazed, the scratch on her cheek even more noticeable for a second, like a big apostrophe. Jack raises his eyebrows and waves Vivian off.

Nicole steps into his office. "Guess she didn't know I followed her."

Nicole is the general manager of the company that wants to buy Schmidt's. She wears tortoiseshell glasses and black pants and always a sweater, even in summer. She regularly drops by to see if Jack has any questions about their offer, and even though he doesn't like anything about DelDine, he somehow doesn't mind her too much. She's easy to be around.

"Busy day," she says, looking around.

"Holidays are pretty busy."

"Don't I know it, guy." Without asking, she scoops up the paperwork from a chair and plops down. "I'm beat," she says. "We're doing a party for Doug Gable Realty at The Pier, and it keeps getting more and more . . . fancy." She tugs lightly on the ring she wears on her necklace. "They're hiring a whole crew for music and video and lighting. What the heck happened to a PowerPoint and CD player?" She rolls her eyes. When she turns to look out the window, the light hits her face, and Jack thinks of something his grandmother would have said: *That one has nice high cheekbones.*

She groans and rests her hands on her stomach and slouches in the chair. "When did people become so high maintenance?"

"You think it just happened?" Jack gives her a polite smile. He needs to finish his list, and he doesn't know why she's here on the day before the busiest day. He feels guilty having his employees see her now that he's seriously considering selling. "Customers have been annoying since the word *customer* was invented."

She puts the arm of her glasses in her mouth. "Did Shakespeare create that word—like everything else?" He notices for a second how pale blue her eyes are, like mist.

"Maybe," Jack says. He glances down at his list, and he gets a sharp pain between his eyebrows. Tomorrow is coming like a hypersonic missile. He looks at her and clears his throat. "So nothing's really new," he says, and tries to sound decisive so she'll get the hint.

But she stays put.

She slips her glasses back on, picks up a *Shore Life* magazine from his desk, and starts flipping through it. Her brown hair is messy today. "I figured." She takes a breath. "I just needed to get away from holiday party planning, Thanksgiving planning, the screech of all the assistant managers. I told them they sounded like porpoises today." She takes off her glasses again and wipes them on her sweater. She points to the magazine. "Hey, look, they're resurrecting the Turtle Trot."

Sometimes Jack can't believe Nicole has reached such a high level in a company that takes itself so seriously. The people she works with would eat a child to get promoted. Soulless, always on their phones, working five in the morning until midnight. Nicole is the most unserious person Jack knows, and he barely knows her. "I don't know what the Turtle Trot is."

She snorts. "How the hell did you grow up here? Remember Skippers in Dewey? They used to have a Turtle Trot every Christmas. You ran a 5K, and then you drank for the rest of the day, and danced, and they'd put out all this fried shrimp and burgers and barbecued chicken. It was *amazing*." She taps her finger on the ad in the magazine. "All the money went to the sea life orgs and the state park. You remember!" she says accusingly.

"Sounds familiar," Jack says. "But in my defense, there are a lot of 5K events around here."

She smiles sadly. "It's where I met *Billy*." She says the name with such care.

"Billy?"

"My husband." Her pale eyes have something in them, an emotion Jack can't identify, but they look frosted for a second. Jack glances at the ring on her necklace. He'd forgotten she used to be married. Her husband was killed in Iraq. She tosses the magazine to the side and stands up. "Okay, well I'll leave you to your"—she looks at his list—"whatever that jumble is."

"Thanks for dropping in."

"Oh, I wanted to ask. Did you look over the packet with your lawyer? It outlines everything—the announcement, the transition, the bonus if it's before the end of the year, the projected plans." She pauses. "Your lawyer is Andie Stone?"

Jack nods. "She's the best. She's married to my friend."

"Thought so," she says. "I do CrossFit with her. Well, to be honest, she kicks ass in CrossFit and I give up and cheer for the rest of them."

"Ah." He looks down at his list. "And I haven't really looked at anything with regard to the sale."

She shrugs. "I feel like you're getting ready, Jack," she says, and smiles. Her eyes have returned to their usual playfulness.

"Me? I'm too young."

She pauses and looks very closely at him, those eyes so intense they almost make him wince. "We all want more than just a job, and if you partner with us, we'll take the burden and give you the gift of freedom." She looks at the picture of his grandmother holding him as she's walking out. "Cute," she says.

"Why do you say *partner*?" he asks. "It's not partnering. It's turning everything over. It's selling and being finished with the business forever."

She shrugs. "Partnering sounds nicer." She pushes the office door all the way open. "And now I'm hiding at Coffee Daze for a half hour." She holds a folder in front of her and looks at him. "Wanna tag along and hide, too?"

"Oh. Uh, no thanks," he says.

He stands and watches her leave, nodding to Sam, to Vivian, to the couple of tables of people who've come for lunch. It feels like it should be evening already, but outside the sun is bright and generous. For a second, and he has no idea why, he almost feels like he should have gone with her.

—

Rehoboth Beach was founded in the 1870s as a site for religious meetings and retreats, and before long, a big hotel was built.

The boardwalk, even though many storms have reconfigured it over the years, was first built in 1873. There was a dance hall in the early days, and people went to movies or restaurants. Rehoboth showed a strong Victorian influence, and often tourists would put on their best fancy clothes (hats and dresses, pinstriped suits) and promenade up and down the boardwalk in the evenings.

A railroad, and later a paved highway, started to bring in tourists from Pennsylvania, New Jersey, northern Delaware, and Washington, D.C., which made Rehoboth busier and more of the Nation's Summer Capital it is called today. But sometimes, in its most quiet moments, you can feel those glimpses of Rehoboth's simple early days.

—That's Rehoboth Beach: A Guidebook

SEVEN

When he was twelve, Jack and his dad were stuck on I-95 for twenty hours coming home from a football game in Baltimore. Freezing rain and a big blizzard and a bunch of car crashes jammed up the road, and everyone had to sit and wait in the cold. There was talk of the National Guard coming to bring food and water, but that never materialized.

Jack still remembers the fading purple sky, and the lines of red taillights in front of them. The stillness of the night, the salt-stained cars, the occasional horn honking as if that would move things along.

He still remembers his father's patient breathing; the way he dumped out his coffee cup and passed it to Jack so he could take a leak, turning his head away politely.

"When's this gonna end?" Jack whined, thinking an hour was too long, two hours the most he could bear.

"When it ends," Johnny said.

—

By two o'clock, the finished pies are piling up, some already in white boxes, taped and labeled. The lunch crowd has died down as they prepare for a busy dinner because no one wants to cook on the night before the holiday, and Jack feels his phone buzz in his pocket.

Looks like my mom won't make it to Christmas, Kitty texts him. *I don't know how to handle this, Jack.*

He glimpses Genevieve out of the corner of his eye, opening the big oven door and checking what looks like a blueberry pie, making sure it's ready, her face worried over what he knows to be more than just pie.

Oh, Ziggy. What's it going to take? Jack wishes he could press a button and make Ziggy see the pain he causes his mother. It can't be too late. Many people turn their lives around. Genevieve always said that Ziggy was the happiest and easiest of all her babies, and Jack is sure a lot of this has to do with grief. Ziggy lost his father when he was ten, and he was left with his mother who tried her best and older sisters who got good grades and always behaved. Jack often imagined him feeling alone in a houseful of women. His dad was the type of guy who never got hotheaded, was always laughing, always poking Ziggy in the ribs or playfully yanking one of the girls' braids, then looking away and pretending it wasn't him. Genevieve said Mort and Ziggy used to sleep in a tent out in the yard, even in late fall sometimes, and she'd hear them laughing until the early morning hours. Jack thinks of Ziggy petting the dog that day, how that boy would not have become this troubled man without the combination of great pain and the pull of powerful substances. But maybe there's more to it. Maybe something they all missed.

He thinks about telling Genevieve to go home, but he knows she'd rather be here. Her daughter and granddaughter, who also live with her, have gone away for the long weekend. He thinks he could offer to get her a hotel room, or tell her she can sleep in his spare bedroom.

He watches Genevieve clench her teeth as she squeezes one of her hands and rubs her knuckles, and he wants to go over to her, hug her even. He wants to tell her it'll all be okay. She has earned her salary for life. Jack will make it work somehow. He can pay her mortgage, even. What good is money if you can't do something useful with it?

But Genevieve hates any kind of charity. Once, a teacher started a GoFundMe to get her granddaughter a new bike because someone had stolen the one she loved (at the time, Jack wondered if Ziggy had sold it), and Genevieve picked up the phone and told them that wasn't necessary. "Please do this for someone else," she said.

Jack walks to the dining room now. He could light the candles for dinner, but it's a little early. He sits down at the corner table they use for silverware rolling and starts twisting up napkins and forks and knives. It's one of his favorite tasks. So simple and definitive, your progress immediately visible. Much restaurant work is like this—him going and going all day long, jumping from one thing to another until the last customer leaves and they put the place back together, only to do it all again the next day.

He remembers Kitty's text. Before he can think about how to respond, Sam comes over, crouching down. Something about Sam always brings out a gentle side in Jack. He can tell Sam was picked on in school. Sam is frail, in his twenties, and last year he got adult braces. He is always nervous, and Genevieve is good at comforting him. Vivian, of course, isn't.

"Mr. Schmidt," he says. "Is there any way we can squeeze in a table of four around three tomorrow?" He grits his teeth. "I've been saying no, but this is Mrs. Florence, who always comes in here with her red hat ladies. Her oven broke, and she's crying." Sam's face is so sincere.

Jack looks down at the napkin in his hand, twisting it around the utensils in one swoop. "Yeah, put them in Vivian's section. She'll get them in and out."

Sam grins widely, showing the metal in his mouth. "Thank you," he says, exhaling.

Jack returns to his thoughts about Kitty's mom, Janet Applebaum. He thinks of what it must be like to know you only have a few weeks left. He remembers years ago, when her husband died right after Jack's dad, how he and Kitty stayed that night in Janet's house with her. At two in the morning, Jack couldn't sleep, and went downstairs to find Janet sitting at the kitchen table, drinking Mr. Applebaum's favorite Scotch. "No one to guard this now," she said, and smiled at Jack, her eyes red.

"Then pour me some." Jack grabbed a glass from the china cabinet and pulled up a chair.

Her hands shook as she poured a little into his glass. He held the glass and inhaled the deep scent, like smoke and medicine. "You know, Jack, I don't know if he was my great love." She paused and looked at Jack with apologetic eyes. "But we *needed* each other, and that was beautiful."

Jack holds a cold utensil, and his eyes feel heavy. He thinks of the Applebaums' dim kitchen, of Kitty alone there with Janet now. He thinks of the concept of needing someone. Over the years he's thought about Kitty almost every day. They were together for more than ten years, and it was comfortable and easy, and at one point he thought they'd get married, but instead they stayed in a holding pattern.

They never completely moved in together. They never talked about the future. Jack knows she thinks it was his fault for his dedication to the restaurant, and maybe something else. "You push people away," she told him more than once. "You don't want to be happy."

But it was more than that, he thinks. Maybe like her mother said about her father, they needed each other but weren't in love with each other. He has always meant to apologize for not being better.

He knows he's considerably messed up, but he always thought things would work out. When he was twenty-two, if you'd told him he'd be a constant presence in this restaurant the way his dad and grandmother were, he would have asked what you were smoking. But here he is.

He regrets Kitty leaving. He wants to tell her that. And he is sorry that her good, sweet mother is dying.

He looks around the restaurant. *It's mine*, he thinks. He forgets that sometimes. It feels like his grandmother's, his dad's even, but never his. He still feels like he's keeping an eye on it until they come back.

"Look what I got, boss." Saul, the cook, comes out of nowhere and glides into the booth opposite Jack. He holds up two shiny new garlic presses. "One for each of us."

"Oh, score!" Jack takes one and inspects it. "A lot better than the last one. Thanks for getting this. Put the receipt on my desk, and I'll reimburse you."

"Think of it as your Christmas gift," Saul says, and stands.

"Good guy," Jack says.

He watches Saul leave and thinks of DelDine. Jack would get one big check, a very big check, and be done with all of this. He could give each employee a bonus and put in a good word for them with DelDine and hope they keep them.

Jack adds the last napkin roll to the small pile he's made. He puts his head in his hands for a second and realizes he hasn't eaten much today. He can smell the beef barley soup from the kitchen, the faint hint of Genevieve's pies. He taps his fingers on the table.

I'm so sorry, he finally replies to Kitty. *Your mother is a wonderful woman.*

He holds the phone and hits send. *I'm sorry*, he writes again.

After Kitty left, he barely saw her mother, except for one day in the boardwalk five-and-ten before it closed. It was a busy summer afternoon about four years ago, hot as hell outside, and one of those times where he felt like a goddamn mole, never leaving the restaurant.

He went outside that afternoon, put sunglasses on, and trudged down the boardwalk. The beach was crammed with people, the lifeguard whistles punctuating the air every so often, the smell of funnel cake and caramel corn in the breeze. You could hear bicycle bells from the street, and Jack took a deep breath, tried to absorb the day.

He walked and walked, looking down at his own pale legs. He was two years away from fifty then. He saw people going into the five-and-ten, a mother standing by her son looking at the hermit crabs in the cage. "Whichever one you want," she said, and kissed him.

He doesn't know why, but he went inside. He felt like buying something, tired of making money and never spending it. He watched people getting sunblock and flip-flops. The faded floor tiles were streaked with spilled soda, and the cash register hammered out prices onto the receipts, one purchase after another.

He saw a big display of beach chairs in the back of the shop.

Overpriced, yes, but so bright—blue and yellow with slings to carry them. And next to them, a mountain of buckets and sand toys. As people passed him, he wanted a slice of whatever they were getting. These people were coming to Rehoboth and experiencing days of perfect bliss: reading books, laughing with friends, holding sandy kids on their laps, feeling the sun on their faces.

Jack grabbed a blue beach chair, the nicest one they had. Fifty dollars or something like that, and he held it against himself, the tag hanging from it. He couldn't explain it, but it felt so *new* and immaculate against him. Like a key to building a good future. It had four positions and a drink holder. He promised himself that one day soon he'd take that chair and sit in the sand and look at the ocean, something he hadn't done in ages. And he'd try to be happy.

"Well, hello, Jack," he heard then, and it was Janet, Kitty's mom. "That's a nice purchase."

"Hey, Mrs. Applebaum," he said, and leaned the chair against his leg as she reached up to hug him. She smelled like the coconut suntan oil she always wore, and she looked so much younger and more refreshed since those days after Mr. Applebaum died. "I needed a new one," Jack said, looking down at the chair.

She smiled. "I thought I was the only one braving tourist central." She held a paperback in her hands—a mystery. She loved them, read one a day by the pool.

He glanced back in the direction of the restaurant, as if he could see it through the walls. "I just needed a break." After he said this, she stared at him for a few seconds and nodded.

She walked alongside him toward the cash register. She stopped and picked up an ashtray with *Rehoboth* written in the center and balanced it in her palm. She picked up one of those beer can koozies with a palm tree on it and squeezed. "How are you managing, Jack?"

He let his shoulders relax for a second. He imagined pulling the chair open and plopping down in it right there. He wondered how long he could be gone before the restaurant needed him. "We're doing great. Busy as ever. Couldn't ask for more."

"Not the restaurant," she said carefully. "*You.*"

"Oh. Not bad," he said, and avoided eye contact while he handed the chair to the guy behind the counter. He made the go-ahead motion and smiled, and she put her paperback down by the cash register. He shooed her when she tried to give him money for it. "No, no, my treat," he said.

She patted his shoulder and took her bag. "Thank you. It was lovely seeing you." She looked at his beach chair. "Enjoy it," she said. She wore her sunglasses on her head, and placed them over her eyes. He wanted to ask what Kitty was up to, if she had met someone, if she was as happy as she thought she'd be, away from here, away from him.

He took the beach chair back to the restaurant and hung it over a hook in an upstairs closet, where it still waits.

Every once in a while he catches a glimpse of it, behind a broom, underneath a raincoat some customer left awhile back, and the bright blue calls out to him. He always pauses for a second before quickly closing the door.

—

Vivian brushes by him now, a cleaning bottle and rag in her hand, and Jack hears Sam on the phone again, saying, "I'm so sorry, but we're all booked." In the back of the kitchen, he can see Genevieve and wonders for the tenth time that day how he can help her, what he can offer. He takes out his phone again and writes Kitty: *Is it okay if I come see your mom? She has meant a lot to me.*

Come by tonight, she replies, so fast that Jack's not even sure if she read what he said.

EIGHT

The restaurant closes at ten, and he finalizes the register numbers and slides the money into the deposit bag, which goes into the safe. Nothing is off today, which is a relief. If he disables the promo codes and gives the crew some type of speech, maybe that will nip it in the bud. But he still needs to figure out who was stealing. *Maybe all of them*, says a voice inside Jack, and he shakes his head and thinks of how much Kitty hated when he was cynical.

He can't imagine any of these employees stealing from him. "Big day tomorrow," he calls out, and he helps Vivian mop the rest of the dining room so they can all get out of here. Sometimes he feels like a high school coach. Saul and Ernie and Smokes and Paulette go over the list for the kitchen stuff, and Vincent, a shy guy in his thirties who is the best dishwasher Jack has ever had, nods goodbye as his wife pulls up outside.

Tomorrow, after such a big day, beyond their wages and tips, Jack will hand each of them a hundred-dollar bill for their hard work, as he does every year. The restaurant stops serving by three o'clock, and they're cleaned up by four so they can still have Thanksgiving dinner with their families or friends. Jack will just go home to sleep, an aluminum pan of leftovers out on his counter. Andie and Deacon invited him to dinner at their house, and he had said yes so they would stop needling him, but he's going to write Andie in the morning and say he can't make it. The restaurant does this to you: you work so hard and so long that it makes you unfit for normal interaction.

When they've all left, he goes back to his office to turn out the lights and lock up. He hears an odd sound that he recognizes instantly and can't quite place. A squeak. A turning of something. Maybe it's just the heat, the freezer?

He's about to close his office door and switch off the light and scan the rest of the restaurant when Genevieve appears and startles him. He hadn't seen her for the last hour, and assumed she'd left a little early. "The final ten pies are done," she says. Her eyes are puffy, and the frown on her face stabs him.

"Genevieve." His desk lamp makes shadows on the wall, and above them, he hears the rain they've been forecasting pinging the tin roof. "What can I do for you?" He offers the hotel idea, or for her to stay at his house.

She waves her hand to dismiss his suggestions. She looks down at the floor and shrugs. "There's nothing," she says. "It's wait-and-see time."

"I think you should take tomorrow off," Jack says. "We'll be okay."

She shakes her head. "I have not one desire to do that."

"I know. Okay." He coughs nervously. "Well, you can just hide back here if you want, whenever you want."

She nods and squeezes her eyes shut, but the tears roll down her face anyway. Jack hugs her. Her hair tickles his chin, and her glasses dig into his collarbone. She sobs and sinks into him.

"Maybe we should call the police."

"Tuh," she says. "The police."

He knows. He knows. They've never been much help to her.

When Ziggy punched out a bouncer at a club in Dewey, they just drove him to her house and told him to get some rest. When his friend said Ziggy had stolen his watch and phone, the police showed up, collected them, and labeled it as a misunderstanding between buddies. Ziggy didn't seem all there, Genevieve confessed. Eyes wide, staring at nothing. Jack wonders if it would have made a difference if he told his dad years ago, when Ziggy first started to get quiet after Mort's death, that Jack noticed a change in the boy, that he saw something familiar in him and somehow knew he was screaming inside. Would it have changed his course if Jack had brought it to someone's attention? But he said nothing and Ziggy got worse.

"It'll be okay," Jack says, and he keeps saying it, the rest of the restaurant dead quiet. He doesn't know what he or she can do, but he keeps hearing himself repeat the words anyway.

She nods and walks away, and he listens to her footsteps and the murmur and surge of the ice machine. The rain pounds harder on the roof, and he realizes what that noise was before she came in here.

The safe in the utility room down the hallway by the walk-in freezer, where his dad said it was out of the way. It was the sound of the safe door closing.

NINE

From the window he watches Genevieve's taillights as her car creeps away, and he looks at his own lonely car out front in the first parking spot and feels so tired. The restaurant mostly dark, he walks to the safe, and his stomach flips as he thinks about recounting the money. His hands shake as he punches in the code. He places his fingers on the safe lever, but he doesn't turn it.

He doesn't want to know right now.

Let's get through tomorrow, he thinks.

—

When he told Kitty earlier that he wouldn't be done until late, she replied, *Time doesn't matter here at all. Come even if it's midnight.*

It might be getting close to that time, but he looks down at his clothes and decides to run home to change first.

Is Genevieve the one stealing from him? All these years, he's always been able to trust his crew. People calling in sick who weren't sick, a few fibs about tips when it was time to share with the bussers and host, having to tell Vivian to cool her hotheadedness. But mostly, *mostly* they've been good.

But Genevieve? It's unthinkable. She is the bones of this place.

He's never, ever not trusted her. And that son of hers making her life so miserable breaks his heart. She wouldn't steal. She would never.

—

He focuses on the rain on the windshield, the rhythm of the wipers. Sometimes he's okay, and sometimes the loneliness, especially this time of year, maybe because of the dark coming so early, sinks into him.

His house was the first big purchase he ever made. On the other side of town, in the Pines, five blocks from the ocean. An old woman lived in the house for sixty years, and when she died, they found squirrels in the attic had chewed through electrical wires. The roof was covered with moss, and there were rotted floorboards and a crumbling chimney. The cottage was in ruins, and Jack's dad said, "You'll lose your shirt trying to make it decent." But Jack looked at the collapsed house, the tall pine trees around it, the way the sky seemed bluer on that street, and he was determined to make it work.

He was in his mid-twenties, right after he decided to stay at the restaurant for a couple of years (he told his dad he wouldn't be there after he was thirty—they even shook on it). A few investors were at the auction, but most people seemed to feel the way Jack's dad did, scrunching up their faces during the brief walk-through. When the auctioneer said, "Sold!" and pointed to Jack, he held his wrinkled, sweaty check for a down payment in his hand. He couldn't believe he got such a good property for a reasonable price (in the nineties, this was still possible—not anymore), and little by little, over the years, he's fixed it up.

He's replaced kitchen cabinets, sanded and varnished the hardwood floors, put on a new screened porch, repaired the holes. He left the windows open day and night to air it out and crossed his arms as a crew reshingled the roof and an electrician got the place up to code. Something about the house always comforts him.

Jack called the space above the garage his studio.

"What exactly happens in this studio?" Kitty had asked, smiling.

"It's where I'll put model ships in bottles when I'm retired. It's where I'll write novels and learn to play the guitar. It's where I'll carve tiny wooden sandpipers that I'll sell on the boardwalk."

"So it's staying empty?" she said.

And it has. Jack has never even brought a chair up there. All these years, and no activity. Just spiders and dead moths.

In his house, every piece of furniture is secondhand—from yard sales, thrift stores, from things people put out on the curb—so the whole place feels like a broken-in T-shirt.

He remembers as a kid seeing Rory, the old woman who lived here before him, walking the streets, a purse over her shoulder, a kind smile on her face. She was beloved in the town, wearing baggy sweaters and skirts, and the people at Steelo's Pizza always gave her a balloon when she ate there, which delighted her. Her parents were old money—they had a pharmacy and café in town in the 1920s and '30s—and when Jack moved into the place he found in an upstairs closet a box of old silver goblets and a clock that looked like something from the *Titanic*.

He leaves his car running, and when he opens his front door, his cat, Harry, nudges him. "Hey good-looking," he says, and scoops him up as he tosses a pile of mail onto the kitchen table and turns on a few lights. The house is drafty, and Jack can hear the rain on the roof. He fills up a glass of water from the refrigerator and takes a deep breath, thinking about seeing Kitty, poor dying Janet.

He shakes some cat food out of the bag, and Harry purrs as he crunches it. Jack's stomach flip-flops as he walks into his downstairs bedroom. He usually sleeps upstairs in the winter and downstairs in the summer because upstairs is always warm and downstairs is cooler. It's an idiosyncrasy a single person can afford. Jack pretends it's like two houses.

He'll probably start sleeping upstairs soon, and most of his winter clothes are up there, along with warmer pajamas. He feels like a bear or squirrel, tucking himself away for the winter.

He takes a deep breath. He doesn't have the words for Janet, for Kitty either. And his bed looks so ready and comfy that he just wants to climb into the rumpled sheets and put his pillow over his head and sleep until the morning light peeks in.

He finds a nicer pair of jeans and a light cashmere sweater his dad gave him. It's pilled in a few places, but he doesn't mind the way he looks in it. He stands in the bathroom and brushes his teeth and splashes some water on his face. Goddamn, his eyes. Don't they sell a cream to fix this? He is unshaven, grisly looking. The restaurant, the restaurant.

Once, he noticed Vivian studying him. "Don't take this the wrong way," she said, "but you look like someone famous, right before they went to rehab. Or like Tom Hanks in *Cast Away* when he was bigger, *before* he went to the island."

Jack had nodded. He kind of knew what she meant. "At least you didn't say Elvis in his later years."

She narrowed her eyes and shook her head. "Okay, Gramps, it's not the 1950s."

He rifles through the medicine cabinet and sprays some cologne. He dips his fingers in a thing of hair paste he bought the last time he had a good haircut. The sky through the skylight has an eerie glow from the rain. He pats the paste into his messy half-wavy hair and tries to smooth it out. His reflection looks back at him, and he shrugs.

"I'll be back, buddy," he says to Harry, but the cat doesn't look up. He texts Kitty that he'll be there in fifteen minutes, and he finally adjusts the stove and microwave clocks that he hasn't changed since daylight savings ended a few weeks ago.

On the bookcase are all the books he keeps buying that he never reads, mostly classics: *Moby-Dick, Their Eyes Were Watching God, The Sun Also Rises, My Ántonia.* On the fireplace is the stack of cruise brochures and European tour pamphlets he picked up from Rehoboth Travel a couple of weeks ago, thinking this winter when Schmidt's is closed for a couple of months as they've done every year since his grandmother opened it he could take a vacation, instead of doing his usual nothing.

He thinks of Genevieve and her son. His throat tenses. He imagines having to call the police about her stealing. Would he let it get that far, or would he just tell her that he knows? *Please stop. You don't need to.*

And then he leaves the house, the porchlight shining on his steps on his way back to the past.

TEN

He pulls up to Janet's house, and he's surprised to see a lit wicker pumpkin on the porch, orange pillows on her two white rocking chairs, and a gourd wreath on the door, as though he's gotten something wrong. This isn't the house of a dying woman but of someone who has kept up with the seasons and is ready for what's next.

He can't imagine she's awake, so he taps lightly on the storm door, and through the curtains of the small windows, he can see someone make their way toward him. When Kitty pulls the door open, he's taken aback by how beautiful she looks, her hair a bit longer, her eyes with more mascara than he remembers, and she sees him and shakes her head. "Jack," she says. Instead of inviting him in, she steps out and pulls the door shut behind her. "You still have the Jeep," she says, and smiles quickly.

"Hey," he says. "Yeah, if it ain't broke, right?"

She hugs him, and he stays frozen as she shakes her head. "Oh, Jack. It's awful," she whispers, and then he rubs her back the way he used to.

"I'm so sorry, Kit. She is a one of a kind." She trembles as she cries. "You know that, right?" He feels her nod against him.

She stands back and wipes her face. "You look nice," she says, and shakes her head again. "Mom said I'd be surprised how good you still look."

Jack shrugs. He tries to think of the last occasion he saw Janet. Definitely a few times since the five-and-ten. Maybe at the grocery store? The car wash? "She always had a soft spot for me."

Kitty crosses her arms and looks out at the street. "She would have traded me or Ray-Ray for you any day."

"Nah." Jack puts his hands into his pockets. The rain has stopped, and the wind has picked up a little, drying everything and making it feel crisp. He can see the bright moon and so many stars scattered over the rooftops.

Kitty turns and looks at him. "How've you been?" she finally says. "Andie says you're still a workaholic."

He rocks back on his heels. "Did you expect anything different?"

She shakes her head. "I just hoped for progress." Her eyes are so kind, like she has missed him.

He's about to tell her that he's thinking about selling the restaurant, just to see her expression, but he doesn't. "I'm living."

She shakes her head. "We're all dying," she says, and looks toward the house. She takes his hand then. "Come inside. She'll love seeing you."

Jack plants his feet for a second. Her hand on his, warm and smooth, stuns him, and he feels like he's not ready to see Janet, to say goodbye.

He takes a deep breath. He swallows the lump in his throat and steps through the door with her.

—

"Hello, stranger," Janet says, and Jack is stunned because she's sitting at the dining room table, not lying in a hospital bed.

He doesn't know what to say, but with Janet, he always trusted his instinct. "Has there been some mistake?" he asks, and gestures toward her.

She laughs, and it's raspy. "It won't be long. I'm getting more and more slumped over here. I feel like the witch in Oz after the water hits her."

"Well, you look terrific." He smiles, and Kitty stands beside him like they're a couple again. The painting of ducks flying over a marsh above the living room sofa settles him, and he notices the fire crackling, the brass fireplace tools hanging from a rack. The table next to the sofa is stacked with all her paperback mysteries, and then he notices a machine on the coffee table next to the *TV Guide* that looks like a nebulizer.

Janet snaps her fingers. "Kitty, get us some Scotch, yes?"

Kitty's shoulders relax. "Why not." She goes to the sideboard and takes out the Scotch, the same kind they drank the night Kitty's dad died. Kitty crouches down and pulls out three crystal glasses. "I'm going to have ginger ale. Scotch burns my throat."

"Lightweight," Janet says. She holds a pen, and Jack looks down and sees a nearly finished *New York Times* crossword. She looks up as Kitty pours her some liquor, and then back at the crossword. "My last one, probably."

"Nah," Jack says, and he realizes his coat's still on, his hands in his pockets.

"Sit," Kitty says, and she goes into the kitchen to get her ginger ale. He hangs his jacket on the dining chair and plops down next to Janet. She does look slumped over. He thinks of that day in the five-and-ten and how good it felt to find someone who knew him in the sea of strangers.

Janet looks over at him like she wants to say something important, but instead she stops, her eyes alert but with regret behind them. She motions for him to pour himself some.

"Cheers, Jack," she whispers, and he holds up his glass and clinks hers. She flashes him a smile before she sips, and then she winces. "That's the stuff."

"You don't have to be brave." He doesn't know why he says this.

"Thank you, dear." She holds the glass and looks down into it. "It's heavier than I remember," she says, and puts it down. Her wavy hair is still the blond-gray it always was. Her sweatshirt says *Bethany Beach.*

Sitting on the chair, he feels so tired. The liquor tingles but in a good way. He listens to Kitty put ice cubes into her glass, listens to the clock in the kitchen that plays nature sounds every hour: crickets, frogs, owls. He traces his finger in the ridges of the crystal. His lips make a sound as he parts them to say something hopefully helpful, Janet looking at him, but now Kitty's back, putting a bowl of pretzels in front of them, her chair scraping the wood floor as she yanks it out. "How do you feel?" she asks Janet, and she puts a hand to her head.

"I don't feel ready," Janet says, and shrugs.

She finishes the rest of her Scotch, grabs a handful of pretzels, and groans. Jack thinks of Kitty's sister, Ray-Ray, and wonders why she isn't here, but he doesn't ask. Things were often tense between her and Kitty. "You could go back to Oregon and come back in a few weeks when I'm sure." She starts laughing then, and Jack laughs, too. He stops when he hears the wheezing sound she makes.

"Mom," Kitty says. "I think you should lie down."

"I do, too," she says, and points to the newspaper. "I'll finish *you* later."

Jack helps Kitty move Janet to the couch and get her set up there. "Miss Stubborn here won't let me get a hospital bed," Kitty says.

Janet rolls her eyes. "Hell no I won't. I love this sofa. I always felt safe here. All these years in this house alone, I just slept on the sofa at night. It didn't feel weird, and it doesn't now."

Jack smiles at her as she pulls her blanket up to her chin.

Kitty runs her hand through her hair. "I said we should get a chair lift for the stairs, but she didn't want that either."

"I'd hate it," Janet says, and does a thumbs-down.

Jack smiles. "I can't get over how strong you look . . . and the crossword, the Scotch." He pauses and searches for something that will make her smile. "You're good at this whole dying thing. Probably the best."

She smiles, and he can see her eyes are tired. "I am, aren't I?" she says. "Kitty, where did the heating pad end up?"

"Probably in the den," Kitty says, and walks to the room behind the kitchen.

Janet turns to him suddenly. "Jack."

"Yes," he says, crouching down to hear her strained voice.

"Don't give up on her, okay?"

He looks toward the den where Kitty has disappeared. "I'll try my best."

"She loves you," she whispers. "Always, always has."

"Ah, I don't know," he says, feeling the flush creep over his face.

"I'm serious," she says. "It's not too late . . . for either of you. A lot of the stuff people worry about—it's silly, Jack. But being there for someone, being someone's partner." She props her head up and seems to get a burst of energy. "I could always see in your eyes the pain you carried, Jack, all the, the *stuff* that weighed you down." She reaches out and touches his face, and he feels his eyes open wider. "You're allowed to be happy now. You've earned it." She blinks. "Know that it's a possibility, okay?" She gives him a weak smile. "There, I said it." She closes her eyes.

"I'll try," he whispers. He's not sure if she hears him. He takes a step back and watches her as she drifts to sleep.

Kitty stands there a moment later, the plaid heating pad in her hands. "Just like her to send me on a wild goose chase." She wraps the cord around it and puts it by Janet's feet.

"I should get going. Busy day tomorrow."

She nods. "I'm so glad you came by," she says, and she walks over and grabs his coat. "It's weird being here," she says, and when he takes the coat from her, her hand lingers against his for a few seconds. The house is dim, and Janet snores softly.

Kitty walks him to the door. She clears her throat, and her eyes look helpless. "I didn't want to leave."

He looks at her, and his head swirls. Maybe from the Scotch. Still thinking about everything from today, thinking about Janet's words. "What?"

She rests her head against the doorway. "I haven't been happy there. It was a mistake. I don't get the people out west. I'm out of sync with them or something. I should have stayed here." She bites her lip. "Even if things with you didn't work out, I should have stayed."

Jack opens the storm door, the air feeling so much colder now (his dad used to always say that Thanksgiving brought down the temperatures so you could store your food on the porch). He looks at Kitty, the room behind her lit by a few lamps, the sofa in the distance with her dying mother breathing softly, their Scotch glasses still on the dining room table. Kitty's eyes are the same color as the liquid: amber almost, catching the light. She looks scared. He grips her shoulder. “I wish I hadn’t made you leave,” he says. He bends down, and she stands on tiptoes to kiss him.

“You don’t have to go,” she whispers, squeezing his hand.

He looks beyond her into the house. “Get some sleep,” he says, and kisses her forehead.

“Happy Thanksgiving, Jack,” she says, and stands still as he walks away, the doorframe centering her like a photograph. He starts up his Jeep, and the steering wheel is freezing cold.

He swears he can still see the color of her eyes as he drives away.

ELEVEN

He remembers that night being stuck on I-95 when he was twelve, and how cold it got when his dad said they'd better turn off the car to save gas.

He remembers wishing his mother was home waiting for them. That would have made it seem less terrible. Sometimes being away from the house was the worst, because he expected her to be there when he got back. When he was home, and he felt all the quiet sadness, it was easier to accept that she was gone.

He wanted to tell her about the night stranded on the highway, his dad's coat over him in the back seat, the glow of the taillights slowly turning off one by one, the black sky and white mounds of snow. He remembers his dad's extra pair of socks on his hands, the sound of him finally snoring; he remembers hearing a few cars idling, especially a big tractor trailer that hovered over them.

The next morning, he figured things would be solved. He always thought mornings solved everything. Like when his mom still lived with them, and she would cry and take one of her drives at night, but in the morning, Jack would wake up and things would seem peaceful, his mom making herself a cup of tea, his dad outside chopping a pile of wood for the woodstove.

But that day he woke up in the still car, his mouth and cheeks so cold, and though his dad smiled patiently, his eyes looked worried.

Outside the car, some people were standing around, and up ahead, a bakery delivery truck opened its doors and started passing out cupcakes and cookies and loaves of bread.

Jack's dad's eyes lit up as though they were watching a surprise circus come to town, and the two of them opened the car doors, sticking for a second in the freeze, and rushed toward the truck. His dad ushered Jack in front of him, and Jack took a bag of sliced bread, and it felt soft and promising in his hands, like something he could always hold.

—

"Seize the day, motherfucker!"

It's Thanksgiving, five thirty in the morning, still dark, just the glow of the lamps on the boardwalk, the heavy keys jingling in Jack's hand, and here is bloody Deacon in shorts and a sweatshirt and an annoying hat with a tassel on it, jogging in place.

Jack sips the last bit from his coffee tumbler. "You're a piece of shit," he says, seeing his breath in the cold air. "You could be in bed with your wife, and you're scampering around at dawn like a loose puppy."

"Hell yes I am." Deacon's eyes are animated and wide awake. He doesn't stop moving. "Join me for a quick jog."

Jack looks down at his Crocs, and he imagines them slapping the boardwalk, Deacon not out of breath at all, keeping up a full conversation while Jack gasped. He shakes his head. "You're grotesque," he says, and motions him inside. "Want coffee? I need more."

"No. I'm doing ten miles today, so I gotta hit it hard."

Jack glances into the restaurant, and it's settled and peaceful, the light from the back of the sign making scattered diamonds on the hardwood floor. Vivian and Sam laid out the tablecloths last night and got the fake Christmas tree up yesterday, left it plugged in.

Jack feels the seconds slipping by. The first reservation is at eleven, so he has to make sure the early round of turkeys, which they got ready to go last night, are in the big oven right away. They cook three fourteen-pounders first, which will be done by ten and will last the first hour or two of reservations. The others will go in at seven and be done by noon. "Well, enjoy yourself, my friend."

Deacon holds the door for him. "I heard you visited someone last night," he says.

"Jesus," Jack says. "Does news really travel that fast? That was just a few fucking hours ago."

"The news cycle with ladies is instantaneous, man." He smiles. "Why the hell didn't you stay the night?"

"Complicated." Seeing all the tables set, the napkins folded in small boats, the water glasses standing at attention, makes Jack feel relieved. He almost feels like today won't be too bad. Bearable, even. "She didn't really want me to stay. She's just sad, you know?"

He nods. "You still like her? Think you could lure her back here?"

Jack imagines the turkeys already in the oven. He imagines their skin browning, the onions and carrots and celery in the pan sizzling in the drippings. "I've never lured anyone anywhere," he says. He scratches his chin. "Plus—" He is about to confess something, maybe because he's tired, but he stops.

"Plus what?"

"Nothing."

Deacon sighs and frowns. "You won't be able to handle the rejection if it goes bad." He lifts one eyebrow. "You act so pissy and

Eeyore-ish, but you're actually fragile, right?" He clears his throat. "*Right?*"

"Don't pretend you know me." Jack shakes his head.

"Don't pretend I didn't bull's-eye it. Oh, and Andie says I'm not to accept no for dinner tonight."

"I already texted her. I told her I'd be too tired, and probably stuffed from eating in between sittings. Just please tell her I appreciate it but I can't."

"Did she write you back and say it was okay?"

"No."

Deacon's eyes widen, and he purses his lips. "Then you're *not* excused. You call her if you want out. I'm not telling her I failed." He claps Jack on the back. "Later, man," he shouts, and Jack watches him disappear into the fog, the rhythmic sound of his sneakers on the boards.

—

Saul is the best turkey carver, so he and Jack are slicing the first batch to get every last bit of meat, and Paulette, who does prep, is whipping potatoes and taking out the giant pans of sausage stuffing, which makes Jack salivate for a second when he smells it from across the kitchen.

A couple of years ago, Genevieve set up a pie station for the customers who preordered them to go, and it worked so well now they come in the side door to pay and don't interrupt the flow of traffic.

Every so often Genevieve and Jack exchange glances, and she looks nervous as she hands customers change and bags up their cheesecakes and pumpkin pies. Jack thinks of the sound of the safe closing. All those years, all the trust he's placed in her. He's let her make her own hours. Would she really steal from him? How many other details could he have missed?

"Go home," he whispered to her a little while ago, talking like a ventriloquist through his teeth as he stood beside her.

She shook her head. "It's easier here," she said in a low voice, and waved the next customer to her station.

"I'm already sick of turkey," Saul says now. He lifts the meat into a giant pan then sharpens his knife. "I feel like the grease is in my skin."

"I could eat turkey every day," Jack says. He sees Vivian walk by, her nails painted orange, and she groans when Saul asks her to stir the pumpkin bisque. "If it's not too much trouble," Saul calls, and she smirks.

She rubs her throat. "I need a hot toddy or something."

"A hot *toddy*?" Saul says, and laughs. "I didn't know Daddy Warbucks was here."

"Dickhead," she says, and flicks the arm he's carving with.

"Watch it," Jack says, louder and less friendly than he means to, and they all snap to attention.

Sam walks by with six pitchers of water on a tray. "Behind you," he says, and Vivian grabs a monkey dish and ladles some bisque into it. She blows on it before she samples it, and Jack looks at the clock. Fifteen minutes until the first reservation. They'll be busy all through the weekend, and already his damn worthless feet ache.

Holiday parties, New Year's Eve, New Year's Day, and then he closes the doors until April. Unless he sells to DelDine, in which case it'll be the last time he does any of it.

Trying to imagine being finished with the restaurant feels exciting and scary—like living without having to ever worry about rain or snow again. He looks around at the crew, and can't imagine not seeing them every day.

He glances down at the turkey carcass below him, the stainless counter smudged.

All that money from DelDine.

He stretches his neck and rolls his shoulders. On the ceiling, he sees a water spot and some cracks. He can still see his grandmother pointing out flaws to her maintenance guy. He holds his electric carving knife and keeps carving away, the meat falling, his crew choreographed in their jobs around him. He is both nothing and absolutely everything here.

—

An hour later, things are going okay. Customers are laughing, clinking their wineglasses together and buttering their rolls and saying the soups are delicious. The room of two hundred people is buzzing, and the waitstaff—Vivian especially, her scratch covered with concealer—are charming in their ties and dress shirts, carrying trays of steaming turkey on platters, gravy boats, and bowls of sides like candied carrots and roasted brussels sprouts and mashed potatoes.

For Thanksgiving, Schmidt's serves everything family style to replicate the experience they're skipping at home to come here.

"Save room for pie," Jack hears Vivian say to some sweet old people, and the music in the background, instrumental Christmas carols, is pleasant.

Sam methodically clears tables, and in between seating the large parties, he fills water glasses and assists the servers with getting the whole meal to the table, nudging a dad or uncle with a small bowl and saying, "I bet the cranberry sauce goes here, right?" When Sam's not doing anything else, Jack sees him make small talk with people in the waiting area, and feels grateful he is on the team. Once in a while, he is gripped with an emotion like that—special gratitude that an employee landed in this place at this time. Jack has felt that for so many of them. He hopes Sam is happy here.

—

Jack is cutting the last of the turkeys, listening to the sound of the final potatoes being mashed, when he sees Genevieve rush toward his office.

He motions for Saul to take his place, and hurries back to find her sobbing into her hands in the corner near his filing cabinet. "*What*? What happened?"

She looks at Jack. "He took my car," she says. Her volume rises. "He's up to something awful, I know it." The sight of her wounds him, but he also feels a stab of pain thinking about Ziggy. What if this is it? What if he ends up dead? That poor kid.

Jack tries to comfort her, his hand meekly on her shoulder, but she jerks it away, clutching her heart now and suddenly doubling over, looking terrified, like she can't breathe.

He kneels beside her and shouts, "Genevieve, can you hear me?"

Now she is gasping, and he's dialing 911 and trying to remember first aid training, balling up his sweatshirt like a pillow under her head. "Can you hear me?" he asks again.

TWELVE

The paramedics come through the back door and none of the customers seem to notice. Genevieve has oxygen on her face, and Jack pulls Vivian and Sam aside. "I need you two to be in charge," he says. "You both know everything you need to do to keep this place afloat until the end of service."

Sam's face drains of color. "But what if?"

Vivian steps in front of him. "We'll be fine, Schmidt," she says. "Take care of Ma," she says, looking past Jack at the two women administering to Genevieve.

"Thanks for handling it," he says, grabbing his coat and walking out with the paramedics as they wheel Genevieve toward the transport.

They are about to close the ambulance door, but Genevieve is pointing furiously at Jack, saying something he can't make out.

"What's that, miss?" The paramedic removes the oxygen mask for a second.

"He's family!" Genevieve says, and points at him, and the woman motions for Jack to climb inside.

—

The doors close, and Genevieve reaches her hand out for his, her fingers so cold. Jack holds her hand tightly and stares out the small window. He can see the sky is perfectly blue, the restaurant and beach fading away as the truck speeds down Chesapeake Street.

He feels a loss looking out at the quiet day that he can't put into words. Genevieve blinks at him as her breath fogs up the mask. Her eyes are unfocused, but they glance in his direction. He braces against her stretcher as the ambulance coasts over bumps and rushes toward the highway.

"You're okay," Jack whispers. "Hang in there, Genevieve. You're doing great." Does the money even matter?

They speed past the outlet stores that will be packed tomorrow for Black Friday, past other restaurants with full parking lots—an IHOP, a new steakhouse that looks like Frank Lloyd Wright designed it, DelDine's crown jewel The Pier—and the movie theaters with a few people in line. He tries and tries, but he can't get her hands to warm up as the ambulance hurries toward the hospital, the sirens crying.

—

Rehoboth Beach is a town where the sun is always bolder, a place that carries the memories of a busy and fun summer all year long. White benches line the boardwalk, and a bandstand at the top of Rehoboth Avenue has live shows. There is a farmer's market once a week from spring until fall, and three parks right in town.

During the summer, the town buzzes with people walking the streets and setting up chairs on the beach, but in the fall and winter, it is just as fun to visit for events like the film festival or Halloween parade.

There is nothing better than a quiet weekday in autumn in Rehoboth—no parking meters to pay, very few tourists. You can walk around and see the seasonal shops with their signs that say See You in Spring, or you can eat dinner at a quiet year-round restaurant with no wait. It might be windy, but it never seems depressing, even in midwinter.

Frequent visitors feel that their lives are divided into Rehoboth time and non-Rehoboth time.

—That's Rehoboth Beach: A Guidebook

THIRTEEN

Tears are rolling down Genevieve's face as they pull up to the emergency room doors. "Jack," she says through her oxygen. "Don't call the police."

For a second, this frustrates him because that is exactly what he was planning to do, even just to track down her car and have someone stop Ziggy, help him. But if he were a parent, he thinks, he would understand. He *does* understand, because Ziggy was never all bad. He used to sit at the bar and order a root beer float when he was seven or eight. He used to ask Jack how to whistle. Jack would protect his own child in the very same way.

—

It's nearly two thirty when Jack's Uber drops him off. He pulls open the restaurant side door, and the kitchen sounds calm. He hears Vivian say gently to one of the teenage bussers, "Run this to table 33, sweetie." She is setting up a tray with half a dozen cups of coffee, and he realizes how badly he could use one of them. She freezes when she sees him.

"She's okay," he says.

Vivian slaps her chest and sighs. She shakes her head. "Couldn't you have texted?" She blows a bubble with her gum. "Shit, I thought she was flatlining and you were trying to spare us." She wipes her eyes. "Oh, our sweet Ma."

"Yeah. Just some rib cartilage inflammation, which can feel like a heart attack, they said."

Jack doesn't tell Vivian that they also said Genevieve was probably having a panic attack. When he left, they had given her a sedative, and her daughter Rose had come to sit beside her, kissing her hand every so often. "She didn't want me to call the police," Jack told Rose, Genevieve's most responsible kid who lives almost an hour away.

"She never does," Rose said. "I worry about him, too, but this isn't going to end well." She picked up her phone and dialed the police on her own. "I hope they bring him in and start taking seriously what a problem he is," she said as she waited for someone to answer. "My mom can't take this."

Vivian lifts her tray now, the coffee cups quaking, and looks at him. "That's a relief." She grabs two white creamers from the cooler. "You still should have texted me. I was worried sick."

Jack nods. *I don't think about stuff like that*, he wants to say. "You're right, Viv," he says instead, and starts to fill the empty water pitchers.

Sam walks by with a handful of dirty tablecloths, and his face relaxes when he sees Jack. "Oh, good. Is Genevieve all right?"

"She should be fine."

He smiles. "It's weird without you two here," he says.

A couple of servers brush by Jack, and he hears one of the kitchen guys say something about his kid. Vincent, the dishwasher, fills up the ice bay of the soda dispenser, dropping a few stray cubes onto the floor that he gently kicks under the tower. Out in the dining room, a baby cries, and some old people laugh. Someone gives a toast, and

Jack hears Vivian thank a table that's leaving. "You were an awfully nice group," she says.

—

An hour later, they are cleaning up. Vivian and the other servers have stripped the tables down to their usual wood for tomorrow's lunch. Jack lets a handful of the workers take home pies, and others fill up to-go containers with stuffing and rolls and turkey and sides. "Don't waste anything," he says, and drinks another cup of coffee, black, and thinks about poor Genevieve, the way she collapsed in his office, that awful pained look on her face.

Her child, Jack thinks. Her only son. He turned into someone no one recognized. Suspended from school. Stealing. Even in junior high, the principal called Genevieve every couple of days. Did he miss having a father? Did it fuck him up? Jack wonders for a second if Genevieve took money from the restaurant to get him out of trouble. She said she would sit him down and ask to hear his side every time there was a problem at school, but didn't know what to do the day when he burst into angry tears, screaming, "Mom, I'm just bad, okay?"

Sam adds Christmas centerpieces to each of the tables, and Vincent hangs small red stockings with each employee's name on the big wall. Jack gives everyone who was there today cash in an envelope, and Saul tells him he and the guys are going to the Lucky Toad for drinks and asks if Jack wants to join them.

"Very flattered. But you don't want me cramping your style," Jack says, thinking for a second that it would be nice to just be one of the guys and laugh over beers.

"Suit yourself, boss," Saul replies, and grins.

They all start to disperse, and Jack looks at his crew, young and old, some of them changed out of their uniforms, a few of them, like Vincent, in a jacket and tie because he's going to his wife's aunt's house. Paulette is going to Vivian's for dinner after she goes home to change. Jack texts Rose to make sure Genevieve's all right. He stares at his phone for a few seconds after he sends it, and Rose doesn't write back.

"Thank you, Mr. Schmidt," Sam says, and waves to Jack, and a couple of the servers walk out with him.

"Gotta rest up for Black Friday, Schmidt," Vivian says, carrying a pie. He can see Vivian's scratch showing through now, but it's healed a lot since yesterday. She wears a tank top and holds her white uniform shirt and coat over her free arm.

"You're not on the schedule tomorrow, though, right?"

"No way," Vivian says, furling her eyebrows. "I'm resting up for shopping. A group of girls and I get up at 4 a.m. and hit the stores hard."

"I think I'd rather work here."

She looks at Jack with something like pity. "Well, go relax now," she says.

He switches off the lights and holds the door open for her. "Thanks for covering today, Viv. You and Sam really stepped up." His feet throb, and he feels a headache forming. He can't wait to go home and change into his favorite T-shirt with the ripped collar. How luxurious it will be to just melt into his big chair in the living room, Harry sleeping on his lap, some holiday movie like *White Christmas* or *Home Alone* on the television.

Vivian is the type of person who can't take a compliment. She rolls her eyes. "No problem," she finally says. "Just so Ma's okay."

He wants to say Genevieve will be. He wants to think of a way to fix all this for her as he stands there outside his restaurant, the light almost lost from the sky, a few seagulls flying in formation over the boardwalk. "Good luck tomorrow," he says to Vivian. "May the discounts be in your favor."

She shakes her head and walks away. "Cut to me coming home with a freakin' air fryer and that's it."

FOURTEEN

There is one problem with his plan of going home and having a hot shower and slipping into his wonderful shabby clothes and eating the trough of leftovers he's carrying in two Styrofoam containers.

Jack knows he'll sink into the chair and be snoring in minutes. Outside the night will get black, and he'll wake around midnight to trudge to his bed, getting up in the morning and going back to the damn restaurant tomorrow that he should just sell and be done with.

The problem is that he never called Andie to make it clear he wasn't coming to their Thanksgiving dinner that starts in forty minutes. Well, he did text her, but she never wrote back. And Deacon said that wasn't enough.

He thinks about just texting Deacon, but he knows what he'll say. *Bullshit, man. I'm not delivering* that *message. Your place at the table is set. Speak to your lawyer yourself.*

If Jack calls Andie, she will be breathless, finishing up everything and fixing people drinks, rushing around. If he says he's too tired, she'll say, "We're not going to make you do sprints. Get over here." And if he doesn't show up, it'll be a whole thing, Deacon coming by the restaurant tomorrow and saying, *Someone's pi-issed at you.*

Christ. He can't go.

His brain hurts. Genevieve's daughter still hasn't written back, and he just wants to forget everything. He pulls up to his house and the sky is pink, the sun blazing its last call, and his little bungalow looks like something he doesn't ever want to leave.

But there's no getting out of this.

He should have invented other plans. He should have stayed at the hospital with Genevieve.

Years ago, Jack's dad suggested to Genevieve that Ziggy could come into the restaurant. "He'll straighten out, and we can all keep an eye on him." Johnny Schmidt always thought the restaurant could solve anyone's problems. But Ziggy showed up twice and said he thought some of the waitstaff was laughing at him. Then he said he might sue Johnny because he slipped in the parking lot and hurt his elbow. An eleven-year-old! "Sorry, Genevieve," Jack's dad finally said. "I guess it's not gonna work." But Jack often thought about Ziggy alone at home, those long days after school with his sisters off at marching band practice or cheer, and he wondered how he was coping.

Now Jack sees Harry in the window, pressing his furry face against the screen, and rushes inside, jumping into the shower for two minutes just to let the hot water rinse the sweat and grime and turkey grease off him.

He's not even hungry, but on the other hand, he thinks, a guy like him is lucky to have friends who care like Deacon and Andie do. He takes two Advil for his headache, drinks a big cup of water, and throws on his corduroy pants and black button-down, his unruly hair semi under control.

"Sorry, buddy," he says to Harry, and scratches his head. He shakes a few fish-shaped treats in front of him as he leaves.

He opens his liquor cabinet and finds a new bottle of Baileys he bought a couple of months ago when he had a date who he thought might come back to his place but didn't. He finds one of those sticky bows in his bottom desk drawer and puts it on the bottle. It almost looks like he tried.

—

He gets to the house five minutes before five, and he takes a deep breath as he rings the doorbell. They live on a golf course, but Deacon hates golf. He bought a golf cart a year or two ago, and he and Jack drove around the neighborhood in it, drinking Deacon's favorite bourbon and talking about life. "We're such posers," he said, playing Led Zeppelin from the small radio.

Now Andie comes to the door, Evie in her arms wearing a small velvet dress. "Happy Thanksgiving," Jack says, and he shows her the bottle.

"Jack," she says, and puts her hand to his face. "Deacon said you'd bail on us, but I told him you wouldn't."

"Despite any contrary communication you might have received, I wouldn't dare," Jack says, and winks. He clutches Evie's little arm, and she looks at him and then back at Andie. Andie wears a red and black checkered silk blouse, nice wool pants, and high heels. Her dark hair is swept up, and she wears deep red lipstick. She has a certain elegance no matter what she's wearing. She's ten years younger than Deacon, and they work for the same law firm. While Deacon specializes in wills, her area is commercial businesses, so she's represented Jack anytime he happens to need something done. Over the years he and Kitty dated, she and Andie became close.

"Come in, come in," she says, and Evie watches Jack from over Andie's shoulder.

"Shit, he made it!" Deacon calls from across the room, a group of his friends and a few older aunts and uncles turning in Jack's direction. "I lost that bet."

Jack waves to him. "Happy thanksgiving, *Deek*," Jack says, and glares, his polite way of calling Deacon a similar-sounding word.

"There you are, Jackie," he hears from behind him, and Deacon's dad, Carl, is squeezing Jack's shoulder. Carl was a contractor for many years and then served as the president of the builders' association. For an eighty-year-old, he has a grip like a vise. He is taking Evie from Andie now. "Have you seen this buttercup lately? Doesn't she get prettier every second?"

Evie looks at Jack wide-eyed and reaches out and grabs his shirt collar. "She sure does," Jack says. "How've you been, Mr. Williams?"

He bounces Evie, picks up a glass of white wine, and sips it. "I'm holding my own."

Deacon's mom, Evelyn, whom Evie is named after, has gotten really bad with dementia, and Carl decided last summer to put her in Pine Creek, a memory care facility. "I keep glancing across the room when I'm at something like this, thinking I'll see her, and then I realize she's not coming back. It's a loss, Jackie. A big loss." Right then, he seems to scan the room, as if he forgot she wasn't there again.

Jack doesn't say anything. He just looks at Carl and nods, Evie closing her eyes for a second and then looking up at Jack. Carl puts his wine on the counter by the cheese tray and glances at her. "Well, I'm going to see if Deacon wants me to change her out of this dress before dinner," he says, and shrugs, and Jack pats his back and watches him go. He can see Carl walking with Evie, and the way his arms shift from Evie getting heavier. After conferring with Deacon, he takes the baby out of the kitchen and down their long hallway, and Jack feels something like envy.

Carl loves his son's family, but his loss shows as he walks. Even though he lives alone now, he had something big and perfect for many years. Jack watches him and wants the thing Carl's missing.

—

Jack knew they wouldn't eat right away. Deacon and Andie are all about the appetizers and the chitchat. The "let me freshen your wine" and "come see my new outdoor brick oven," or "look what we did to the family room," Deacon grinning as he presses a remote control, and all the skylights and windows disappear under dark shades like it's the Avengers compound.

There are about twenty people at the house, and Jack has been kissed by aunts and made small talk with neighbors and caught up with Deacon's cousin Sylvie and her wife, Daisy. Sylvie has a restaurant in town called Jetty, and Daisy owns the local paper, *Cape News*. Jack goes to get a little more wine, and he takes in the room: candles flickering everywhere and a whole station of hors d'oeuvres with grapes and figs and oranges that look like they're from a medieval feast. All the people in their merino wool sweaters and sport coats and dresses and skirts are like something out of a catalog.

Deacon is surrounded by five people at all times, telling a story that will end with him doubled over laughing, Andie rolling her eyes and shaking her head across the room and smiling. Jack can see the dining room from where he stands, and the table is set with Andie's grandmother's china, the napkins folded in fans, a fire crackling in the fireplace.

Jack feels lucky to be here in such a full place, but he's overwhelmed, like he can't possibly make it through this whole night. He wants to pull Andie aside and tell her thanks but he's got to run. He thinks about Genevieve and wonders if she's out of the hospital. He thinks of Kitty and Janet and what a terrible night it must be for them. He could have stayed there with Kitty last night and held her. When they kissed, it was like no time had gone by. Maybe Janet was right.

He's dated a handful of women since Kitty, but nothing serious. They all felt wrong, the conversation forced, the kisses weak. He usually ended up sleeping at their houses because he didn't want to bring them into the sad world of his bungalow. He felt embarrassed by his life, by his bachelor furniture, his pitiful groceries in the fridge.

Does he miss Kitty? Is that what this is all about? He's too tired to figure anything out. Sylvie is asking him something about storage at his restaurant.

"Oh, yeah, we have a ton of storage. After the storm in 1962, my grandma rebuilt everything the way she always wanted. She got to reconfigure the dining room and add a second floor," he says, and Sylvie smiles.

"Was her life divided into before the storm and after?" she says, her wife, Daisy, slipping off to help Andie wash some glasses.

"Actually, she did talk about it that way. It was almost biblical to her." Jack has a memory of sitting in her living room, his grandmother and her best friend, Agnes, side by side on the sofa, exchanging stories about the flood, telling Jack about the downed trees, the sand all over Rehoboth Avenue, the slow cleanup and recovery.

Sylvie crosses her arms. "I'm glad we're closing down this winter. The last few years have been nonstop. The weeks never begin or end."

"You definitely need a break," Jack says, and then he's thinking about the permanent break he's considering and how simple his life would be. He could even have dinner parties like this, couldn't he? What would stop him?

As if she can read his mind, Sylvie leans in. "Have, um, the restaurant bullies approached you?"

Jack swallows. "DelDine?"

She nods. A lot of the small restaurant owners steer clear of DelDine. Too corporate. Too out of line with the indie business philosophy.

"Oh, well, you know, they're always putting their nets out, but um, I try to keep them at bay." Jack clears his throat. "They'd take over a McDonald's if they could. How about you?"

"Same," Sylvie says. "That Maurice is just awful." Maurice is the president and owner of DelDine, a bloated man without a neck. He is famously unlikable.

Sylvie leans closer. "Once he had Nicole Pratt deliver a handwritten note to me that said he admired Jetty and could do great things for it." She rolls her eyes. "*Let's talk soon*, he said. Like, go to hell, you know?"

Jack nods, feeling his palms sweat. "Yeah, that's how I feel."

"Is this the restaurant section?" someone says now, and Jack turns to see Nicole herself, wearing the same clothes he saw her in yesterday, her hair wet and combed into a short ponytail. She gives them a big smile.

He and Sylvie exchange surprised glances. *Speak of the devil.*

Nicole gestures at her water goblet filled to the top with red wine and swirls it around. "Can you tell it's been a damn day?"

"How are you, Nicole?" Sylvie says politely.

Though they technically owned competing restaurants, Sylvie and Jack and their fellow owners had seemed to strike an unspoken truce and united front when DelDine first exploded on the scene. If Sylvie only knew how often Jack lets Nicole into his restaurant, how she just invited him out for coffee yesterday.

Nicole doesn't seem to notice Sylvie's polite disgust and gulps her wine. "Ahh," she says, and whistles. "Whoo boy."

"It's a surprise to see you here," Jack says, and smiles.

"I'm full of surprises," she says. Her eyes sparkle, and she winks at him, and for a second, he feels like he's in a trance. She pops a small crab-stuffed tomato into her mouth. She looks at him and Sylvie and laughs like a maniac. She mock-slaps his arm. "Remember, Andie and I are CrossFit buddies?" She shakes her head. "I told you this yesterday when we were hanging out."

Sylvie looks at Jack and cocks her head to the side. *Hanging out*? she mouths.

"Oh, that's right," Jack mumbles.

"Andie told me this morning to come by if I felt like it." Nicole pushes her eyeglasses up on her head now. "When I got home tonight, the quiet of the house kind of screamed at me, and you know what, I felt like it."

"It's a nice place to be," Jack says, and then he notices Andie is calling everyone to their seats. Sylvie picks up a relish tray and brings it to the table, and he sees Evie in a soft turkey shirt and colorful striped pants, Deacon holding her up to the crowd like he just caught a touchdown pass.

Jack feels a wave of tiredness wash over him, and wonders what his employees are doing, Genevieve especially. Is she in a dark hospital room by herself? Or being led out of the car to her daughter's house?

He reaches into his pocket and checks his phone to see if there's any news, but nothing.

Carl, Deacon's dad, carves the turkey at the counter, and Jack's about ready to offer to help him when Nicole grabs his sleeve.

"I'm sitting next to you, Jack Schmidt," she says. "And that's final."

FIFTEEN

Nicole is odder than Jack thought. She interrupts people's conversations, turning to tell Deacon's aunt she grew up in Pittsburgh when the aunt mentions the city.

"Here we go, Steelers," Nicole chants. She puts her two pointer fingers up like drumsticks and winks. The aunt and the woman she's talking to nod politely.

Nicole has no inhibitions. She reaches across Jack several times to grab something, and she loads up her plate over and over. "Fabulous," she says, and does the chef's kiss gesture. At one point, she dips a piece of her dinner roll into Jack's gravy, and he stares at her in disbelief.

"What?" she asks.

He finds himself unable to stop watching her. He's not disgusted the way someone else might be. It's like she's a one-woman performance. Her confidence is unshakeable, and every so often, she winks at him.

There are a dozen conversations happening, and Andie is blowing on mashed potatoes for Evie. "Such a big girl," someone says, and then Deacon is clinking his glass with a butter knife and everyone stops.

"I almost forgot," he says. He holds up his wineglass. "To family and friends, the best gift of all." He pauses for a minute, and Jack sees the fun slip away from his eyes. He screws up his mouth and blinks. "To my mom, who made a million Thanksgivings perfect."

"Hear! Hear!" Carl says softly, and he looks down at his plate.

"To our beautiful baby," Deacon says, tapping the tray of Evie's high chair. She drops the teething beads she's holding and looks delighted. "And my partner in crime." He squeezes Andie's hand, and she gives him a wide smile that makes Jack ache. He has an image of them clearing the plates later tonight. Of Andie standing in their bedroom and taking off her rings. Of Deacon reading in bed and snuggling close to her.

Deacon's still giving his toast, and people are still listening, except for wild Nicole, who keeps talking to Jack the whole time. "These toasts always make me feel like crap," she says, and swats his arm so he turns to her. "I mean, good for them, but . . ." She snorts and points to herself. "Can you all let some of your aura rub off on me?" She sighs loudly, and Deacon's aunt turns to her and glares.

Jack pretends not to hear Nicole and tries to focus on Deacon, who has gone uncharacteristically quiet. Evie makes a babbling noise in the silence. "To the always-amazing Williams-Stone family." Jack raises his glass, and everyone at the table claps.

Deacon looks at him, and Jack blushes, knowing he's just made himself a target. Deacon smirks and gestures toward Jack. "If anyone is looking for an attractive business owner with a heart of gold, a *crushing* work ethic, an expired passport, and a full message mailbox, my man Jackpot is your guy."

Everyone chuckles, and Andie slaps Deacon's arm. Carl, who is going for seconds, shakes his head and tousles Jack's hair as he passes by.

"Cheers," Nicole says, and clinks Jack's glass, even though he's not holding it.

—

Jack's grandmother had been in business for just eight years when the big storm of 1962, a three-day nor'easter, hit Delaware hard. Most of the boardwalk collapsed, and hotels and the rides and games pavilion toppled onto the beach, some of it dragged away by the ocean. Dunes were washed away, and the highway was covered in mountains of sand. People died all along the East Coast.

Jack's dad was a couple of months away from finishing college, and he came to check on Hazel, whose friend Agnes stood beside her as they surveyed what was left.

"We're done, Johnny," she said, kicking a broken dinner plate.

The restaurant, according to what Jack's dad told him, looked like someone dropped a bomb on it. Every window was broken. Wet sand was scattered in what was left of the dining room. Agnes stood beside Hazel and tried to reassure her, but Hazel said she was going to take whatever the insurance company offered and make a run for it. "I can be a teacher or a secretary. Maybe I'll go to nursing school," she said, and crossed her arms.

Jack could picture it. The collapsed restaurant. Two middle-aged women trying to make sense of the destroyed coastline, all the houses and businesses pummeled and in splinters. And there was Jack's dad with his almost-degree, his clean-shaven face and youthful energetic blue eyes, the Chevy Bel Air Hazel had given him for his twenty-first birthday idling in the middle of the road.

Johnny had told Jack the sky was so clear after the storm, and the ocean had retreated and looked smooth as a lake. He said he could envision a newer, better Schmidt's, and decided at that moment that it was his calling. That he could make a life out of being needed there.

He stood between Hazel and Agnes. "We can do this," he said. "We'll get it all back. Hell, Ma, we'll fix all the things about the place you didn't like."

Hazel shook her head, and Agnes looked at Johnny surprised, but to this day, Jack still imagines the scene: rubble everywhere, but the new-blue sky and valiant sun shining through. And he imagines that deep down, they couldn't help but believe Johnny's promise.

—

Deacon is putting Evie to bed, and Carl is drying dishes. Jack helps Andie take apart the large table, and Sylvie and Daisy hug everyone goodbye. "This was great," Jack says to Andie, and she puts her arm around him.

"I'm so glad you came. I know how tired you must be." She smiles and gives Jack the *wait one minute* finger. "Do me one last favor," she says. Jack looks at his watch, and it's 9 p.m. He can't believe they have Black Friday lunch tomorrow. Too many shoppers in town, out and about, not to be open. He wants January to be here so badly, to be done with it for a couple of months. Or to just sign Nicole's papers right this instant.

He realizes Nicole must have left without saying goodbye, but that doesn't surprise him. *Born in a barn*, his grandmother would have said.

Andie comes back with a grocery bag packed with leftovers, and Jack raises his eyebrows. "Would you please, please drop this off for Kitty?" She holds up her hand. "I'm not trying anything, I swear.

But I can't stand the thought of them not having a nice meal. I think Janet still has an appetite. So I made them each a plate, and put a few slices of pie in there." She shrugs. "Only if you don't mind."

He takes the bag and feels its weight. He can't imagine walking up those porch steps again. It feels impossible. He takes a deep breath and smiles at Andie.

"No problem," he says.

SIXTEEN

The porchlight flicks on before he knocks, and Kitty comes outside the same way she did last night. "Happy Thanksgiving, Jack," she says, and her eyes are red rimmed.

"Hey," he says. "Yeah, happy Thanksgiving." He pushes the bag toward her. "From Andie."

She takes the package and holds it against her stomach. "She's the best." She glances toward the door. "Mom's sleeping. Seems like she's sleeping more and more."

"I'm so sorry." He swallows. "When's Ray-Ray coming home?" Kitty's sister Ramona is a guitarist in a semi-successful indie band that tours the country.

Kitty shrugs. "She's doing her best to get here by the end of the weekend."

"Your mom'll love that."

"Yup, she loves her little wildflower." Jack has the sudden urge to touch Kitty's cheek, to hold Kitty and try to comfort her. She looks so sad; maybe these habits come back easiest at vulnerable times. He can't stand her eyes so red, how somber she is. A car drives by, and the rain starts again, and he hears the way it patters on his Jeep's roof. It feels damp and cold, and he rubs his hands together.

"Well," he says.

She looks back at the glowing windows behind her. "Yeah." She nods. "Thanks, Jack, for running this over. Busy day, I bet?"

"Crazy," he says. He's about to tell her about Genevieve, but decides not to. He wants to say how seeing Deacon's dad missing Evelyn gutted him; how watching Deacon and Andie and Sylvie and Daisy—all those couples—made him feel so singular and separate and down. He wants to ask her how people like her and him and even Nicole got on the outside of that. *Is there something wrong with us?*

He wants more, he wants to tell her, and he wants her to understand. He wants what his parents didn't get to have. He doesn't want his life to be over. He shrugs and just stands there, and the rain seems like someone flipped a switch to high because it starts falling in sheets, the wind gusting, the last of the oak and poplar leaves blowing down in her driveway, his car running.

"Why did you get married?" he blurts out. He wasn't planning on asking, but it just popped to the surface.

She tilts her head back. "I think it felt nice to have someone who wanted to." She looks down and shrugs. "At the time, I mean, it did." She swats the air. "But it all went bad so quickly. Out of this long relationship with you, then engaged in a month and married for less than a year." She shakes her head. "It wasn't wise, but it felt good at the time. Cozy or something. I just wanted to be cozy."

He puts his hands into his pockets and nods. "Yeah. Who knows why we do what we do." He looks at the rain then and shrugs. "I guess I better go." He's still thinking about what she said—about having a person who wanted to marry her. "I'm sorry, Kitty." He stares at her, and he feels like she can see right into him.

"I'll get you an umbrella," she says.

He shakes his head and is about to say he doesn't mind getting wet, but she's already gone inside and popped out with a big golf umbrella, wearing an old pair of her mother's rain boots. "Here," she says, and he gives her half a smile. He steps down from the porch, and she holds it over his head.

"Now don't *you* get wet," he says, and when he goes to take the umbrella from her, his hand on top of hers for a second, her fingers as smooth as he remembers them, she doesn't pull her hand away. She looks into his eyes.

"I'll walk you to the car," she says.

"You sure?" She nods, and they keep their hands together on the umbrella handle, their steps slow and coordinated, his shoes splashing the puddled concrete, a few maple seeds pelting the umbrella and falling to the ground. They walk side by side toward the car, and Kitty moves closer to him, the whisper of smoke coming from his exhaust, the headlights illuminating them.

When they get to the driver's door, Jack opens it, and she stays there. "Enjoy the food," he says quietly, but she just nods. He glances into the car and looks back at her.

"Jack," she says, and she rests her head against his chest, the rain hitting the umbrella, his feet wet, the leaves tumbling along.

"You'll get through this," he tells her.

She holds the umbrella steady and stands on her tiptoes to kiss him.

Her lips feel like something he'd forgotten. Something right and warm and easy, and they kiss and kiss, his hand squeezing hers as the wind gets under the umbrella and lifts it for a second.

He imagines them floating away together.

She pulls him against her. "In the Jeep," she whispers, and he knows what she means because this isn't the first time she's said this to him. She's pulling the door open now, and inching her way inside. The dome light on the Jeep's ceiling is like their small sun, and the car is their planet, and Jack closes the umbrella, and drops it in the driveway, and the light is still on them as he shuts the door and lets their world turn dark.

—

When Thanksgiving ends, Black Friday brings enthusiastic shoppers to the outlets on Route 1 where they stand in long lines at J.Crew and Le Creuset, and downtown Rehoboth transforms into a holiday scene. Almost every business sees an influx of shoppers throughout December, and merchants offer hot apple cider and Christmas cookies, the smell of a pine candle or simmering oranges and cranberries greeting eager customers. Every tree and shrub along Rehoboth Avenue is covered in red and green and white lights, and by the bandstand is a towering tree, which gets lit up after a few rounds of carols by the mayor and townspeople.

On the boardwalk, appearing seemingly out of thin air one day, is Santa's house, and he keeps regular hours when children can visit. Up and down the boardwalk are glowing displays of dolphins and starfish and turtles, and every weekend, the town offers horse-drawn carriage rides. The holidays are a magical time, and even on an idle Wednesday, you will see a customer leaving Green Awning Books, a new novel under her arm, a gingerbread latte in her hand, smiling like she's found her way into a Hallmark movie.

—That's Rehoboth Beach: A Guidebook

SEVENTEEN

Vivian gets to the restaurant first, and Jack nods to her and then looks puzzled as she punches her code to clock in. "You're off today, I thought."

"I was," she says, and scowls. "But my sister's a crazy bitch, and she messed up me and my friends' Black Friday plans. I don't want to get into it." Vivian's dark eyeliner makes her look even more intense. "*So* I thought you could use me." She doesn't wait for Jack's response and finishes her PIN, and she is on the clock.

Jack shrugs. "Sure, I can."

She looks at him and seems about to say something, but then changes course. He wonders if he somehow looks different after last night and feels his face redden. He clears his throat and unwraps a cough drop.

"Is Saul in today?" she asks.

"I think so. How come?"

"Just wondering." She smooths her lip gloss. "How's Ma?"

He holds out his arms. "Your guess is as good as mine. I'm hoping no news is good news."

She twists her hair into a tight bun. "Was this shit Ziggy-related? He's such a scumbag." She narrows her eyes. "I'd really like to hammer him for all the misery he's caused Ma."

"He's her son," Jack says, "And we don't know what he's been dealing with."

Vivian rolls her eyes. "Please. If he hurts sweet Genevieve, he should pay."

—

Things are already getting busy around 11:30, and Jack helps Vincent with a tub of dishes he's just cleared because a couple of the bussers are out. Vincent had shoulder surgery in late summer, and Jack still doesn't like for him to strain too much.

"Thanks, sir," he says, and wipes off a table. "Going to the tree lighting tonight?" he asks. Jack hears him, but doesn't answer right away.

"Probably not," he says finally, and Vincent goes to check the condition of the bathrooms.

He's thinking about Kitty and the back seat of his Jeep and how her body felt exactly the same as he remembered, even if he's too old for a back seat anymore, his hips and elbows hurting. He's wondering what this all means. They didn't talk afterward. She just kissed Jack goodbye, picked up her umbrella, and walked back to the house.

He's holding the heavy bin of dishes and lost in thought when Sam is behind him—he moves more quietly than anyone Jack knows—tapping him on the shoulder. "Mr. Schmidt," he says, and Jack turns.

"Yeah, buddy?"

Sam looks nervous. He often does. Jack never asks him if things are okay at home. He knows at one point Sam was taking classes at the community college, but doesn't know if he still is.

Sam is clenching his teeth, about to talk, and Jack wants to punch anyone who ever bullied him. Jack charged out one time and stood nearby when he heard some dicks making fun of Sam's high voice, but Jack probably didn't go far enough to look out for him. *You're not the god watching over the ship*, his dad used to say. *You're just the captain, trying to steer it safely.*

Sam takes a deep breath now. "Genevieve's . . . son is here," he finally says. "I think he's drunk or something."

—

Ziggy is standing by the coat room, peering inside. He's tall and lean with his head shaved, cuts and bruises on his arm, and a black T-shirt that says Action Park. It's faint, but Jack can still see a flicker of the young boy who would have done anything for a puppy. Jack can smell the booze from this far away, and as he gets closer, he can see Vivian coming out of the bathroom, drying her hands on a paper towel.

"The hell are you doing here?" she says.

Jack puts his hands out. "All right, let's keep it down."

Ziggy sneers. "Who are you?"

"Your worst nightmare," she says, and she reaches into her pocket.

Jack puts a hand on her arm. "It's okay, Vivian."

She glares and doesn't move. "We'll see."

"*Jack Schmidt*," Ziggy says, and reaches out like he's going to hug him, stumbling.

Jack takes a deep breath. He tries to summon his dad, who could charm anyone and de-escalate any situation. All these years he has felt a pull to Ziggy's pain, a parallel connection. But this guy, this version of Ziggy, is never what he pictures. "Ziggy, good to see you. Been awhile."

His eyes are bloodshot, his pupils dilated. He is anxious, his foot tapping, his hand shaking a container of Tic Tacs. He starts scratching his arms. "Definitely has." He takes a deep breath. "Is, uh, my mom here?"

Jack shakes his head. "She's not, sorry."

He groans. "Gimme a break," he slurs. "She's *always* here."

Something about Ziggy's tone breaks Jack's heart. He looks terrible standing here, and Jack imagines the young boy saying his mom's always gone. Jack realizes he's clenching his teeth. He wants to say, *She's not here because of you, because she went to the hospital, because she's falling apart over you*. "She wasn't feeling well yesterday." He clears his throat. *After you stole her car.*

"I need to talk to her. It's an emergency." Ziggy shakes his head and raises his voice. "My sisters are no help." He blows out air. "And I'm sick of their lectures."

Jack sees some customers watching them and takes a step toward Ziggy, trying to quiet his voice so he'll get the picture. "I think you'd better leave, Ziggy. She's not here, and you look like you need to cool down."

He shakes his head. "Who the hell are you, Gordon Ramsay?" He chuckles at his own joke, looks down at Jack's Crocs and starts laughing harder, then stops. "If she's not here then where is she?"

Jack sees uneasiness on a few customers' faces. He waves his hand at them and tries to appear jovial. "It's time for you to go, man." He grips Ziggy's shoulder to lead him out. Ziggy jerks back and throws his arms up. The Tic Tacs make an exaggerated crash as they hit the floor.

Jack hears Sam say something about calling the police, and Vivian shushes him.

"Keep your hands off me," Ziggy says. "I just want to see my mother!"

Jack looks him in the eyes. "She's not *here*," he says, and points to the door. "Leave. Now. Or I'll call the cops." He motions for Sam, and Sam marches dutifully to his podium.

"Where. Is. She?" Ziggy is loud and forceful now, and in that second Jack imagines having to subdue him until the cops come. Would he be able to? Once they had a drunk guy who tossed his barstool and broke three liquor bottles. Jack had to pin him down and sit on him, one arm braced behind his back.

Vivian holds a pepper spray straight out. "Yo, piss hole. You want this in your eyes and mouth, or you want to listen to what my boss is saying?"

Ziggy holds up his hands and glares at her. "I'm going," he says. He looks back at them one more time and smiles, a smile so crooked that it unsettles Jack. He opens the door. "Shame about *your* mom, Jack," he whispers, and laughs, and Jack feels something bubbling inside him that's full of surprise and rage, so raw and real that he needs to head back to his office so he doesn't go after Ziggy and rip him to pieces. *It's the drugs talking. It's not him. It's not him.* He nods to the customers with a fake smile and keeps inhaling and exhaling as he closes the door.

—

A little while later, he calls Genevieve's daughter, Rose, and she answers. "Just got my mom home," she says. She tells Jack about what the doctors said, about how Genevieve needs to take it easy.

"You're at her house?"

"Yeah, we're getting settled." She coughs. "He seems long gone."

"Not true," Jack says, and tells her about the visit. "I'd take her somewhere else right away."

"Shit," she says, and Jack hears her breathe nervously. "Okay, I'll call my friend. She has an empty rental. We can go there for a few days." She pauses. "Sorry he bothered you, Mr. Schmidt."

"I just want to make sure your mom's all right," Jack says. He tells her he filed a police report, and they said Ziggy is on their radar, said he's usually nonviolent, but they will try to find him. Rose said he has a few trials coming up. For theft. Possession of controlled substances. Bad checks.

"I wish I could help him," she says. "He really was the sweetest kid." She sighs. "You know, a friend of mine is a nurse, and she told me once she thought Ziggy had something like prolonged grief disorder after my dad died. Or maybe more like PTSD." She blows air into the phone. "He used to set up that tent they slept in and sit in it by himself like he was waiting for my dad to come back. If we'd try to sit in there with him, he'd holler until we left. My friend said he probably started with the opioids and all that to self-medicate and shut out the pain." Jack hears her gathering some stuff. "It breaks my heart," she says. "I wish we could have reached him in time. He was our baby. All of our baby."

"It's hard to know what someone's feeling if they won't tell you," Jack says.

EIGHTEEN

1989

Alexis was right. He did run into her again. He was in line at the post office, and she was mailing a package. He got her number that time—she used the pen on the chain and wrote it on a change-of-address card.

Maybe because it was summer, maybe because they could only see each other every few days between Jack's shifts at the restaurant, maybe because she was heading back to USC soon to finish up college and start applying to dental schools, everything they did was fast.

They went to the boardwalk, the Delaware State Fair, and the bay, watching sailboats and Jet Skis on sparkling water. They went fishing off the pier. They took the ferry to Cape May and back, playing Go Fish at one of the tables near the snack bar as the boat slowly crept toward the opposite side.

She had Jack over for dinner at her aunt's house in North Shores, Aunt Grace making penne alla vodka and a big salad, and they walked on the private beach afterward, just Alexis and him, watching the sun sink lower behind the house.

Jack was surprised at how urgent her hand felt, how she kissed him the minute the light was gone, how they settled themselves in the sand, watching the moon over the ocean, the gentle waves breaking into whitecaps and glowing, and they couldn't stop. They had gotten close other nights—kissing in his Jeep, her hand on his leg at the movies—but this night was raw, magnetic.

He placed his hands on her waist, and she leaned into his touch. They felt limitless on that giant beach, no one else around, and she yanked Jack closer and closer, lying back, him over her, the faraway glow of the boardwalk rides and bandstand in the distance.

Jack didn't tell her he'd never gotten this far with a girl. He'd done every other imaginable thing, but never this. He had spent the last couple of years feeling like a failure when all his friends, Deacon included, had lost their virginity, and now his moment was here. And it was with a girl he might love.

On earlier dates, when they kissed, he would seize up having someone so close to him. But this felt easy now, maybe because the air was warm and the beach was dark, and they kissed and kissed. She coaxed him, and he pushed himself closer, as though he could move through her, and they stayed there like that, their bodies sinking into the sand, the ocean their tempo, every star above them like dreams they were still young enough to have.

—

They had at least a dozen nights like that, perfect nights he always hoped to repeat. And they did. He couldn't believe his luck. They would eat dinner, help her aunt clear the plates, Alexis looking at him and sticking her tongue out playfully while she dried a wineglass, him putting a platter up on a high shelf Aunt Grace couldn't reach. Outside, the sun would start to fade, and he knew they'd have one of their walks.

Sometimes they were reckless. Jack wanted to risk everything for her. It felt like what he imagined a good drug to feel like. In the dark, the wide open ocean in front of them, everything was okay.

In mid-August, Alexis showed up at the restaurant, and Jack's grandmother was excited to meet her. "You're the future dentist," she said, and stood with her perfect posture and held out her hand.

"We'll see," Alexis said in a disinterested way, tucking a strand of hair behind her ear and not meeting Hazel's eyes.

"Any plans tonight?" Hazel asked, and smiled. Alexis shrugged, and his grandmother picked up a stack of menus and walked away. Jack felt his smile flatten.

"Hey," he said.

"It hasn't come yet," she blurted out. Those big brown eyes of hers were shattered. He knew exactly what she was talking about.

"It will," he said. What the hell did he know? His mom had been gone for years. He didn't have a sister. "It's probably just . . . a glitch."

She got so pale, and started to walk out of the restaurant. He hurried after her. "Hey," he called.

"What if I am?"

"You're not."

"I'm always regular." Her whole body shook. "I'm always on time. Always. Now I'm over a week late?"

Jack wondered if anyone from the restaurant was watching them. He wanted to reach out and hold her face in his hands, but all of a sudden he felt like she hated him. "You're just stressed."

"I can't have a baby," she said. "What am I going to fucking do?"

"I can't either." Wrong thing to say, but he didn't want her to feel alone. "Do you want me to get a test?"

She stared at his face. Almost in disbelief. "No," she said, and started to walk away. "Because then it'll be real."

NINETEEN

Kitty showed up at the restaurant the Monday after Thanksgiving, looking exhausted. "It won't be long," she told Jack, and he pulled her to him as they stood in his office.

"I'm so sorry," he said, and she told him she was just at the pharmacy and needed to get back home because the nurse could only stay until one.

"I'll come after work. Want anything? Soup, cheesecake?"

She shook her head. "Nope," she said, and looked dejected. "I just don't want the next few days."

—

Deacon and Jack have this tradition once a week or so. When Deacon goes to see his mom in Pine Creek, Jack drives him and waits in the car, and then they do some quick errand afterward like taking their watches to get new batteries or buying new toothbrushes from Walmart or running Jack's Jeep through the car wash.

On their way to Pine Creek this time, Jack sees a billboard for a new place where you can throw axes on Route 1, just behind the bowling alley and video arcade. He imagines holding the sturdy wooden handle, arching it behind his back and finally flinging it and watching it soar, the blade landing and sticking in the target.

Today the sun is bright, and the wind pummels the car as Jack waits for Deacon. He scrolls through social media posts on his phone, and finally puts it down.

He lies back for a few minutes and listens to the peaceful sound of the car running, the heat blowing in the vents, and then he looks at the awning of Pine Creek, where Evelyn has been for almost a year. At one point, Carl was going to get them an apartment there together, but Evelyn got very bad very quickly, and the caseworker recommended he stay where he was for the time being. Evelyn needed around-the-clock supervision because she was often getting out of bed and wandering off.

The door opens now, and it's almost four o'clock, the sky getting dark. Deacon comes out, head down, hands in his pockets, and Jack turns off the radio and sits up. Deacon gets into the car, and Jack nods but doesn't ask him anything. Deacon sighs and puts his head back, his fists over his eyes. "Fuck, fuck, fuck," he says, like he often does.

"Sucks, man."

He shakes his head. "It's like she's trapped inside there somewhere." He sits up and grips the dashboard. "Do you know what she said today?" He composes his face and sucks his teeth for a second. "She said I *scared* her." He breathes out. "Just a little, she said."

Jack's about to say that's not her talking, don't let it bother you, and so on, but Jack knows he knows all this, and just has to let him talk. "Man," Jack says, just so Deacon knows he's listening. A van pulls into the circular driveway and drops some people off at the entrance—maybe a day trip somewhere: shopping, or the casino. One old woman sits down on the bench by the door and lights up a cigarette. Jack watches the small flame, the glow of the ember.

He thinks for a second of his own mother and wonders what

she'd be doing if she'd lived to this age. He flicks a piece of lint from the steering wheel and looks over at Deacon again.

"I said *I'm your son*," he says. "And she looked at me so blankly, dude, like she was seeing me for the first time." He puts his hands over his face again and groans. "She said *I hope not*," he whispers, and quickly wipes his eyes. "Fuuuuck," he says, and Jack looks away as his friend opens the glove compartment and finds a napkin.

Jack pulls out of the parking lot and heads down the country back roads that will lead them to Route 1. The field to their left has fresh mow lines and mulched leaves that look like brown and red confetti. They pass mostly dead crepe myrtle trees, and tall straggly shrubs of holly. Deacon stays crouched, and Jack wants to pat his back.

"Let's go throw an ax," Jack says finally, and Deacon looks over at him and lifts one eyebrow.

TWENTY

Janet's funeral is on December 1, the day after Genevieve returned to work and said she didn't want to talk about anything. She had her car back, but she didn't say how. From what Jack got from Rose, the cops had been to the house several times and were still looking for Ziggy.

Jack asked Genevieve the day of the funeral if she could cover for him most of the morning and into the afternoon, and she finally made eye contact with him. "After all these years, you still think you have to ask?" she said, and she went back to expertly pressing her rolling pin into the dough.

It is unbelievably cold on the day of the funeral, which feels right. Necessary, almost. The grass is frozen, and the birch trees are bald and still, reaching into an empty sky. Geese honk and murmur above Jack as he lets his car warm up.

—

Not many people come to the funeral home, and Jack is relieved his black suit still fits. He bought a tie yesterday at Murphy's Fine Clothes in town, an old men's store that's been there since his grandmother's time. It was where Jack got his tuxedo for prom, where he had a suit tailored when he thought he and Kitty were engaged.

Deacon and Andie come to the viewing, Evie babbling on Deacon's lap and every so often nudging her wet giraffe at Jack. "Thank you," Jack keeps whispering, three rows back from Kitty and her sister Ray-Ray and Janet's two brothers who look like old twins.

When the pallbearers, mostly people Jack's age, cousins of Kitty's and guys who worked in her father's hardware store, lead the casket out after a few brief words from the minister, Deacon squeezes Jack's knee. "We're going to head out, bro," he says. "You'll be okay?"

"Oh, yeah." Jack nods and smiles at Andie. He bends down and kisses Evie's little hand. "I'll just go to the cemetery and then back to the restaurant. I won't stay for the family luncheon. It'd be weird."

"Don't think it'd be *too* weird," Deacon whispers, and winks, and Andie nudges him.

"I'm sure Kitty is glad you two came," Jack says. "See you this weekend maybe?"

"We'll be at the Harris party at the restaurant on Saturday," Andie whispers. "So we'll definitely see you."

"That's right," Jack says, and dread creeps over him: all these holiday parties in the next few weeks—so much preparation and planning, so many details that the hosts always want to get right: the colors of the tablecloth, the open bar, the music. Holiday parties are damn good money, but they bother Jack in a way that a regular night doesn't. Maybe because everyone always looks like they've been somewhere extraordinary before the party, and are heading somewhere good after. Schmidt's isn't fancy, but people still show up in nice plaid sports jackets and good dresses and skirts, a sprig of holly on their sweaters. Jack always feels outside of everyone else, sidelined while the world rockets past him like those geese over his head earlier.

He thinks of that blue beach chair that Janet saw him buy, the one he never told anyone else about. He watches them bring her casket by and he sees Kitty tremble, her sister's hand on her back, a tissue balled in her hand. Deacon and Andie and Evie stand beside him as he watches them wheel the shiny wooden casket out, a spray of white lilies and snapdragons on it. Jack can't think of any other way to feel, except lost.

—

He stands in the back at the cemetery, and Kitty and her family sit in the half dozen chairs in their wool coats. People huddle together as the wind blows, and Jack thinks of Janet, who had so much life in her. It all seems too brief, and when everyone throws their flowers onto the casket and the crowd breaks up, Jack makes his way to Kitty.

"Jack," she says, and hugs him. "I was hoping you were still here."

"I didn't want to intrude," he says. He wishes he'd brought sunglasses now, as he has to squint to see her in the bright day.

She wipes her face and nods. "I keep thinking how much she loved the summer," she says. "The pool, the beach, the porch. She'd be in that damn pool from May until October. Warm Novembers sometimes." She sighs. "Winter wasn't her style."

"Your dad called her a snowbird," he says, and gives her half a smile.

She looks over at the stone and stares at their names. "Well, now they're together again, huh? She hated that her name was on here to begin with, like it was waiting for her."

"I'd hate that, too."

"I'm glad you got to see her, Jack." She looks so clearly into his eyes, and Jack knows what she feels, and thinks for a second maybe they can mend everything and find their way back together, like Janet suggested. "I'm so glad you've been here."

"Hey, Jack," Ray-Ray says, before he can reply to Kitty. "Sorry, sis, but I'm freezing. We gotta bolt."

Kitty looks around and hugs her arms to herself, as if she just realizes it's cold. "Come to Marco's?" she says to Jack, raising her eyebrows.

Jack wants to say no. He just wants to return to his restaurant and pour himself a big glass of ginger ale or cranberry juice or even vodka and close his door and not think about anything, but Kitty looks so hopeful that he can't bear to break her heart. "Sure," he says, and watches them walk to the limo.

Did she say Marco's? He shakes his head.

A goddamned DelDine restaurant.

TWENTY-ONE

1989

It was real.

He and Alexis went into the A&P three towns away to get a test, his hand shaking as he paid for it.

Her aunt was at bridge club, so they went to her big empty house, the ocean outside the French doors, a few elementary school kids with their sand buckets dumping pails full of water into a pit they were making, their nanny watching and calling out encouragement.

He felt so far away from the present world, a numbness he'd only known when his dad told him his mom wasn't like other moms, that she needed help.

He remembers his mom's last day at home, hugging her before he left for school. She patted him on the back and kissed his head, and he got on the bus. He can still hear the school bus brakes that day, squeaking. Can still hear the mechanical opening and closing of the bus door at every stop. Can still remember it was foggy and he wanted school to be canceled so he could go home and help her be okay. He could feel so clearly that she was unraveling.

He looked at the bag, the box with the pregnancy test. Alexis took it from him, and he held the white receipt, smudging the ink with his damp fingers.

He followed her when she headed into the small powder room

downstairs, the mirror shaped like a seashell, the expensive hand towels with sand dollars on them. He stood in the doorway, and Alexis glared at him. "I've got this." She closed the door in his face.

He waited out in the hallway, the afternoon sun streaking across the big staircase. He looked at the marble floor and stepped from grout line to grout line, whispering a silent prayer that they wouldn't be cursed with a baby.

They were too young.

They had too much in front of them. She was going back to USC in a week, and the only thing they were supposed to worry about was calling each other from a college payphone, maybe making plans to meet up during winter break.

Everything was so serious now, and she no longer looked at him like she enjoyed his company. A baby? How could there be a baby? How were they even capable of that?

"Three minutes," she said as she came out, the box bent in her hand. "We'll have to throw this away at a gas station or something."

Jack nodded, and that plan made him feel good. That they'd have a future beyond this moment, a future where things were okay and they'd breathe a sigh of relief and pump gas into his Jeep, the doors off, them laughing and relieved that it was just a scare, not the real thing. Because what could they ever do with a real thing?

TWENTY-TWO

The first person Jack sees when he steps into Marco's is Nicole.

Marco's is on the other side of town from Schmidt's, two blocks from the ocean. It has its own parking lot, which makes it supremely valuable as far as real estate goes, and it's been designed to look like an old New York Italian restaurant with breadsticks in cups on red-checkered tablecloths and penny round tiled floors.

The servers wear vests and white shirts and ties, but to Jack, it feels like an Olive Garden that's trying too hard.

"Well, look who it is," Nicole says, handing two appetizers off to a food runner and wiping her hands on her pants. "You here for the Applebaum funeral?" She's wearing the same outfit again (does she have ten of the same sweaters and pants?). Before Jack can respond, one of the other managers rushes up and whispers something to her urgently.

Nicole moves her head back and forth as she listens, and finally looks at the younger woman and says, "Huh."

"Huh?" the woman repeats. Her hair is pulled into a tight braid, and her eyes are serious. Jack can tell she wanted a better answer.

Nicole shrugs. "Yeah, no idea." She chews her lip and the woman looks speechless. "Let me just catch up with my buddy, Mr. Schmidt here, 'kay?"

The manager almost rolls her eyes and trudges away. "If you need to . . ." Jack says, and gestures.

Nicole seems to have already forgotten about the manager. She waves her hand. "*Drama is for Mama*, I always tell them," Nicole says.

She clasps her hands in front of her, then motions toward the back of the restaurant where Jack sees an arched doorway next to two shiny Gents and Ladies gold bathroom doors. "Your party's in the Azienda Vinicola room. Our best, of course." Her glasses slide down her nose, and she reaches up and plucks them off, clipping them onto her sweater collar. "So sorry about Mrs. Applebaum. She came here a lot for lunch, always brought a book with her."

"I wondered why they chose this place," Jack says.

"And not yours," she says, and makes a finger gun at him with a gentle exploding sound.

"Kind of." Jack gives her a patient smile.

Someone walks by then, and Jack doesn't even think Nicole's looking at the person, but without turning her head, she says, "Layla, darling. Use a *tray*, please."

"Sorry," the woman says, and marches back to the kitchen.

"No wonder you sneak out for coffee," Jack says.

"I'd sneak out for booze, but they'd find me on the floor of the Lucky Toad, and that wouldn't be good for business." She pulls out a barstool and slouches against it. Kitty's uncle and aunt walk by, and Jack nods at them.

"Well, I should, um, head back."

"What are you doing later?" Nicole says.

Jack slides out of his suit jacket and drapes it over his arm. He realizes how cold it was outside, how his fingers and face are adjusting to the warmth in this place. He hears Dean Martin playing softly in the background. "Heading back to the restaurant. Busy for the next few weeks."

"Oh."

"How come?"

She shrugs, signing a form without looking at it that the bartender slides in front of her. "I was going to suggest coffee or something."

Jack sees Kitty now, her hand on the shoulder of an older woman he doesn't recognize. He sees Ray-Ray telling an exaggerated story in the room and the buffet setup behind her, a large bowl of salad, shrimp, and oysters on ice. "I still don't know about the sale," Jack says. "I have nothing to add to that discussion, unfortunately."

She puts her glasses back on her face, finger smudges all over the lenses. "Who's talking about the sale?" she says.

—

Kitty has saved a seat for Jack, and he makes a plate for her, not sure if she wants manicotti or not, not sure if she still barely puts any dressing on her salad or if she uses more these days. When he gets back to the table, one of her uncles is in his seat, and he's showing Kitty photos on his phone. Jack puts her plate down, stands there for a bit, and then goes and sits by Ray-Ray at another table.

Ray-Ray has tattoos on her hands, and her eyes are red. "Sit, sit," she says. "Pull up a memory." She holds up her Jack Daniel's and ginger ale for a second and takes a sip. The other people at the table, mostly Kitty's old friends from work, smile at Jack.

Jack moves her leopard clutch out of the way and puts his plate down. He pours himself a glass of white wine from the curved glass decanter in the middle of the table. "This is the trouble table," he says, and gives a weak smile.

"Thanks for coming today, Jack. My mom would've been so happy." She does her mom's voice, the same way Kitty used to do it. "Jaaaackkkkk," she says, and bats her eyelashes.

"She was so proud of you," Jack tells her. "Every time I saw her in town, she gave me an update. You playing in Denver with someone related to Sting or something, and someone you were dating who had pretty eyes but didn't treat you the way she should. I heard about all your awards." Jack stabs some of the beet and apple salad on his plate. "Everyone around here was impressed."

Ray-Ray takes a sip of her drink. "Shit," she says, and sniffles. "Just when I think I've cried the last time."

Jack gulps some water. "Ray, if you ever need anything . . ."

"Thanks," she says, and they both look over in Kitty's direction. "The uncle show has moved on. Should we go join Marcia?"

Ray-Ray calls Kitty Marcia after Marcia Brady because she thinks of her as the perfect one, the older and more together sister. Jack starts to stand up, and Ray-Ray touches his arm. "Are you two finding your way back to each other?"

Jack shrugs. "Who knows." Being in a restaurant makes him worry about Genevieve and everyone else. He should get back there. What the hell is he still doing here in this suit? He looks at how efficiently this place is run, how under a trance all the employees seem, and he can't imagine his staff orbiting in this way. It's too sterile or something. "It's nice to reconnect with her," he finally says. Inappropriate at a funeral luncheon, but he thinks of the way their mouths and bodies felt against each other's, the way she kept pulling him closer the other night in his car. And the two times after that.

But he and Kitty haven't talked about anything. "Who knows," he says again.

—

He doesn't even register it, but Kitty has her arm through his as they're leaving the restaurant, so many people offering her condolences, and it's like over the last few hours, he's gone from sitting at the back of the funeral home to being her fiancé again. "I'm so glad you've been here," she says as they walk out, and she's holding the bill for the restaurant in its black check holder.

"I can cover this," Jack tells her, taking out his wallet.

She shakes her head. "My mom had a funeral account with precise instructions."

"All set?" someone says, and Jack sees it's Nicole. For some reason, he feels his ears get hot, his cheeks get red. She looks at Jack and nods.

"Yep," Kitty says, and hands her a credit card. "It was lovely. My mom would be so pleased."

Nicole smiles. "She was our best customer," she says. "Let me just go run this." She heads over to one of the point-of-sale stations.

"Do you know that woman?" Kitty whispers.

"Yeah," Jack says. He's just about to tell her that she's the one who's trying to persuade him to sell Schmidt's, but he doesn't feel like sharing that today. Maybe because it's her mother's funeral and she's exhausted. Or maybe for another reason. "Her name's Nicole," is all he offers.

"Strange bird," Kitty says.

"You think?"

Kitty looks at him and grimaces, and now Nicole's coming back, her glasses on top of her head, a noticeable black smudge on her cream-colored sweater. She looks down. "Damn ink," she says, and hands the credit card, pen, and the receipt pinned to a little clipboard back to Kitty. "Thank you very much for your business, and from all of us at Marco's and DelDine, we're so sorry about Mrs. Applebaum." She looks toward the dining room. "I can still see her sitting over there, a Mary Higgins Clark or John Grisham novel in her hands. And always three beverages: tea, water, and some Scotch."

"Sounds like her." Kitty laughs and signs her name. Jack can't help but hope she's leaving a good tip. "Here you go then."

"Many thanks," Nicole says.

"Thanks," Jack says to Nicole, and she gives him a professional nod.

He waits for her to ask him about coffee again—nervous that Kitty will be annoyed by it; or worries Nicole will spill the beans about the restaurant sale, but she just holds the clipboard in front of her, clasping her hands and smiling . . . not really a smile but a polite squint. Kitty's arm holds Jack's, and he nods to Nicole without knowing why he feels bad as they walk out.

TWENTY-THREE

That night, he pulls up to Kitty's house, and Ray-Ray's car is there. Kitty's in the living room going through some drawers below the China cabinet. She has vases and small crystal bowls and a pile of tablecloths all around her. "Hey," he says, bringing in a big tomato pie from Steelo's in town. "I didn't know if you guys were hungry."

"Thoughtful," Kitty says, and smiles.

Ray-Ray is drinking wine and listening to some of their father's records. Earl Thomas Conley is playing. She comes over to Jack and takes the pizza from his hands. She smiles pleasantly, her eyes puffy. Jack forgets sometimes she's almost forty. She was always Kitty's little sister, just back from college or touring Rome or London.

"The records are all yours," Kitty calls over to her. "Take them with you next week."

"Do you have to do that now?" Ray-Ray says, and rolls her eyes. "And what do you mean *next week*?" She opens the tomato pie and selects a corner piece. "I'm leaving tomorrow."

Jack looks at the two of them and waits for Janet to appear to smooth things over the way she always did. Jack sees her reading glasses on the hutch, her purse and the pile of condolence cards next to them, and he feels like they've been abandoned.

Kitty stands now, holding something that looks like a bookend: a wooden ship. "*Tomorrow?*"

"Yeah. I have to get moving. We start a new gig next week, and we're booked up through New Year's." She bites into her pizza and licks her fingers.

Jack's stomach does a small flip. He watches Ray-Ray pour more wine, and Kitty holds her bookend as though she's about to sail it across an imaginary sea.

Kitty shakes her head. "Fucking ridiculous."

"Is there more of that wine?" Jack says, and no one answers.

"What's ridiculous?" God, he'd forgotten how they used to fight. Janet could expertly redirect things, bring up a good piece of gossip that would get their attention.

"*This.*" Kitty gestures widely. "*This* all has to be done. Who's supposed to do it? Me, I guess."

Ray-Ray walks toward the kitchen. "What else are you doing?" she says under her breath, and Kitty's eyes widen. Jack hears Ray-Ray opening some cupboard doors, and stands next to Kitty. He wants to help her stay calm, but doesn't know what to say.

"Are you getting rid of those bookends?" he finally asks.

She sighs and hands him the small ship, and he goes and looks for its match.

—

That night, in her bed, Kitty wraps her arms around him so tightly that he almost can't breathe. She reaches her hand inside his shirt, and he doesn't move but she doesn't stop, so he finally starts kissing her. "I need you," she whispers, and she hugs him and cries against him, and then they are kissing again, and she keeps saying, "I need you, Jack."

—

She isn't in bed when he wakes up before six.

Just once, he would like a day where he doesn't have to be at the restaurant. But he also doesn't know what else he would do if he didn't have to go there and check the soda syrup levels and fill up plastic cups with cocktail sauce and salad dressing and keep replacing all the butter packets. Who else is he besides that restaurant?

His back hurts from Kitty's childhood mattress. He slips on jeans and a sweatshirt and walks past Ray-Ray's door, and it's quiet. The small clock Janet has in the upstairs hallway moves its pendulum back and forth. Jack looks at her bookcase with the giant fern on it, and he thinks that it needs to be watered, and the heat needs to be kept on this winter so the house doesn't freeze. Come April, the yard will need to be mowed and weeded, and the whole thing overwhelms him.

When his dad died, he felt such a relief when the house in town where Jack had grown up sold, the same way Johnny must've felt when he sold Jack's grandmother's ivy-covered colonial.

Jack finds Kitty sitting on the back sunporch with a space heater running. She holds a mug of coffee and stares out at the small backyard, barely lit by the early sun. Leaves are scattered everywhere from the cherry tree, and a little bunny hops by and hides in the boxwood. "Morning," Jack says, and she turns toward him.

"Hey." She seems so young in her flannel pajama pants. She has her hair in a bun, and she looks annoyed.

"I've got to get going," he says. He thinks he should really grab some coffee before he does. He could sit a few minutes with her.

"Yup, the restaurant," she says.

"What else?" He gives her a friendly smile, but her face doesn't change. He keeps thinking they need to have a talk. That he'll tell her he might sell the restaurant, and maybe she'll want to move back to Rehoboth like she said, or maybe he could go see what Oregon's like for a while.

"Do you love me, Jack?" she says, and he freezes. The bunny outside darts away, and the yard looks so still and ruined, as if spring will never set it right again.

TWENTY-FOUR

1989

Alexis had a friend named Courtney whom she worked with at the dental lab that summer. Courtney had gotten pregnant around Christmas from a guy she said was a psycho, and she told Alexis about a clinic not many people knew about.

Alexis stared out the windshield of Jack's car and didn't look at him. "Courtney said I'll be so relieved. She was." She sipped some tea from her Styrofoam to-go cup and told Jack Courtney could take her.

They had gone to a new café that was selling bagels, which were a rarity in Delaware. Jack's shirt had sesame seeds on it, and Alexis looked at her toasted cinnamon raisin and didn't seem to know what to do with it. He watched tourists come in and out of the bagel shop with big paper bags. He drank some of his orange juice, and he thought of the Hemingway story they read in his lit class last semester: "Hills Like White Elephants," about a couple at a train station deciding if they should get an abortion. Jack's professor told them they never say the word *abortion* in the story because it was taboo at the time, but Jack remembered how tense the dialogue was, and he felt like Alexis and he were living out the same scene. He remembered the man saying, "It's the only thing that's made us unhappy," and he wondered if this pregnancy was the thing that had ruined them, and once she had the procedure they could go back to what they were before. "I want to take you," he said. "It's something we need to do together."

She held her white plastic knife and started spreading cream cheese on her bagel. She shook her head and sighed and stuffed the bagel into its waxed paper. "I don't want you to," she finally said. The early morning sun peeked out behind the movie theater to their right, and up on a big ladder, someone changed the names of showings on the marquee.

He reached over and held her hand, and realized what strangers they were. Her hand felt rigid in his, like something that never really fit. There had been times this summer that he had told himself he could leave everything for her: college, the restaurant.

He'd imagined transferring to USC, and them getting an apartment. They had seemed like something that needed to last, a new song that he didn't want to stop listening to. But this news had made them strangers, and they weren't pulling together and figuring it out; they were like a broken sculpture that couldn't be glued.

He wondered how his parents had felt. His mom and dad weren't married when she got pregnant, and had only known each other for a couple of months. He wondered if they'd considered driving and driving and finding someplace that would get rid of their problem. He wanted this problem gone, but he knew no matter what, they wouldn't go back to their old selves. Her eyes had lost something when she looked at him, and the halo that seemed to be on them all summer—the halo of youth, of chance, of free nights in the sand—was extinguished. "I should be there," Jack said. "It's my fault, and it's not fair for you to have to go on your own."

"I won't be on my own. Courtney's coming. Remember?" She looked at him, her face free of makeup, her bangs in her eyes. "What are we even doing, Jack?"

For a second, he thought she meant about the baby. In his mind, he tried to imagine being a father. Working at the restaurant and holding a baby on his lap while he did the schedule or itemized food and labor on his dad's ledger pads. "I don't know," he said.

"We're not even a couple. We were just having fun." She looked irate. "And now this."

His stomach twisted. "And now this," he repeated. "I'm sorry." He paused. "We could . . ." But he didn't finish because he didn't know what to say. They could be a couple? They could try to have this baby? They could pretend this wasn't true and still have fun for a while? He kept thinking of that positive test: the blue liquid in the small tube. He couldn't even think about something growing in her that was part of them.

He just wanted them to hold their breath and have it gone. *It's the only thing that's made us unhappy.*

She looked down at her belly, and Jack did, too. She wore a navy hooded sweatshirt with a pocket in the middle, and he thought of the word *baby*. How absolutely odd that she and he, two kids, could make something viable. He wanted to pretend it didn't happen. "I'll take you and I'll pay for it," he said.

She shook her head. "Courtney knows the drill." She had a sad look on her face. "I think I should get home now."

TWENTY-FIVE

"I've always loved you," Jack tells Kitty. "I never stopped missing you."

She doesn't respond, and he stands there in the silence and hears his words echo in his head. He doesn't know where this awkwardness has come from, but maybe she's realized this isn't her home. In his heart, he felt like it would end sooner or later, and she'd want to get back to her new life. Wouldn't she? He walks to the kitchen to get coffee. When he comes back, she's biting her nails.

"I found out something last year, Jack, and it was wrong not to tell you." He can see the regret on her face, and his chest feels tight. He almost feels sick because she looks that upset. She puts her coffee down and walks toward him.

"Kitty, you don't have to tell me," he says. He gets a familiar feeling from when he was young and his dad told him something about his mom. He remembers how he always wanted to wrap up bad news in insulation and stow it away somewhere he couldn't feel it. His throat tightens.

He wants to leave. He doesn't want to hear whatever she has to say. He wants the hum of the restaurant refrigerator, he wants Vivian to come in loudly, snapping her gum. He wants the sizzle of the grill, the customers smiling as he unlocks the front door and they file in. He wants to feel settled, watching Genevieve flour the stainless counter. His heart races. "You've had a rough couple days, and you're tired."

He doesn't know why he's so worried, but her expression is one he's never seen. It makes him want to pass out. She looks like she's about to tell him the worst news.

"I'm sorry, Jack," she says, her face crumbling. "I'm sorry I didn't tell you sooner." She buries her head against his chest, and he can feel the wet warmth of her tears. "I'm so sorry."

"Tell me . . . *what*?" he says slowly. He looks at his coffee on the small table. He thinks about leaving it there and just driving away. He's dressed. He can just leave.

She shakes her head and doesn't say anything, just cries more. Jack wiggles free and holds her out in front of him. "*What*?" he says again.

She doesn't look him in the eyes. "She never did it," she finally says.

"*Who*?" The pressure in his head is too much. He wants a bottle of Advil. He wants Janet's Scotch. He wants to hear Paulette dumping ice into the beverage station, Sam turning on the music.

"That girl. That girl you were with. *Alexis*," she says carefully.

"What about her?"

And then he knows. Like a house collapsing, brick by brick, on top of him. Like a hammer to his ribs. Now his knees are nothing—just wobbly and unsteady. His ears are ringing. This never entered his mind. The possibility—never once.

She says the words Jack knows are coming. It feels so clear all of a sudden, like in some way he already knew. And his head is like a piñata that's been busted open.

"She never had the abortion," she says, and Jack can't tell if he's sitting or standing.

—

That night on I-95 with his dad, he doesn't remember how it ended. Life is like that.

You felt stuck for so long it seemed impossible, and then all of a sudden, the cars started up one after another like the items clicking to life in the Mouse Trap game, and they all just crept away.

They were stuck there, and then they weren't. The sky was gray, and his dad looked over at him and winked. *Told you.*

Jack remembers leaving the place their car had stayed still for so many hours. He remembers the feeling of his teeth unbrushed, his lips dry, his stomach half hungry, half full of white bread. He remembers watching the cars pull away, navigating around some that had been abandoned, the trash people had left on the side of the road, mostly wrappers, some soda cans, too.

He remembers almost feeling sad for a second that he'd never see that group of people again.

But they were out of it. They were out of it.

TWENTY-SIX

1989

On the day of the appointment, he dropped by her aunt's house after work. "Hello, dear," her aunt Grace said. "I'm afraid Alexis isn't feeling well, but she'll be glad to see you." She pointed upstairs. "She's been working too hard." She smiled, and there was something behind her eyes that looked like she might have known what they'd done, but he wasn't sure. He felt guilty.

And relieved.

He was relieved, definitely. They'd done the thing. They could move forward now.

He walked up the large staircase slowly, his hand holding on to the polished railing, and at the big window at the top of the stairs, he could see the ocean and cottony clouds in the sky. He thought of the little thing they'd made, gone before it became anything, and he felt awful in a way, but also, not.

He remembered sitting with his mother years ago and watching the news and seeing protesters at a clinic, and his mom shaking her head and saying, "Rich women have always had abortions available to them. It's just a few cells." She held a cigarette and blew the smoke in a slant. "Let these protestors pay for doctor's bills, school lunches. Let them help all the starving children who aren't loved." She had reached over and kissed Jack's head.

He got to the top step and was glad to return to his old dreams. He was too young. She was too young. They needed to be in better places, didn't they? What right would they have to bring a baby into their confusion?

"Hey," he said when he opened the door of her room. Not so long ago she was leading him into this bedroom when her aunt was at a benefit for the art league, and they were loud and wild in this bed. Now, the shades were pulled down, and Alexis looked pained. He imagined she had an ice pack across her middle, under the blanket.

Jack had brought her a small violet plant, and softly touched one of its fuzzy leaves.

He also had a quart of chicken rice soup from the restaurant, which seemed stupid, but he felt like he needed to give her something. He had money in an envelope, too, for the procedure.

She didn't sit up, and he put the violet on the nightstand. It looked weak, rumpled from the journey. "I love violets," she whispered, but she didn't look at him.

"And I brought soup." He didn't say anything about the envelope of cash. He waited for her to meet his eyes, but she wouldn't look at him. "You okay?" he said.

She took a breath. "I will be." A line of sun came into the room through the pulled shade and she put her hand up to shield her eyes. "I'm going back to California on Monday," she said.

"Already?" He'd forgotten summer was almost over. They had been so paralyzed by the pregnancy that he assumed once they'd done this, summer would be reset.

"It's time, Jack," she said. "Isn't it?"

He swallowed. "I don't want this to be over."

He stood closer to her and pushed the hair out of her eyes. He felt so unskilled, as though each step he took was making her hate him more. She could only see him now as the person who'd ruined her life. He put the soup down, the money down.

He wanted to hug her, to sit next to her, but it didn't feel right. They seemed to have lost any ounce of couplehood. He loved her. He thought he did. They were so close to being something limitless, but now the balloon had deflated. Had she wanted him to convince her to keep the baby? Had she thought ending it was a mistake?

He knew she insisted he not go with her, but all of a sudden, he felt he'd failed a test, he'd abandoned her when she needed him. Jack thought of the courage it took for her to get dressed that morning, to walk into that clinic and give them her name and answer the questions the nurse asked.

He thought of how she must have felt as they started the procedure, how she must feel now. He thought of the favor she did for him, she did for both of them, by taking care of this, and he felt so sad and empty.

"Does it hurt?" he finally asked.

She looked up at him and shook her head. "I just want to rest," she said, and turned away.

TWENTY-SEVEN

Kitty's eyes are wide. She keeps twisting her fingers together. *How? How could she know this? How the fuck could this even be?* Jack wonders.

He thinks about Janet. He wants her to be here. He wants her to tell him Kitty's not serious, she just had a bad night. None of this is true. It can't fucking be. He is sweating. From the coffee? He's so goddamn jittery.

He looks down at his arms, his feet. They aren't real. The floor looks wrong. The outside looks like a fake backdrop. He thinks about waking Ray-Ray. He feels like he needs a witness, like he's staring up at the sky and watching a UFO blink at him.

"What are you saying?" he asks slowly, and he is queasy. His forehead is clammy, and his hands shake. She tries to reach for him, but he jerks back. "Tell me," he says.

He can still see Alexis in bed that day at her aunt's house, and from that image, he always knew how someone looked and felt after having that procedure. Since that day, he was always so, so careful. He never wanted to hurt anyone like that again.

When Kitty doesn't answer, he starts rambling. "She *had* the abortion. I know she did. She was sick afterward. She was holding her middle, the place where it was."

He feels like some idiot on a soap opera. He is bad writing. Who the hell gets duped like this?

They had a problem, and they took care of it. *She* took care of it. She wanted Courtney to bring her. She wouldn't let him fucking come with her. What the hell was this?

Kitty shakes her head. "Last spring, I was visiting my mom, and I went to Ocean City with a bunch of friends. We did a pub crawl."

Jack takes a breath. "Okay." She bites her fingernail again. She looks down at her coffee and swirls it around.

"Well, Jeannie brought some friends from her new job, and one lady was named Courtney. We were drinking and laughing, talking about failed marriages, failed relationships, and I ended up talking about you and the restaurant." She is wiping her eyes now, and she sniffles. "Courtney said she knew you, that you and her friend Alexis were together one summer in college. She said it had to be the same guy.

"I said it's definitely the same guy, and I told her I'd heard about Alexis." She puts her hands to her face, and Jack can see she's trembling. He wants to comfort her, seeing her like this. He wants to tell her just to stop, to not say another word. She takes a deep breath. "I had had a lot of vodka, and I said I knew what happened with you two, and she got this weird look and didn't say anything. When we went to the next bar, some of the girls went to play darts, and Courtney bought us shots, and said, 'I know a secret about your guy that would wreck him.'" Kitty looks at Jack, and whispers, "I said he's not my guy anymore. And then she told me it never happened. It was just so weird I didn't know whether to believe her."

Jack shakes his head and sits down on the arm of the big chair. The space heater blowing its lukewarm air annoys him. He looks out at the yard, and he sees their pool covered up, leaves and acorns on top of the stretched blue vinyl. He sees the spot where Janet used to lie in her chaise longue, drinking her wine cooler. "She was making it up," he says, his stomach churning. "I don't know why. I didn't know her. Some sick joke."

"No," she says, getting up. "She said Alexis didn't have the abortion that day. She couldn't go through with it. She pretended she did. Courtney kept in touch with her. Alexis never said a word to anyone, just flew back to California and told her parents she was pregnant, told them she didn't know who the father was, and she, um, she *had* the baby, Jack."

His brain is a jumble of questions, but nothing makes sense. "Kitty, she did not." He holds his hand over his mouth. "There was never any baby." He realizes how hard he's breathing now. "It didn't *exist.*"

She stands in front of him, and the tears fall down her face. "I looked her up, and I found out. She did have a baby. April 1990. A boy."

She starts to sob. "I came home drunk that night, my head spinning, and I woke up the next day and wondered if it really happened. I was here for a few more days, and I kept telling myself that if I ran into you, I'd say something, but I didn't run into you. I kept thinking about it and thinking about it, but I didn't tell anyone: not my mom, not Andie. I buried it so it couldn't do any harm, I think. I just kept thinking it was so long ago, and you went all this time without knowing, maybe you didn't want to know." She is sobbing now. "I'm so sorry," she whispers.

His hand covers more and more of his mouth. He wants to disappear behind it. "Of course I'd want to *know*!" he whispers, his throat hurting. He sinks down. "I have a *son?*" He shakes his head. "No." Nothing adds up. He mentally counts the years, but he keeps getting stuck. It was so long ago. But a pang in his heart. An undeniable truth. "He's so old, and he never knew me."

"Unless maybe it's a mix-up. Maybe there was another guy, a little later or something," she says weakly.

His shoulders sag. "You were just waiting to run into me? You couldn't call me, text me? Anything? You *know* me, Kitty. We were together for a lifetime. You *know me.* You knew I'd want to know!" He has a flash of speaking to a counselor in high school. *You constantly expect to be let down.* The woman had said these words like they would be a comfort. Jack told his dad he never wanted to go back there. Now he takes another breath. He can't get a handle on this. It's like someone told him he's not real, that his life isn't real. He has a son who never knew him. Tears slip down his face. He shakes his head.

She cries. "It's been torturing me, Jack. The more time went by, I just couldn't tell you. It got worse and worse."

Jack nods. He is looking at her, but not seeing her. He tries to speak, but he can't think of any words.

"Say something," she whispers. "Please." Jack just stares through her. He doesn't want to yell at her the day after her mother's funeral, but he doesn't want to be near her anymore. He thinks of Alexis now, and wants to drive all the way to her house and beg her to tell him this isn't true.

A son. A son who never knew him.

Ray-Ray is standing in the doorway now in an oversized T-shirt and sweatpants. "What's going on?"

Jack shakes his head. "Nothing," he says, and walks past her. He grabs his coat and car keys.

"Jack," Kitty says, rushing after him. She reaches for his arm as he opens the front door.

"Please," he tells her, his voice loud for just that second, and he looks at her hand and then into her eyes, as if he's never known her in any way, as if she's a stranger now, and Kitty lets go.

TWENTY-EIGHT

When he gets home, his place is freezing cold, and Harry is crunching his food. Jack realizes his teeth are chattering as he stands in the middle of his dusty house.

He is scrolling through Google when he almost gasps. He finds her obituary. From last summer! "Alexis Johnson Hammersmith, 51, of Sacramento, California, and Henderson, Nevada."

Oh.

He can still see her in that bed, the look on her face like she'd lost everything. He had been so impressed with her courage.

His stomach is a pit of nothing, and he feels like he's in some bizarre dream. He kicks off his shoes, and the cold of the floorboards sinks into his socks.

I hate her. I loved her. She's dead. Alexis is dead.

Why? Why couldn't she have told him? Now she's gone and he can't ask her anything. They were young and happy for a few minutes, and she's nothing anymore. He only knew her as someone smart and beautiful with her whole life ahead of her, and now his heart aches for what they could have had.

> . . . survived by her husband of twenty years, Todd Hammersmith, and three children: Patrick Johnson, of

Newport, Rhode Island, Lara Hammersmith of Cape May, New Jersey, and Michael Hammersmith, of Elko, Nevada.

He reads it over and over. Reads how she had a dental practice in Sacramento for many years and then got her master's in school counseling, how she worked for ten years at a private school in Nevada. He reads about how donations can be made to the breast cancer society, how she was active in her local museum and library, how every year she organized the holiday tree lighting in their town.

He can't stop thinking about her. He wonders why she stopped being a dentist and became a counselor. Did she get burned out? He wonders where she met her husband and if they loved each other. He wonders why the move to Nevada, and if she was at peace with everything in her last year. He wonders when she first felt the lump in her breast. Did she know she was going to die, or was she sure she'd conquer this? "Alexis." He can't help but say her name. "Why?" Why did she do this without him? He feels lonely, left behind. A familiar, familiar feeling. He thinks of her plane landing in California. He thinks of all the times he thought about her over the years.

He lets his mind wander to the baby. Why didn't she go through with the abortion? Why didn't she tell him?

Patrick Johnson.

Jack says his name, and he googles it, but there are too many results.

He adds Newport, Rhode Island, and a LinkedIn profile comes up: Patrick Johnson, information security analyst. There on Jack's phone in a suit and tie is a guy with a sunburned face and dark hair. Jack pinches the screen to zoom in, and halts.

He has my mom's eyes, he thinks. *He has my mom's same exact green eyes.*

TWENTY-NINE

He doesn't go to the restaurant that day.

Genevieve covers for him, and he doesn't do anything but find out as much as he can about Patrick and Alexis. Sometimes he just sits in the silence of the house and thinks about calling Deacon and asking if he wants to throw an ax again. And then he thinks about calling Patrick at work and saying, "I have a crazy story for you." But he doesn't call anyone. He just stays in his chair.

Finally, he dials Nicole that night, and she answers on the first ring. "Well, hello," she says, a laugh in her voice. "What can I do for you, Jack Schmidt?"

Jack cradles his phone between his ear and shoulder, and paces back and forth in his kitchen. He picks up an apple and grabs a paring knife, slowly cutting the apple's skin away in one continuous red strip.

"I'm ready to sell," he tells her. "I'll sign the paperwork tomorrow."

—

As winter approaches, many of the boardwalk businesses operate on a nice-day policy, playing it by ear and deciding to open if the weather looks promising. If the sun is out and the crowds are decent, you might see Happy Cones open on an idle Wednesday in December, or Tony's Eats pry off the plywood and plug in their cash register on New Year's Day.

In this way, it seems Rehoboth Beach is a place that's never closed off to possibility, and winter is only as long as the span between when you last played Pac-Man at Zonk's. Steelo's Pizza and Green Awning Books are open 364 days a year, and no one in town lets their bike tires go flat because a bike ride is never more than a couple of weeks away.

Rehoboth is a place where all you need is one sunny day to make the magic of summer return.

—That's Rehoboth Beach: A Guidebook

THIRTY

Jack barely sleeps. Harry is across his legs, and he keeps folding his pillow trying to get comfortable. He mutes Kitty so her texts stop coming in, and he almost goes to a hotel because he's worried she'll come by. The night is long and still, and he hears an ambulance and a car backfire and something that sounds like a dog howling.

He finally gets up at six and stares out his back kitchen window at the ivy on the ground and the pine trees, the sunken picnic table he should replace. When his coffee finishes brewing, he sips it black and shakes his head.

He has to get to the restaurant, but he doesn't feel like he can do anything today. He picks up his phone and texts Genevieve.

Any chance you can open for me again? Just one more day.

A few minutes and nothing. Finally, *I'm sorry Jack, but I can't come in today. I'm very sorry.*

Are you okay?

He sees the three typing bubbles come up after a long pause. *No.*

He gulps the rest of his coffee, throws some clothes on, and grabs the restaurant keys and car keys. He calls Vivian as he walks to his car. She sounds groggy and pissed off. "Any chance you can open for me?" he says. "Genevieve doesn't seem right."

She groans. Pauses. Then groans again. "Yeah. But only because it's Ma." He hears a guy's voice in the background. "Not your business," she says to him.

Jack tells her he's leaving the keys in his mailbox. He goes over the procedure of the morning items, asks her to call Sam or Saul and one of them will probably come in to help her. He tells her he should be in before lunch. He hangs up and his phone's ringing.

"Where the hell are you?" Deacon says. "Second day in a row, no Jackpot."

"Sorry." He wipes his eyes and tries to focus. He starts his car, and it feels extra cold. "Um, Vivian's going to open."

"Why, you and Kitty having omelets in bed?"

"No," Jack says flatly. "Not even close." He can't believe Kitty hasn't told Andie about this.

"Oh."

"I'll call you later."

"Where are you?" he says. Jack hears Evie say something that sounds like *bubble.* He hears the wind through the phone.

"Driving to Genevieve's," Jack says.

Deacon clears his throat. "My phone's in my hand," he says. He always says this; it's one of Jack's favorite Deacon lines.

Jack hangs up and can picture Deacon standing outside the closed restaurant, holding Evie in her little fuzzy hat, the two of them just waiting there on the boardwalk like a postcard.

—

Genevieve lives about fifteen minutes from Rehoboth in an older development with nondescript homes and hardly any trees. Over the years, Jack has driven her home if her car was in the shop, or another time he came by when she had baked all the pies at her house because the restaurant oven she normally used was being repaired.

When he pulls up to her house now the screen door looks like someone kicked it in. Her car is there, the driver's door dented and smeared with red paint as though swiped by another car. Jack puts his hands into his pockets and tries to listen. It all seems quiet.

He walks up the concrete steps and through the broken porch door. He is about to knock when he hears her scream. Shit. He should really call the police. He has no skills to handle this. He puts his fist down and decides not to knock, decides to call someone, when the door swings open, and Ziggy is there, a gloating smile on his face.

"Ziggy, is everything all right?" Jack says.

"*Oh*," he says sneering, glancing back into the house. "You called boss man in for help."

"Ziggy, I'm just making sure your mom's okay." Jack rakes his hand through his hair and tries to look nonthreatening. "And you *too*, of course." He takes a breath. "Ziggy, I know you're a good guy, and all this, this isn't you, okay? How about you let someone help you?"

Ziggy blocks the door, but Jack peers past him. He can see Genevieve's face looks swollen. "She's fine," Ziggy says.

"Did you hit her?" Jack says, rage building that feels like it's coming from a hundred powerful turbines. Why has Genevieve let all this go on this long? How the hell can that ever be okay? Because when it's your own family, you keep hoping for the best. You live in disbelief and hope it passes. Something pulses through him then, maybe that he's running on fumes from no sleep last night, maybe Kitty's news, maybe his brain collapsing from not being able to make sense of any of this, but he's about to grab Ziggy by his shirt and jack him up against the wall, and he's barely ever been in a fight. *Ziggy lost someone, too. He lost someone, too. Think of the boy with the puppy. That sweet little kid.*

"She's fine," Ziggy says again, and he closes the door more, his long, lanky body wedged in the opening.

"Genevieve," Jack calls, and he pushes at the door and steps halfway inside.

"You're not listening, asshole," Ziggy says, and he pushes Jack's chest. Jack knows he should call the police.

He knows better.

"Let him in," Genevieve says, and she sounds humiliated.

"Your mother works so hard," Jack says. "And you make her deal with all this bullshit. You're better than this, man." Jack picks up his phone now, but Ziggy swipes it.

"Hey!" Jack reaches for it. "I'd think carefully."

Ziggy smiles and shakes his head. He holds it up in the air. "Say *please*," he says, a small drop of spit flying out with the *p*, and that's when Jack lunges at him.

He knocks into Ziggy so forcefully that the door swings open all the way, and Jack sees the house is a wreck. Broken picture frames everywhere, glasses and plates. It looks like someone threw the kitchen chairs against the wall, and the back door looks worse than the front.

"What the hell is going on here?" Jack says, but Genevieve is screaming, and Ziggy in one second has his arm against Jack's neck as he slams his knee into his stomach. "Ziggy, we can help you."

"Mind your business," Ziggy says, and he punches Jack in the mouth, Genevieve begging him to stop. The punch stings, and Jack feels like he could puke from the knee to the stomach. He imagines shredding Ziggy to pieces, but with Ziggy's arm on his neck he struggles to breathe.

"Call the police," Jack calls to Genevieve, gasping.

"*She* knows better," Ziggy says, and he looks back at her and smirks. Jack notices Genevieve's granddaughter peeking out of her bedroom.

"Close the door," Genevieve shrieks.

"Ziggy," Jack says, and he releases his arm for a second. Jack struggles for air. "Stop this shit. Please. You need help. Let us help you. You'll get yourself put away."

"You think so?" Ziggy says, and he pulls a knife from his pocket. Jack's stomach drops, and Genevieve screams louder, a scream so earsplitting that Jack's head buzzes for a second. The metal of the knife gleams in the light, and Ziggy is smiling again.

Though Ziggy's hand shakes, though his eyes look unfocused, Jack has never seen someone hold a knife with such purpose. He imagines it digging into his skin: his neck, his chest. Would it feel like glass, or fire? Tears come to his eyes, and he wishes he knew a way out of this situation.

Ziggy looks at Genevieve, whose face drains of color, and he smiles. "Tell him your secret," he says to her. "Tell Jack."

Jack can't breathe, and thinks he's going to black out soon. He imagines knocking the knife to the side. He realizes his hand is moving, trying to grab something. Ziggy's arm, the knife. Anything. He never thought he'd die like this. He thought he was guaranteed a long life. He thought one day he'd figure everything out. He knows in seconds Ziggy will gut him and he'll look like some movie victim: haunted, the life leaving his eyes.

I have a son, Jack thinks, *and I never met him*. His eyes water more. He gasps and pulls at Ziggy's arm. Snot runs out of his nose.

Ziggy laughs, and Genevieve is behind him, bawling, grabbing at him, but he's a strong bastard. He flicks her away without any effort. Jack will die from not breathing, or from the knife. One or the other. He hears the TV come on in the other room where the girl is. A kid's show with a happy voice. Ziggy releases his arm for a second and looks into Jack's eyes.

"She is stealing from you," he whispers, his breath smelling of cigarettes and metal and beer. "Your sweet angel *stole* lots and lots of money from you."

Jack's eyes meet Genevieve's, and her face falls. "That's not true!" she screams. "That's not true. I *never*," and her voice cracks on that last word.

Maybe because of the thing with Kitty, maybe because he might be dead soon, but Jack looks at her face, and he doesn't believe her. He shakes his head. He's so fucking sick of being disappointed by people. He can tell from her expression that she knows exactly what he's thinking.

With Ziggy's arm off his throat, Jack can breathe a bit better. He thrusts his arm up, just missing the knife, and grabs Ziggy's neck using strength that comes from a locked-up place he didn't know existed. He slams Ziggy's head against the wall so hard it dents the drywall and knocks a small painting to the ground. Jack grabs his hair and does it again. He is choking on air still, and his neck aches. He looks at the knife, limp and hanging to the side, and thinks for a second he might kill Ziggy.

But Ziggy's smile returns, and he knees Jack again. He wiggles out of Jack's grip and raises the knife and holds it steady, in line with Jack's neck.

He mimes slitting Jack's throat, and keeps laughing, clearly high.

"Go ahead," Jack growls. He doesn't recognize himself. He is nothing now but adrenaline and anger. He waits for the blade to cut through him, and the little girl is crying now back by the bedroom door. Genevieve is saying something, but Jack doesn't understand her. He thinks of his dad. His mom. He wishes he could have met

Patrick. Is Patrick also this angry, growing up without a dad? Jack's heart sinks. In his final moments, he feels like he failed in so many ways. This can't be it. What the fuck is even happening? The knife is against his throat and the blade tickles him, and Jack tries to look away from Ziggy's wild eyes.

"Please," Jack whispers, choking.

Ziggy digs his arm into Jack's throat harder, and he lowers the knife to his chest.

Jack's heart is beating so loudly he feels like Ziggy can hear it. They will find him on Genevieve's floor. Ziggy will kill her, too, maybe. Will he kill the girl? Jack hopes she will flee and forget all of this. He imagines the blue sky, the brown grass, her little shoes running and running.

Jack looks at Genevieve, and her eyes are so hurt, so broken, and she keeps pleading with Ziggy, words he doesn't even understand through her sobbing. He looks into her eyes, and remembers everything she's done for him, how in so many ways she has been his only family since his dad died, and Jack gives her a half smile because maybe it's a big misunderstanding, and if she did steal, she needed to, and Jack forgives her, and she stops saying anything, and Ziggy grips the knife harder and Jack realizes he's crying.

Jack wishes Patrick could know he was thinking about him in these final seconds. He wishes someone could tell Patrick he was the last thing to cross Jack's mind. He tries to look into Ziggy's face. He wants to tell him he knows, he *knows*. He wants to say he remembers the puppy, and that was everything. Such pure love, such an unblemished view of the world. Ziggy didn't deserve to have his dad taken away. Patrick deserved his dad, too. *You were always good*, he wants to say. To both of them.

He feels tears on his cheeks, and Ziggy's eyes are dilated, and he's laughing again now. Jack wonders if he can possibly survive this. Maybe Ziggy will just cut him superficially, won't damage any organs. Maybe he'll just need stitches. His brain is saying to jam his knee into Ziggy, to figure out a way to tackle him.

He is wishing the little girl or Genevieve would break a lamp over Ziggy's head. Maybe the girl called the police back in the bedroom. Or her mom or aunt, where are they? Jack is almost blacking out, maybe from not enough oxygen, maybe from being paralyzed with fear, when he sees a big figure behind Ziggy.

Deacon with a metal baseball bat, clutching it like a hero.

His eyes are so wide, and he looks at Jack, and before Ziggy follows Jack's eyes and turns around, the bat clangs against the back of Ziggy's skull, making a noise Jack will never forget.

He feels Ziggy's arms sag, the pressure of the blade release, and sees Deacon's face, perfect and clean shaven, his eyes so focused on the hit, like when he played baseball, like when he would throw a dart at a bar and get a bull's-eye, like at the boardwalk, when he used to swish a basketball perfectly into the net.

Jack wants to say something, but he is stunned, gripping at his throat and trying to breathe, Genevieve wheezing, the little girl wailing.

Jack looks at Deacon and wants to hug him, but he feels himself fall to the ground in a crash.

THIRTY-ONE

Jack is in a big, bright hospital room, and he has been checked by three people in the last hour. One nurse is the father of a kid who used to work at Schmidt's, and he updates Jack on everything his son has done since high school. Jack nods and whispers in his hoarse voice, "Please say hi for me," and the man smiles and walks away.

Deacon and Andie left a few minutes ago, and Jack was told the police will be here shortly to ask some questions, but for now, he lays his head back against the white pillow and tries not to think about how raw his neck and throat feel, how close he came to dying. He mouthed to Deacon today, *I owe you one*.

Andie rubbed his shoulder, looking proudly at her husband. "He always has good instincts," she said.

"You owe me a lot more than just *one*," Deacon said, and winked, and then he said, "Fuck it," and bent down and kissed Jack's head. "Just glad you're okay, buddy."

As he lies here alone now, he tries to understand what happened. He didn't tell Andie and Deacon about Kitty and Patrick, but he asked them not to say anything to her.

He asked Deacon to call Vivian and tell her to close down for a couple of days with a sign that said Closed Due to Family Emergency, but she responded that the restaurant was no sweat and a handful of them could keep it open and Jack shouldn't be such a martyr all the time. Jack laughed, which hurt his chest and ribs.

"You should either fire her or promote her after this," Deacon said.

Jack thought about Genevieve then and wanted to ask how she was, where she was, but he decided to wait and ask the police when they came. Outside his window it is cloudy and gray, some of the buildings decorated with Christmas garlands and lights. He wants to call Patrick right now, but he doesn't trust his bruised voice or his emotions. The high school counselor was right, he does feel let down—by everyone except Deacon and Andie, and Vivian.

He pulls the sheet up to his chin, and his head throbs. He closes his eyes for a second, and he is drifting into a peaceful sleep. He even hears himself snore for a second. He hears the beeping in the hallway and some of the hospital staff bantering about the Ravens and how well they're playing this season. He sinks his head into the pillow, and then he hears someone clear their throat.

He opens his eyes, and there under the fluorescent lights is Nicole, with four or five Mylar balloons and a box of candy. "What the—?" he whispers.

"If you're trying to get out of selling, it's not working," she says, walking right up to him, like she's not afraid of someone so bruised and foolish, like hospitals don't scare her. "My oh my, Jack." She tsks and shakes her head. "Aren't you a sad sight."

"Don't I know it," he whispers.

She puts the balloons by the window and pulls up a chair. Her high cheekbones seem to shine. "I was worried," she says, and smiles at him.

He looks at her and wants to say something funny and tough, but the sight of her warms him, and for a second tricks him into thinking he's okay. Like he can't feel his injuries. He opens his mouth to talk, but there are no words. Just his eyes opening wider, his shoulders relaxing. He feels himself smile.

PART TWO

January 3
Patrick Johnson
231 Kingsley Road
Newport, Rhode Island

Dear Patrick,

I don't know how to start this letter, which is why it's taken me several weeks to begin. I don't know what you know, but I just found out about you, and I still can't believe you're real. Based on recent news, I think I'm your father. (This feels ludicrous for me to put in a letter, but I thought it best to give you some time before I attempted to call.)

Also, I am sorry for your loss. Your mother was a brilliant, fun, complex, beautiful person. I hope you are close to your sister and brother and that you are all there for each other.

I thought I would have the right words, but I don't seem to. I can be reached at this address, or at (302)-555-2551. If it works better, I even check email occasionally: schmidtdining@gmail.com.

I'm not trying to be a burden by asking you to reach out, but I am not sure what you know yet. I'm happy to tell you everything from my end.

And I realize how odd this all is. In this day and age, it seems impossible not to know something or to have had both of us not show up in some ancestry DNA test. I'd like to talk with you, but I understand if you need time to adjust to this idea.

I know this is strange, but maybe we can try to catch up.

Yours truly,
Jack Schmidt

—

You know you've made it through winter when clumps of daffodils gather around mailboxes, when forsythia, like yellow stars, bloom to liven up the forgotten brown trees. All of a sudden, the empty ponds have ducks in them again, and residents name these ducks: Scotty and Louise, Hansel and Gretel, Lucy and Desi.

If you stand on the bridge by the elementary school, you will see life returning to Rehoboth: robins in every tree, snapping turtles lifting their ancient heads out of the murky water, looking for bread.

Downtown, you feel the hum of spring, of store owners hosing off their sidewalks and the Main Street Association planting baskets of hyacinths and tulips. Though winter is short and bearable in Southern Delaware, spring still feels like an awakening, a time where no one can tame their excitement. You will hear the familiar sound of trolley tours; you will smell caramel corn in the air. The shop windows will say Help Wanted: Waitstaff; Opening Soon; New Spring Hours.

Unfortunately, in little time, the crowds will return. But spring in Rehoboth is so perfect that it's worth it.

—That's Rehoboth Beach: A Guidebook

THIRTY-TWO

It's a nice day in April when Jack waits in the car for Deacon, the white rhododendron bushes behind the main building drooping next to pink crabapple, and two blue jays hopping around in the brown-green grass.

Deacon smiles when he gets into the car. "She was good," he says.

"Shit, that's great," Jack says.

Deacon drums his hands on the dashboard. "She pointed right at me and said, 'You remind me of a song.'" He smiles, a big broad smile, and his face lights up. "She started singing 'Here Comes Peter Cottontail.' Just out of the blue." He breathes deeply. "She used to sing that to me all the time."

"She remembered."

He nods. "It was pretty cool."

Jack puts the car in reverse, and just lets the good silence linger for a minute. He wonders which way he'd rather have it—his mom gone so early, or a piece of her staying around for years. He looks at Deacon and feels a touch of envy, and then he can't get the Peter Cottontail song out of his head. *Hippity-hoppin', Easter's on its way.* "Where to, my friend? Should we check out phone upgrades?"

Deacon sits back and looks straight ahead, a twinkle in his eyes. "I think today calls for ice cream."

"Not the post office?" Jack asks, looking at his pile of bills without stamps.

Deacon shakes his head. "Ice cream," he says, crossing his arms and smiling.

—

Jack thinks this all feels like the next season of a show that begins after the cliff-hanger, and everyone looks a little different: different haircuts, maybe tan or more relaxed from a vacation, and the viewer at home is trying to figure out what happened as the time went by, and where their favorite characters are.

This morning he's on his way to the restaurant.

It opens again in a few days. The crew will come back the Thursday before Easter, and they'll open on Good Friday. Here Jack is, key in hand, like winter didn't happen. Like he didn't just spend three months hibernating and recovering mentally and physically and trying to figure out what the hell he should do. He slept a lot—tried to sleep, he should say, staring at the window from the sofa, the light hurting his eyes, or staring up at his dark ceiling in the bedroom.

He tried a meditation app called Tranquil, and thought it would calm him, but it didn't. He couldn't even do the three or four minutes a day. He kept hitting pause, kept scrolling Instagram or looking at this guy he discovered on YouTube who tames feral cats, and another lady who builds intricate sculptures out of pasta. He did what he always does in winter: loaf around. He wondered where the days went.

He learned to bake pies. From YouTube, also. When Genevieve didn't return his calls, didn't show up at the restaurant, he googled a recipe for apple pie out of desperation and arrogance, and he wanted to see if he could get anywhere near the kind his grandmother used to make.

He couldn't. The dough was a mess, stuck with butter, and he couldn't roll it out to save his life. It burned on the bottom, the apples still raw, and he took a picture of it and sent it to Deacon.

Is that roadkill? he responded.

—

Jack parks his car and looks at the restaurant, a massive hunk of shingles and siding on the corner, the Schmidt's sign faded. He thinks of the storm in 1962 that leveled the place, but he thinks of all the hurricanes and tropical storms and lightning and snow that haven't been able to hurt it. He gets out of his car, stretches.

Right before Christmas, he bought Deacon and Andie a gift certificate to the Hotel Azul on the boardwalk, one of the fanciest places with a three-level dining room that looks out over the ocean and suites with four-poster beds. He told them it was for saving his life.

"Maybe we'll go there when Evie turns ten," Deacon said, and slipped the gift certificate into his back pocket.

"No," Jack said. "I'll watch her for you, and you two can enjoy a night to yourselves."

They were all in their kitchen, and Deacon had just poured Jack a beer. "*You?*" He cleared his throat. "Sorry." He looked at the foam of the beer, waited for it to dissolve a bit, and then poured the rest of the bottle into the glass. "But *you?*"

Jack took a breath. "You can trust me." He looked at Andie to gauge her reaction, and she smiled and nodded, warmth in her eyes like she was impressed. "I know I don't understand a fraction of what you two know, but I'll do whatever you say. I'll rock her, feed her, play with her. Read her stories." Jack can't say why he thought he would offer this. He wanted to repay Deacon for coming to Genevieve's that day, because Jack knew he'd be dead if Deacon hadn't. He wanted the gesture he gave them to be a big one, something beyond money. He wanted to tell Deacon and Andie he'd do anything for them, and he thought they'd appreciate a night away.

"Tell you what," Andie said, and Deacon glared at her, but she went on. "If you don't mind tag-teaming with Deacon's dad, it's a deal."

Deacon handed Jack the beer. "Unless something comes up," he said, his lips pursed, but Andie scowled at him.

"They'll be fine," she said, and Deacon dropped it.

So the days came and went, and the holidays and January and February came and went, and then Deacon finally called one day to say he made the reservation for a night in April. Tonight. "You sure you can handle it? We can just take her with us, Jackpot. It's no biggie. I mean, my dad can be weird."

"I'm looking forward to it, buddy," Jack said.

So tonight Jack will meet Carl at the house right before dinner, and Andie and Deacon will be on their way. Now Jack puts the key into the restaurant door, and someone taps him on the shoulder. "Almost time!"

He turns around. "Nicole."

"Tick tick tick," she says, and grins, her glasses on a plastic chain around her neck. Her hair has grown out a bit, and she looks happy and earnest in the midmorning light.

"Is that a bomb you're imitating?"

She smirks and holds the door for Jack. "The timer until your free days," she says. They walk inside, and the chairs are up on tables, and the floor is freshly waxed. Jack touched up the paint in a few spots, and they are getting some big food deliveries in the next few days leading up to Easter opening weekend. Nicole looks around. "Brrr," she says. "Still cold."

"Yeah."

She shakes her head. "What on earth will you do come June?" She opens up her folder to show Jack something. "I'm so envious of you, Jack."

"Envious?" Jack shakes his head.

He wants to tell her he feels like he failed. He wants to say he hated to see his crew's faces when he broke the news to them right after New Year's. He wants to say he should have just boxed up his stuff that last week instead of agreeing to the phased transition model outlined in the contract. *All yours*, he should have said.

"Yes, envious." She rifles through the paperwork. "You can go to Switzerland. You can take foxtrot lessons. All this money and no commitments. No alarm clock, Jack! Hell, you can open up a new restaurant if you want." She points her finger at him. "Don't you dare, buster." She starts laughing now. She hands Jack some more documents, and he wants to tell her he never reads them. He gives them to Andie and she makes sure it's all shipshape.

He looks at Nicole in her tiger-striped sweater and thinks for a second about Patrick, who never responded to his letter. Who never got in touch with him. Jack has nothing to do when the restaurant's gone.

He plods toward the back to turn the heat up and starts doing inventory. "Tick tick tick," he finally calls out to her, and she laughs.

THIRTY-THREE

That evening, Jack pulls into Andie and Deacon's driveway and parks behind Carl's Lincoln Continental. As he wipes his feet on the doormat, Carl opens the door. "Here's my coconspirator," he says, and Jack braces himself for one of Carl's shoulder grips that turn his nerves to Jell-O.

"You think we can do this?" Jack says, and smiles, and hears Deacon upstairs asking Andie about a phone charger, and Andie's heels on the hardwood floor.

"We'll be fine, Jackie," Carl says, and he takes Jack's coat and hangs it on the antique coat rack in the foyer. "We're grown-ass men." He winks at Jack and grips the back of his neck, sending a jolt down Jack's spine.

"Is the whole crew here now?" Andie says, walking carefully down the stairs, Evie looking happy in her arms.

"My babycakes," Carl says, and Evie kicks excitedly. Then she turns to Jack and grins. It feels like an accomplishment that she knows him. He wonders if she imagines the aquarium at the restaurant for a second. He looked at the fish today when he went over some papers with Nicole, and he realized they never stipulated in the contract what happens with the fish.

He doesn't want DelDine to have them, but are they furniture and fixtures, as stated in the agreement? He wants to ask Andie right now, but she is dressed up for a nice dinner, a black dress and a diamond necklace. Her perfume is light and expensive. Carl takes Evie from her. "Come here. Charge my old batteries."

Andie smiles at them and slings her tote bag over her shoulder. Deacon trudges down the stairs now with a big rolling suitcase.

"You going for a night or a week?" Jack says, and he smirks.

"Watch it, Schmidt." He sets the suitcase down by the door, and Jack looks around their house, a few lamps lit, the television on in the den, and feels lonely all of a sudden. Like he doesn't want his friends to leave. Deacon brushes his hands together. "Sorry if we need to pack more than jogging pants and a frayed T-shirt." He looks Jack up and down disapprovingly.

"Far be it from me to judge," Jack says, and nudges the big bag with his knee. "Take all the costume changes you need."

Andie winks at Jack. She shows Carl, who has watched Evie a million times, the food she has in containers ready to go. She reminds him he has the doctor's number in his phone, says that Evie doesn't need a bath tonight. "Just a warm washcloth to her hands and face before bed."

"Got it," Carl says.

"And how about we order you guys a pizza or something?" Deacon says.

Jack holds up his bag. "No need. I got us a salad and chicken parm from Steelo's, and I, um, baked a pie."

Deacon's eyes bulge. "A pie?"

Jack nods.

"You can . . . do pies?" Andie says.

"I've been trying."

"Bullshit," Deacon says. "You sent me a pic that looked like rocks and sludge. You've improved that much?"

"Watch that mouth," Carl says, laughing, and covers Evie's ears. Deacon looks at him and grimaces.

Jack shakes his head. "You know I've been cooking since I was in high school. A pie isn't so far-fetched."

"There's a big difference between microwaving string beans and being a pastry chef."

Jack takes the pie out from its carrying case. It's a lemon chess pie he's been practicing. The crust is a little too brown but looks decent, and the pie is topped with fresh whipped cream and a lemon peel in the center. "Voilà," he says.

"You made this?" Andie says. "*You* or Barefoot Contessa?"

"My oh my," Carl says, looking at Evie. "We're going to feast!"

"Looks all right?" Jack asks.

"It looks like you didn't fucking make it," Deacon whispers so Carl doesn't hear.

"I swear I did." Jack looks down at the pie, and tries to see what they see. Maybe YouTube has helped him. He's watched every video of Pie Lady Pam, and he's started to enjoy the sound of her instructions and her expressions. *Oh pitter pat.* "And I never microwave string beans, jackass," Jack says through his teeth.

"Save some for us," Deacon says as Andie hugs Jack.

"Have fun," Jack calls, and Carl distracts Evie with a yo-yo while they leave.

"Well, here we go," Carl says.

Jack watches their car pull out of the long driveway, just red taillights, and thinks how nice it must be to have what they have. Someone who knows you, listens to you, tells you when you're going too far. Sticks up for you. *Someone to make a pie for.*

—

The first couple of hours go rather smoothly. Carl reads Evie's favorite board book to her over and over again about farm animals going to sleep, and Jack sits on the floor with her and watches her do her activity table that sings songs and lets her move buttons and switches up and down. It buzzes and clicks, and Evie is delighted. Carl feeds her baby carrots and chicken and mashed potatoes in her high chair while Jack does their dinner dishes and makes a pot of decaf.

The hours pass slowly, but Jack's pleased they have a grip on things. While Evie sits in her high chair, she plays with a set of plastic keys, getting her food all over everything. "Messy little baby," Carl says, and kisses her. She giggles.

Jack notices how present you have to be in every moment with her, and how you constantly have to be thinking ahead about what you'll do next. It is 7:00 when Carl takes her out of her high chair, and Jack stands behind him and wipes off her mouth and hands.

Her eyes fill with tears, and she seems to be looking around for her parents.

"No, no, don't cry," Jack says, his stomach twisting. Carl bounces her, and Jack starts singing "The Itsy-Bitsy Spider" and doing the motions with his fingers. She pauses for a second and watches Jack in surprise. Carl brings her over to the floor and takes out a big set of blocks that all fit together. She is still crying, and she doesn't want to be put down, so he gets to his feet again in a surprisingly agile move and walks her to the window. "Here now," he says, "let's look and see if we see the moon."

Jack can tell she understands those words, so she pauses her crying again as he points out the window. "Look, look," he says, and her eyes are so big. "Trees. Sky. Moon."

"Maybe we could put on *Sesame Street* or something," Jack says, but Carl shakes his head. "They are a *no* on TV," he says, and raises his eyebrows.

"No Cookie Monster, no Bert and Ernie? Man, I gotta talk to them."

He shrugs. "I've tried."

Jack goes over to her shelf of toys and picks up a little pair of maracas. "Look what I have here, Evie Boo." He shakes them to the left and right and does a weird dance that should embarrass him but doesn't.

She looks over Carl's shoulder and smiles. Carl brings her now and surprisingly, she keeps smiling as she sits on the floor beside him. Jack hands her the maracas, and she shakes them and laughs. Carl sits on the big chair by the fireplace, wedging a pillow behind him. "My old bones," he says, and groans.

"I got this," Jack says, and he and Evie are stacking blocks and shaking those maracas. They pass them back and forth, and she giggles at Jack's reaction when she hands them to him, so they keep repeating it. Jack reads that farm book to her one time, two times, and he is letting her turn the pages. At one point, when he's reading, she turns around to look at him, and her eyes are just so real and beautiful. He swears he can see the moon in them that she watched from the window.

—

Later, Carl gets her into a clean diaper and pajamas, and he turns on the white noise machine in her bedroom. He expertly gives her a bottle in the rocking chair, and Jack goes downstairs to straighten up the toys and finish the dishes.

When Carl comes down, Jack will cut them each a piece of pie. Maybe they will have a glass of wine. Maybe play a quick card game, or just sit back and watch TV and fall asleep, like an older version of Bert and Ernie. Jack feels strange like he always does when he's not in his own house, but it's comfortable here, and he's glad they could do this for Andie and Deacon.

He thinks of their night away, how thrilling it must feel, but also how they must miss what they have here.

He thinks of Patrick, all those nights as a baby and child getting put to bed by someone else. He wipes off Evie's high chair. He hopes Patrick is happy.

He imagines if things had been different. Not if Alexis and he had been together, but just if he'd been in that boy's life. He imagines reading to him; Patrick in the back seat of Jack's car in a small hat and ski jacket, looking at Christmas lights. He imagines there would have been something he could make that Patrick liked, a soup or a drink, that no one else could.

Maybe it's from holding the baby so much, maybe it's because winter was long, but he misses the son he never met. He sits back on the couch now and laces his fingers behind his head and vows to find a way to meet Patrick.

THIRTY-FOUR

"We're all in this together," Nicole says the Thursday before Easter, but it doesn't feel that way. They open tomorrow for the new season, and Jack is training the few new servers and getting reacquainted with Vivian and Sam and Vincent and Paulette and Saul and the rest of the crew. He doesn't have time for this transition period. He's not sure how he'll work with DelDine for two months, and now he wonders again why he agreed to turn it over slowly.

He should have just packed up his stuff in January and never looked back.

"I don't need to be in this together with anyone when I put new paper towels in the bathroom," Jack tells her, and her eyes light up. Jack has noticed more and more how unflappable she is. She is clear and firm with her employees, and she has this quiet authority, but she doesn't have an ounce of a temper or let anything derail her. She never sweats either. Not one drop.

"No paper towel committee?" she says, and laughs.

She is asking Vivian something now, and Jack sees Vivian look at him and wrinkle her nose. Nicole has promised to keep all Jack's staff, but he doesn't know how long some of them—Vivian mainly—will last. Sam is being trained on an app they use at the host stand called Simply Seat, and he looks pale and frustrated. Sometimes Jack just wants to hit reset and have this be his place again, but he thinks about summer, all those evenings open, all those mornings he can sleep in, and he thinks of that beach chair hanging in the closet, the tag still on it, and how the first morning he's free, he will carry it over his shoulder and walk past the pine trees and leaning wooden fence and look at that giant ocean.

He'll just sit there and stare out at the horizon, and the sun will warm him and the sand will feel luxurious against his feet, and this will all be worth it.

Nicole is inputting things into the computer system, and the servers will have to carry these little smartphone-looking devices around and put the orders right into them, communicating directly with the kitchen. Jack's stomach tenses, so he goes back to his office, the one place they're not allowed to touch until his last day in June.

Saul is carrying a Styrofoam box of fresh scallops from the delivery truck, and he pops his head in. "Won't be the same without you, boss." He gives Jack a half smile, and Jack's insides sink, but he pretends to laugh it off.

"Who knows, buddy. You might give up cooking to be the next AM." Two assistant managers in V-necks accompany Nicole every so often, and Jack's crew all make fun of them, calling them bots. They say *AM* like it's repugnant.

"Lucky me," Saul says, and a minute later, Jack sees him take out his pack of cigarettes and go out the back door. Since Nicole oversees almost every aspect of DelDine restaurants, Jack doubts she will spend much time here after the transition. He wonders who the manager will be, and how they will treat his crew.

He thinks of Genevieve for a second and wonders what she would say about all this. He mailed her a final paycheck in January after she never returned to work, but he didn't hear anything back.

Ziggy was taken into custody, and Andie said she thinks he will do at least a year once he's tried and sentenced. Jack already put in a security system at his house, something he never thought he needed.

Every once in a while, he thinks about the missing money. He thinks of Genevieve and wonders what's true. He can still hear the safe that night before Thanksgiving, such an unmistakable sound.

Why would she steal? He would have given it to her—any amount. Even in her last paycheck, he added an extra thousand dollars. He can't stop thinking she is family, and you shouldn't give up so easily on family, should you? It hurts him if she did this, but she has been by his side all these years, the best of the bunch.

—

When his dad died, Genevieve was the first one to come to Jack's house. She rapped on his door, opening the screen door before he got onto the porch.

"Oh, my poor Jack," she said. Jack hadn't cried at all when he left the hospital. He had held his dad's stuff—his favorite Eagles hat, a cactus someone had given Johnny, two limp balloons—and walked to his car. It was early spring, and the sky was hazy and the street smelled like earth. Jack was just so alone, and after the long drive home, there was Genevieve, and she took Jack in her arms.

"We will be okay," she said, and rubbed his back. She was crying, and Jack was crying, and the *we* part made him feel so much better.

She walked right past him and into his house. She took her shoes off by the door, picked up his phone, and ordered a pizza.

She pulled some photos out of her purse of Jack's grandmother wearing a paper crown on her birthday, and his dad carving a Christmas ham for the restaurant, a silly expression on his face that he often made, and one of Jack, young and shy with the old handwritten server orders pinned behind him to the stainless steel rack, standing between Hazel and Johnny, giving the peace sign.

He held the photos and looked at them. "What do we do now?"

She put her hand over his and squeezed his knuckles. "We'll keep thinking about them. We'll keep the restaurant alive."

THIRTY-FIVE

Jack's phone buzzes that afternoon as they prep for opening day tomorrow. It's Kitty.

Since that morning at her house, she's called and texted him repeatedly, but he can't talk to her. He feels betrayed that she sat on this news so long, but it's something else, too. Something he can't put his finger on. Two days before Christmas, she knocked on his door, and it was dark and drizzly, and she stood there with no coat on, just an oversized wool sweater, and Jack didn't unlatch the screen door.

"Talk to me, please," she said.

Jack shook his head. "I need more time." He paused. "Okay?" And she bit her lip and nodded. He went inside and crossed his arms and watched her from the window. She got into her car under the streetlight and pulled away.

Now she writes, *My mom's house closing is tomorrow. I'll be going back to Oregon. I'm sorry for everything.*

He studies his phone in his office. He hears Nicole make a joke about the customer always being wrong and telling Saul his jacket is misbuttoned and reminding him about presentation. "Yeah," he hears Saul reply flatly as he sharpens his knives. Jack braces himself for a moment, knowing Saul's the type who can only be pushed so far before he snaps. Jack wonders about him and Vivian, especially—if they will be able to play that DelDine game or if they are both too strong-willed to buckle. The oven timer dings, and the dishwasher surges. He hears Saul clear his throat, and one of the AMs says the music should be a bit lower. Jack looks at Kitty's text. *I'm sorry, too*, he replies, and he slips the phone back into his pocket.

—

Everything is set for tomorrow, and some of the crew have gone home. Jack and Vivian are in the small area on the second floor of the restaurant, throwing away stuff from filing cabinets and packing up old framed pictures that used to be on the restaurant walls. Jack wasn't planning to start this project today, but when he told Vivian about it, thinking they would tackle it in a couple of weeks, she suggested they take a bite out of it.

"What do you want to do with these?" Vivian asks, holding up a stack of yellowed place mats.

"I think those are from before the storm." Jack scratches his chin. "Toss 'em."

She rolls her eyes. "Maybe donate to the Rehoboth Museum." She cracks her gum. "They love stuff like this."

Jack shrugs. "If you want."

"Philistine," she says.

She takes out a big box, and Jack can smell the mildew and dust. "What the heck is this?" she says. She lifts up what looks like a binder, and Jack has a memory of his dad in the early days, when Jack was a teenager, holding this binder. Jack can still see it sitting on the table behind his desk, next to the expensive camera Johnny bought but never really used.

Vivian starts flipping through it. "Oh my God, it looks like a sketch of the first place." She pages through it. "An early menu. Coupons from the 1960s. This is cool shit. Don't tell your girlfriend Nicole, or she'll steal it all."

"You're hilarious."

She smirks. She turns another page, and Jack recognizes pictures of his grandmother next to her friend Agnes. Vivian looks closely at it. "Were they, like, a couple?"

"Who?"

Her face is pensive. "Your grandma and this woman. Were they together?"

Jack looks at the photo. "My grandma wasn't gay," he says. "She had a husband. He died when my dad was young."

She gives him a look. "No one said they *were* back then, did they?" She turns and wipes some dust on her jeans. "Just sayin' she and this chick look close."

Jack looks down at the photo, and he sees Agnes's hand on his grandmother's shoulder. He has a sudden memory of walking into the kitchen at his grandmother's house, saying something like, "It's so hot out today," and she and Agnes separating quickly, Agnes straightening some cookbooks on the shelf. Jack hadn't thought anything of it, and his grandmother had poured him iced tea and talked about her garden, but now . . .

"Look at this," Vivian says. "A matchbook. 'Schmidt's: Fresh Seafood and a Good View.' Ha!" She presses her finger to the name, and Jack thinks about how a family's history is like a puzzle—the assembled pieces show the whole image, but no one pays attention to all the small pieces: a blur of green, the shape of a corner. *What was the deal with Agnes?* he wonders, and then he remembers Agnes at his grandmother's funeral, sadder than anyone else. What a good friend, he had thought.

Did he miss all that?

He stands up then, and his back hurts, and he opens the other closet and sees his beach chair hanging there, the bright blue not faded one bit. The five-and-ten is no longer on the boardwalk, but if he leans close to the chair, he can still get the scent of that big open store, smelling of magazines and sunscreen and balsa wood and taffy; he can still see Janet's face that day. "Enjoy it," she told him.

THIRTY-SIX

When he gets home that night, there is a big yellow envelope propped against his screen door. He recognizes his name in Kitty's handwriting. He stands there for a second, and there's a perfect warm spring breeze, and he thinks he could almost just go for a walk, late at night like this, his feet stepping on fallen pine needles and broken shells. He turns fifty-three next week, and Deacon wants to have a party, but he's not up for it.

The air smells like salt and magnolia, and he picks up the envelope and bounces it in his hand. He doesn't want to read a note from her. He doesn't want to think about Kitty anymore. *We all make mistakes*, Andie had said to him.

Of course we do. But if Kitty loved Jack, she would have known what this would do to him. He hasn't stopped thinking about Patrick and what he owes him and what was taken. Kitty only played a very small part in that, but after all their time together, she should have told him what she'd learned. But it's more than that. It's as though he realized they weren't meant to get back together, they were just fooling themselves, bound by not wanting to be alone.

What bothers him even more is that maybe they never really knew each other, and that's why they never talked much about his mom, why he never told her about wanting to sell the restaurant, why he wonders even now if she didn't think knowing about Patrick would change him in a significant way.

Forgiveness is hard for you, isn't it? that counselor he never went back to asked.

He goes into the house and doesn't see Harry anywhere. He clicks his tongue for him, but he doesn't come. The curtain blows lazily in the dining room, and Jack stands there and opens the envelope. He reaches inside and finds a small box. He opens it up and sees Kitty's dad's cuff links, two gold knots that he always wore. The other item he recognizes right away: Janet's leather bookmark she always used. It's worn at the edges, and he holds it in his hand and feels bereft. A sticky note is on it in Janet's handwriting. *For Jack*, it says.

He thinks of all the words she read, sipping her drink, the pool or ocean in front of her. He thinks we are all just small things, each person just a sum of days, and he feels good that Janet wanted him to have this.

He wonders if the cuff links were her idea or Kitty's, and maybe he will write Kitty and thank her, just a quick text, but he is thinking about Janet and living and dying, and all of a sudden, Harry nudges against him and startles him, and Jack realizes he should get to bed. Big day tomorrow and all that.

April 20

Dear Patrick,

I won't bother you again, but I want you to know, if I'd known, I would have done everything I could for you.

I'm so sorry.

Yours truly,
Jack Schmidt

May 15

Dear Mr. Schmidt,

Please stop writing.

Sincerely,
Patrick Johnson

THIRTY-SEVEN

Jack holds the letter, studying Patrick's handwriting, and feels like an idiot.

The glee. The goddamn foolish glee he felt when he saw the return address. But what did he imagine? That he was going to suggest they build a race car together? That Patrick was going to plan a trip here, or encourage Jack to come up to Newport? The two of them walking along the cobblestones, sharing stories from the past or stumbling upon commonalities: *You drink your coffee black, too? You can't whistle either? You hate mayonnaise and mushrooms?*

Did Jack imagine the relief? The connection? Did he imagine Patrick and him staring at the sailboats in the harbor, a perfect spring day where they'd come together? All those years disintegrating as if they haven't mattered. The feeling that it was Jack's turn with Patrick now.

How did he think this would go?

But yes, that's exactly what he hoped for.

—

"Fuck him," Deacon says. They are at Coffee Daze in town, 6 a.m., and Jack can feel the energy of Memorial Day coming in a week and a half, seasonal businesses opening, shop owners sweeping off their sidewalks, flags going up, garbage cans and boardwalk benches being set up by the town.

"He's just a kid."

Deacon shakes his head. "He's a grown man. So *man* up, right? You didn't *know*. If you had, it would've been different." He leans back in his chair, sips his espresso, and puts his arms behind his head. "He should be pissed at his sketchy dead mom, not you."

Jack holds his dry biscotti and thinks of Kitty telling him one time about a psychological fear of holes or patterns of holes—like a beehive or lotus flower. He dunks the biscotti into his coffee and bites the end off. He cracks his knuckles a few at a time and doesn't look up. "I just wish it could be different. He's out there, I'm here. I thought we could at least meet."

Deacon rubs his jaw, looks at the barista shooting steam into a drink and stirring it with a long spoon, and then back at Jack. "He got to have a family, Jackpot. He *had* a mom. His stepdad was not you, but he was probably okay." Deacon takes a deep breath. "My mom's in rough shape, and she'll probably be gone soon. My dad's okay now, but eventually he'll be gone, too. I don't know if I'd be in the mood for a brand-new parent to show up." He downs the last of his drink and stands. "But still, fuck him and his rudeness. *I'd* at least be polite."

Jack looks up at him. "So what do I do?"

"Forget him," he says. "In a month, you'll be swimming in Scrooge McDuck's cash pond, baking your pies left and right, probably signing up for a singles cruise, most likely annoying the hell out of me on a daily basis. Who needs Patrick whatever his name is."

Jack waves to him as he goes. Getting Deacon to sit still is always a major feat. He leaves his drink and the rest of the biscotti and drops a big tip. Back to work.

—

"Saul quit," Sam tells Jack as soon as he walks in the door. It's eight thirty in the morning, and all his employees had a DelDine training meeting at seven—DelDine likes to have breakfast meetings so it doesn't interfere with the rest of their operational day.

"What?"

"I was shocked," Sam whispers. He taps his fingers on Jack's office doorframe. "He just raised his hand in the middle of some AM's presentation about customer satisfaction and said he quit."

Jack stacks some of the papers in front of him into a random pile. "He didn't say anything else?"

Sam shakes his head. "They looked really upset, and asked him for feedback on his decision, but he just said he's not interested in this"—he makes air quotes—"'*shithole* company.'" He coughs. "He said they're unbearable, and then he just walked out." He does a walking motion with his two fingers. "Vivian looked impressed, and it seemed like she was going to get up and leave, too, but she didn't. She kept watching the door after that, like maybe he might come back."

Jack shakes his head and picks up his phone. "Like effective immediately, or is he going to give us a week or two?" He knows Sam doesn't know—he's just trying to sort this out. Jack looks for Saul's number on his list and dials. It rings and rings and nobody answers. He knows none of his crew check their voice mail. He hangs up and texts him. *Call me ASAP.*

Sam turns around, and Nicole appears beside him. "Can I speak with you for a second?" she says to Jack.

Jack motions her inside. "Thanks, Sam," he says. His eyes look sad, like a kid watching his parents walk away on the first day of school.

Nicole closes the door and shakes her head. "Heard about Mr. Rowan?"

"I just did," Jack says. "What the hell happened? He's worked here since he was a kid. Amazing cook. Knife skills, great precision. A good communicator, too. He could hold his own in a New York restaurant."

"I thought *you'd* fill me in."

Jack looks down: his phone's vibrating, and it's Saul. He turns his phone over and doesn't answer. "I have no idea. He never quit on me. Never even threatened to. What kind of cult stuff were you presenting?"

Nicole moves a box and sits in the big leather chair. "The cult stuff doesn't start until June 15, mister." She takes off her glasses and rubs her eyes. "It seemed to come out of left field."

"Well, I'll talk to him. He's a purist. Hates anything artificial. He's a good guy, though, so you shouldn't write him off."

She shakes her head. "Sorry, he's *donezo.*" She looks down at her glasses, frowns, and slips them into her shirt pocket. "DelDine has a zero-tolerance policy for quitting or no-shows."

"You're serious?"

"Why wouldn't I be?" she says. She doesn't blink.

Jack groans. "Ridiculous."

"It's how we do it." She stands. "I hope Mr. Rowan doesn't inspire anyone else. Vivian was looking at him like he slayed a dragon."

"Hopefully you told them all it's one strike and you're out. That you can't be human or have a moment of weakness. Can you tell the higher-ups I said that's a stupid way to govern? If you get Maurice Engel on the phone, I'll tell him myself."

"Will do," she says, and walks toward the door.

"I'll at least try to get Saul back until I'm gone. And then hopefully he can find something else."

"Here?" she says. "That's not possible."

"What do you mean?"

"He *can't* work here anymore. He's done."

"For me he can."

She sighs. "You might want to check the contract."

He knows the final contract is somewhere in his email but hasn't looked at it lately. "*I* can't decide who works for me?"

"Jack," she says.

"Nicole."

She sighs. "We're *partners* now. DelDine has been committed to retaining your crew. They'll be eligible for promotions, other restaurant opportunities, even in our Philadelphia or Ocean City locations." She twists her fingers. "But we have to decide together who works here, even while you're still on the floor. And Mr. Rowan can't come back."

Jack's phone is buzzing again, and he knows it's Saul. A headache pulses between his eyebrows. He holds his hand over the phone. He opens his mouth to say something, and it's a *Star Wars* quote. "This deal is getting worse all the time," he says.

Nicole turns to leave and pauses. "I don't suppose you want to go grab coffee," she says, looking back hopefully.

"I already had some," Jack says, and he watches her leave.

THIRTY-EIGHT

The next day, Sam stands in Jack's office door again, right as the lunch rush is winding down. "A woman's here to see you," he says. "She says it's important."

Jack is in the middle of responding to many points in a long email from Andie about the final terms of the agreement. "What's her name?"

"I'm not sure. Laura or Layla or something. With a hammer in her last name, I think." Sam blushes. "Sorry, I should have written it down. She's dressed pretty fancy."

Jack closes his laptop. The name sounds familiar. "Is she like in sales or something?"

He points at Jack. "Could be," he says. "Should I, uh, tell her you're busy?"

Then it hits him. "Hammersmith?"

Sam snaps his fingers. He always looks so unsettled, and Jack keeps wanting to ask him how things are at home, but the days pass and he doesn't. "That's it."

Alexis's daughter. Patrick's half sister. Jack stands up and smooths his hair. "You can send her back here."

In a moment, Lara Hammersmith is standing in front of him.

She is young and on the short side, with long dark hair, and looks nothing at all like Alexis Johnson. Jack tries to smile and clears a space for her to sit, gently closing his laptop. "Hello there," he says, pretending he doesn't know who she is. She wears a blazer and pants and a silk blouse with ruffles.

She smells like expensive shampoo and carries a big leather purse. She blots her face with an antique handkerchief. She is in her midtwenties, maybe, but has rosy cheeks and an old-soul quality to her. "This is so weird," she says, and swallows. She blots her forehead again.

"Okay," he says, and waits for her to talk.

"Here?" she asks, and points at the chair.

"Um, yeah, that's fine." She sinks down and breathes in. She looks at Jack's face. "Unbelievable," she says, and gets tears in her eyes.

Jack clears his throat. "What, um, what's unbelievable?"

"You—that you look so much . . ." She shakes her head. "Wait, let me start over. I'm Lara. *Patrick's* sister." She says the name Patrick so purposefully and slowly—as if there has only ever been one Patrick in the world.

Then Jack notices her eyes, that they are very much Alexis's eyes. Brown, watery, a thousand thoughts going on behind them. "The Patrick you've been writing to."

"I know," he says quietly. He's not sure where the reflex comes from, but his teeth start chattering for a second. "Sorry," he says, and clenches the edge of his desk. "What, um, brings you here?"

She shrugs and heaves a sigh. "You know what? I have no idea. The *ferry* brings me here." She laughs nervously and looks around at Jack's boxes.

He remembers then that she's from Cape May, across the bay.

He imagines her holding the railing on the ferry's top deck, looking out at the perfect blue sky, her long hair blowing. "I'm sorry about your mom," he says.

She frowns. "My dad died a few months after Mom. It's been a weird year and a half." She shakes her head, takes a breath to say something but then doesn't. She holds her handkerchief and busies herself with folding it.

"He's messed up," she says finally.

Jack leans forward. "Patrick?"

"Yeah." She places her big purse on his desk, and he sees a pack of cough drops inside, and a metal water bottle. "I mean, not messed-up psychotic or anything." She gives Jack a small smile. "I mean he always knew he had a different dad, but that fact was like a myth, one we never got close to or questioned. He didn't ever expect the dad to know about him or reach out like that. He's just confused. Doesn't know what to think." She raises her eyebrows. "None of us do, really. Me or my younger brother, Michael. My dad's family, my mom's parents. This is all so weird. Who knew, you know?"

Jack nods. *How do you think I feel*, he wants to say, but she is so well meaning that he just stays quiet. "I'm sorry if I bothered your brother with those letters."

She shakes her head. "The letters were fine. I thought they were fine. I said, *Pat, what do you have to lose?*" She rolls her eyes. "But he's so stubborn. Angry, distant oldest child." She looks at Jack. "Someone called him a bastard once, and he flattened that kid's face." She takes a shaky breath. "But you're *real*. You're right here and real, and my God, I can't believe how much he looks like you." She points to the side of her mouth. "Even those dimples. The look you gave me before. Your ears, too!" She shakes her head. "He's like your Mini-Me."

Jack listens to her words and lets them sink in. There is a part of him out there. "This is new to me, too," he says. "I don't know what the protocol is."

"Yeah, I can tell." She smiles, and she reminds Jack of Alexis again. That light side of her when you could tell her anything. Jack remembers how effortlessly she could joke, how she could just calm him. These memories have been locked somewhere deep and safe, and now they return. He forgot the restaurant existed when he and Alexis were dating. He didn't want to go back to college or do anything but be with her.

Lara holds up her phone to take Jack's picture, and he instinctively leans backward. "Um, what are you doing?"

She puts her phone down. "Oh my God, I'm sorry. I just felt like I needed to capture this." She shakes her head. "Sorry, you're not a zoo animal. What was I thinking?" Her face is flushed.

"It's okay." He wants to ask to see the picture, knowing he probably looks like hell. He imagines Patrick seeing it and being more disgusted than he already is.

"I came here because I live right across the water. I wanted to see what you were like."

Jack scratches his head. He can hear Nicole outside his office going over something with one of the AMs. He can hear dishes clinking as they're being washed, the big mixer whirring. "Does he know . . . Do, uh, you know—that I never knew?"

She frowns. "I'm not really clear on it. What did you think became of the woman carrying your child?" She bites her thumbnail. "I mean, did you think she just evaporated?"

Jack's stomach flips. Does he tell a strange young woman that her dead mother lied about having an abortion? He drums the desk for a second and decides he has no other choice. "She went to, um, end the pregnancy, and before she went back to California, she acted as though, um, she'd had the procedure. I gave her money for it even. But, um, it turns out she never did it. I just found that out a few months ago."

"She told you she had an *abortion*?"

Jack nods. "I was young and dumb, but I didn't, like, ask for evidence. She insisted her friend take her."

She shakes her head. "She came home and hid it as long as she could. She told my grandparents it was a fling right there in LA, that she didn't really know the dad. She said she was going to do it on her own. They didn't speak to her for a while, but when she was almost ready to deliver, they reconciled. My mom and baby Patrick lived with them for a couple years while she finished college and went to dental school . . . before she met my dad."

Jack crosses his arms and stares at her. "I don't know why she did that."

She sighs. "I have never known her to lie," she says, and Jack isn't sure if that's an accusation or just a declaration, but his ears get hot; he won't know what to do if she doesn't believe him. "But she told me about you," Lara says.

"She did?"

"She told me—we talked a lot, especially after she got sick two years ago. She could never talk to Patrick the same way. He gets defensive, and he tries to solve every problem. But she told me Patrick's dad wasn't from California—that he was from Delaware, where she interned at a dental lab for a summer and stayed at her Aunt Grace's. She didn't mention anything about ending the pregnancy or whatever, but she said I should try to help Patrick meet you after she was, um, gone . . . that it might be good for him.

"When your letter came, I had just recently told him what she'd told me. She wanted to do it herself, but she got bad pretty fast, and her treatments were terrible, and it didn't seem right to get into all that. So for his whole life, he thought his dad was basically anonymous, and that shaped his identity. When I told him, I don't think he knew how to unpack the information."

"And she didn't explain why I was never in Patrick's life?"

She looks down at her lap. "She said you were in school, and that you weren't . . . interested." Her eyes shift. "I might have told Patrick that part, too—just relaying what she'd said."

His eyes sting. "Goddamn it." He breathes out. "I would have made it work. I thought if she didn't want it, it wasn't meant to be. She'd been so brave, and I wanted us to be okay. I tried to get in touch with her several times after she left to make sure she was okay, and she shut me out. I probably even have the letter somewhere." He clenches his teeth. "Lara, I promise I never knew."

She puts up her hands. "I believe you, Mr. Schmidt. I'm in sales, so I know how to read people." She smiles pleasantly and shakes her head. "But I don't want to kick up dirt about my mom. I had a difficult relationship with her, and it got better toward the end, and I want it to stay that way now that she's gone." She runs her hand through her long hair. "But I believe you." She whispers the last part as though someone might hear.

"Thanks," Jack finally says.

She holds her handkerchief and looks down at it. "So now what?"

"Help me meet your brother," he says.

THIRTY-NINE

"I actually didn't come here just to see you," Lara says as they walk outside. "I work for Pillar, so I come to the area often to check on our factory store and visit our boutiques."

"Pillar like the handbags?" he asks.

"Yes, and much, much more. We're a luxury lifestyle brand." She looks at him. "I could get you a nice wallet or duffel bag at a discount if you're ever interested."

"Does it seem like I'm into luxury?" Jack laughs, looking down at his sloppy clothes.

She smirks. "I don't know, should I ask you about your beach block property or your successful restaurant?"

"Ouch," he says. He notices people on the boardwalk, and even some umbrellas on the beach. "You remind me of your mom." He pauses. "It's awful what happened to her. I go from being so angry . . . Well, not angry, more confused and disappointed, but then feeling so bad that she lost her life this early. I mean how strange that I'm sitting here with you now instead of her, you know?"

Her face falls. "Don't say anything like that to Patrick. He hates sentimentality." She scribbles her phone number on a piece of lavender paper from her purse and nudges it toward him. She starts to walk away. "Text me if you need anything from Pillar."

Jack looks down at the number. "Thanks." He thinks back to what she just said about Patrick. "So, I might get to meet him?"

"Like it's up to me," she says.

—

After Lara leaves, Nicole pops her head in Jack's office door. It feels odd to have her and the AMs here, like company that never goes away. It used to just be him and the crew, but now he feels like he has a committee around. "Who the heck was that?" Nicole asks.

Jack can never get over how blunt she can be. She wouldn't care if he asked her anything under the sun. "Just someone I know."

"Mysterious," she says, holding her laptop.

"I can't watch a presentation right now," he says. "I have to go meet someone."

"Yikes," she says. "It was only a few slides." Her face looks hurt, but he's still pissed about Saul, so he doesn't care.

"Well, email them to me, and I'll take a look."

She sighs. "I'll do that, but we've got to get some things nailed down. You want this to be a good experience for everyone, don't you?"

He gets up and looks past her out at the restaurant. He watches his busy crew, sweeping the floor and putting away glasses and chopping lemons and mixing up the homemade tartar sauce. Vincent is cleaning all the stainless surfaces, Paulette is peeling sweet potatoes, and Sam is nervously inputting tomorrow's reservations into the Simply Seat program on a tablet. "I feel like they're hostages," he says, and Nicole laughs, but he doesn't look back at her, his car keys jingling in his hand.

FORTY

He meets Saul at the bowling alley and arcade on Route 1. Saul stands outside with his hands in his pockets, and groups of kids with their parents are going in and out. The presummer traffic is getting heavy on the highway, and Saul shrugs when he sees Jack.

"Sorry," he says.

"What are you sorry about?"

"That I couldn't do it." He shakes his head, and Jack stands there and listens to the cars go by. He hears vibrating above them and sees a helicopter alone in the sky. "They were giving their talks about performance and customer outreach and quotas, and I just kind of snapped."

"I don't blame you." Jack looks down at his shoes. "Interesting place to meet, by the way."

A teacher with a line of elementary school kids comes out and holds the door open, telling them to use hand sanitizer as soon as they get onto the bus.

"It helps me blow off steam," Saul says.

"Bowling? I didn't know young people still bowled."

He looks at Jack like his head is bleeding. "No. Laser tag, man."

"Oh. That never looked like my cup of tea."

"You have no idea," he says, and motions Jack inside.

"I have to get back to the restaurant, Saul."

"It's only eight minutes," he says. "You'll feel like a million bucks."

Jack's first instinct is to resist, but Saul is holding a crumpled twenty-dollar bill and looking hopeful, so Jack follows him inside.

—

There's a big line for laser tag, and the whole time Jack is there, he thinks he should leave. The restaurant calls to him, the way it always fills his days. It is hot and loud in this place, the sound of bowling pins falling, arcade games with their electronic jingles. And people at the giant bar laughing and cheering at some sports tournament on the TVs.

Saul tells Jack about his girlfriend who broke up with him, about how his mom in Florida has skin cancer. Two dads with their handful of tweens stand behind them, and the dads look more eager than the kids. Jack crosses his arms and nods as Saul talks. "So what can I do?" Jack finally asks.

He looks at the attendant's station, the red light blinking that a game is in progress inside beyond the door. Saul takes a deep breath. "I don't know, man. I don't fucking have a clue. I feel like I'm falling apart, and I don't know what else to do besides what I've been doing. But the changes just really knocked me over. I didn't want to work for anyone else or have anything be different."

He looks hurt, and Jack feels like he made a decision just for himself when he should've been thinking more about all these loyal employees. Saul and Vivian and Sam and Vincent and Paulette. Smokes and Ernie. Even Genevieve. He let them all down.

The guy calls them inside and runs through the orientation. They strap on heavy vests with blasters and wires attached. Saul and

Jack are on opposite teams, one of them red and the other blue. The dads stand next to them and high-five each other and mime-blast each other's chests.

Now they are running into the huge obstacle course, the music loud, the room dark, and the buzzer signals that they are starting. Jack is running and running and he shoots one of the dads and his vest and gun blink that he's temporarily deactivated. Jack runs up the ramp and sees Saul's green T-shirt, and he spots Jack right as he's shooting at him and hides behind a column. He peeks out before Jack can hide, lifts his gun and gets Jack. The music is loud and furious like a club, and Jack is running around like he's eight years old and playing hide-and-seek, playing kickball, playing something free and limitless.

All these years he hasn't let himself do anything.

He hasn't let himself sit in that goddamn perfect chair because he didn't know what he was beyond the daily call of Schmidt's.

He is so out of breath, and sweat drips down his face, even though it's only been a few minutes. He is laughing and shaking his head, and it doesn't matter that one of the teenagers shoots him, and one of the fathers pops out and gets him as soon as he is activated again.

It just feels fucking glorious.

—

An hour later, Nicole is at her makeshift workstation in the storage room, where she has set up her laptop and a filing cabinet. A small photo of her husband in his military uniform sits on the table she uses as a desk. "Were you . . . mountain biking?" she says to Jack, seeing his red, fatigued face.

"I'm going to need you to take back Saul," he says, not blinking. "And I'm going to need you to look after him."

She raises her eyebrows. "Jack," she says, and sighs.

"If not, I'm pulling out of the deal."

She shuffles some papers and waves her hand. "Fine," she says. "He's back. Tell him to meet with me. But this is his *only* chance."

Jack mock-salutes her. "Thank you, Captain DelDine."

She rolls her eyes playfully. "As if you could pull out of the deal," she says, and goes back to her work.

May 21

Dear Kitty,

I hope you made it back to Oregon safely. Thank you for the cuff links and bookmark. It was thoughtful of you to leave them here. I am buckling up for Memorial Day weekend and bracing myself for the traffic, the packed boardwalk and beach, the water ice booth coming alive next door.

I'm really sorry for ignoring so many of your calls. You didn't owe me anything, but I wish I'd known about him. It just hurts, I guess. I wish you'd told me as soon as you found out, but ultimately, you were just the messenger.

I wish you the best, Kitty. I hope you have peace. I don't think we were meant to get back together, but I think, at certain times, we needed one another, and I'm glad for those times. I hope you are, too.

Jack

FORTY-ONE

It's the Thursday before Memorial Day. Lara Hammersmith meets Jack in the parking lot of one of the outlet stores, and she waves as he pulls up. She is sipping an iced coffee, and she holds her giant purse by the handles. "Howdy," she says, and looks at his Jeep. "How old is that thing?"

"It has some years on it," he says, and smiles. Jack realizes it could use a wash. Maybe a task for his next Pine Creek visit with Deacon.

She looks at her watch. "I have about twenty-seven minutes to help you," she says. She pauses. "But if I take longer, no one ever knows where I'm supposed to be."

"But you still hold yourself to a standard," Jack says. "Admirable." He stretches. "I would have gotten here sooner, but traffic is off the charts already. Tomorrow and Saturday are going to be impossible." He squints in the bright sun.

"Cape May's about the same," she says, and motions for him to follow. "I'm making a pitcher of margaritas and not leaving my house."

Jack is being honored Sunday night by the Rehoboth Beach Main Street Association for the more than sixty-five years Schmidt's has been in business. When they called last month, he asked if they knew the business wouldn't be his much longer, but no one seemed to care. There is going to be a banquet at the town hall with catering by DelDine, of course, and awards to various businesses that have been in town for more than thirty years.

He had texted Lara Monday and asked her if Pillar sold suits. She said no but asked why, and he told her about the award.

Meet me on my lunch break Thursday, and I'll help you. I know a place, she wrote.

I was hoping, he replied.

They go into Threads, an upscale men's outlet store with well-dressed mannequins in the window and a whole section of shoes in a room to the right. "Gray, navy, or black," she says. "Those are your options."

"How about tan?" Jack says.

She shakes her head. "Is it in the afternoon? Is it on the beach?"

"No."

"Exactly," she says. Jack follows her, and she moves quickly, her big purse slung over her shoulder, bouncing as she walks. She grabs a navy jacket and holds it up to him. "Forty-two or forty-four I think, forty-two long probably. You're tall."

"Wow. How can you tell?"

She huffs. "Um, *that's* what I do."

"I like navy best, I think."

"Got it," she says. Jack follows her around the giant store with the polished faux-tin ceiling, the flattering lighting, the occasional full-length mirror. She grabs a few hangers and looks him up and down. "Ideally, we'd get something tailored, but since we don't have enough turnaround time, I think you'll be okay. You're pretty standard."

"Yup."

She hands him two blue jackets with matching slacks. She glances at his face and smiles. Out of nowhere, she pats his shoulder. "You're going to look great," she says, and summons a saleswoman, who looks at the suit. "Louisa," Lara says, reading her name tag. "What do you think: classic white shirt with this, or a chambray blue?"

Jack raises his eyebrows, and Louisa looks at Jack. "I think traditional. Crisp white, Windsor or half-Windsor knot." Louisa nods seriously.

Lara goes to the rack of ties and flips through them. "Ooh," she says, and pulls out a purple tie that she holds up to the jacket.

"Lovely. Bouclé," Louisa says. "Great taste . . . Does he need dress shoes?"

"Yes," Lara says without looking at Jack.

"How do you know?"

Lara turns to him and shrugs. "Guessing. Am I wrong?"

"No."

"I've got to run, but do you have a simple Oxford you can show him, minimal broguing?" Lara says to Louisa.

"Absolutely."

"Thank you." Lara hands Jack two different white shirts and goes back and grabs a belt. "I feel like if I don't add this, you'll tie a rope around the pants or something."

"I'll allow it," Jack says, arms full.

She looks at him again and narrows her eyes as though she's imagining it all together. Jack can see her processing the whole look. "And you'll get a haircut tomorrow, yes?"

"I can."

She grimaces.

"I will," he says. "They'll probably be busy, but the guy at the barbershop owes me a favor."

"Well, then you should be set," she says, and Jack holds all the heavy clothes. It feels hot and still in there, and Billy Joel sings "The Longest Time" over the speakers. "Don't skimp on the shoes, okay?" She winks. "They don't make dress Crocs."

Jack smirks. "How about a nice Velcro pair?"

She shakes her head and feigns exasperation. "I don't joke about these things."

"I'll be fine."

"Brown," she says. "With laces." She gestures toward Louisa. "She'll steer you right."

Jack nods and one of the suit jacket buttons gets caught on the loop of his jeans. "Hey, Lara. Thanks."

"You're going to blow them all away," she says. "Oh!" She digs into her purse and pulls out a tiny box that says Pillar on it. "Here," she says. Louisa takes Jack's bundle of clothes and says she'll get a dressing room ready. Jack looks at the box.

"What's this?"

"For you."

He opens it and there's a tie tack inside. It's a small silver *S*. "Really?" he says. He digs into his pocket. "Here, let me pay you."

"It's a gift."

"So thoughtful."

"Wear it proudly," she says. She punches Jack's arm and walks away, the music changing as the door dings.

"Oh," he calls after her. "Anything from your brother?"

She turns back to him and shakes her head. "No movement on that front." She waves and keeps walking.

"Thanks for trying."

"Any time," she calls back.

Louisa waits for him near a louvered dressing room door. She plays with her keys on a bungee cord. Jack knows he should get moving, but for some reason he is watching Lara leave. He watches her walk, a long shadow to the side of her in the parking lot, and wants to make sure she gets to her car safely.

FORTY-TWO

1982

His mom was getting better. He was sure of it. He had made a mental list of things they would do together. When she was gone, he felt bad that he had started to move away from her, like any almost-teenage boy would do. He was busy with basketball practice and playing Atari at his friends' houses, and he never realized until she was away how often he and his dad had left her alone.

She had started her own business in town, Brighton Bakery, but it never got off the ground. The town wasn't ready for it then, it seemed, and Jack has thought over the years how popular it would have been today. She had giant muffins: blueberry, cranberry-orange, poppy seed. She sold gourmet cookies, homemade croissants. Even delicious chicken and tuna salad and sometimes carrot or potato soup. As Jack sat in his quiet bedroom, he craved her cooking and defrosted every last thing she left in the freezer: oatmeal cookies, Polish kiffles. As he ate them, he realized how sad she had been.

Basketball season ended, and the friends who had kept him so busy before were all of a sudden unavailable. Who wanted to hang out with the kid whose mother had gone crazy, whom the neighbors found outside their house on Stockley Street propped against the mailbox sobbing? The police had been called, Jack's dad had been called, and when Hazel's friend Agnes suggested a place in

Utah because her cousin had gone there and gotten so much better, Johnny didn't ask any questions, and drove her right out there that afternoon.

Jack didn't get to say goodbye to his mom. He got her letters. Letter after letter where she tried to stay upbeat, but Jack could sense the sadness overtaking her. The same way you know rain is coming, just from how the light in the room shifts.

—

The best time to visit is before the end of June, when the weather is pleasant and not humid, and the crowds are sizable but not overwhelming.

Once Memorial Day has passed, the lifeguards are out each day like clockwork; the ice cream places stay open late; and Playland Pier is no longer weekends only.

Take a drive on an early summer night, and you will see front lawns with swarms of old bikes standing at attention; striped towels draped over porch railings; people sitting on their porches with glasses of wine, waving to passersby. Rehoboth Beach is a summer town. Even the locals, annoyed with the parking meters and long restaurant waits, marvel at how alive the streets are, how happy everyone else is to get away. Even the locals get excited about the baskets of nectarines at the farmer's market, the sweet corn and cantaloupes at the grocery store.

Take it all in. Rehoboth in early summer is an oasis. Go to Dewey and order a tableful of crabs with two pitchers of beer. Take a drive to Bethany and watch the sunset over the lit-up Inlet Bridge. Hop onto the trolley and listen to the laughter of children, the conversation of grandparents, the chatter of teenagers. Walk the length of the boardwalk and listen to the happy splashes in the hotel pools. Get a funnel cake and watch the sea dragon at Playland Pier glide back and forth. Play a quick round of mini golf. Not to experience Rehoboth Beach in summer is to be robbed of something pure and real. What are you waiting for?

—That's Rehoboth Beach: A Guidebook

FORTY-THREE

Jack is at the hardware store. He's walked there this Friday after Memorial Day, the first nice day after a cold start of May, to get an air filter for his heat pump. He also has the small bolt from the refrigerator at the restaurant, and he knows that's not his problem anymore, but it needs a nut and washer, and Collin Brothers has a whole wall of screws and bolts that you can dig through to find the size you need.

The bell dings as he heads inside and the two guys who work there offer to help him right away. He tells them he's good and finds the air filter and tucks it under his arm. He's trying to match up his bolt with its correct top when he sees Nicole and one of the assistant managers—Shelly or Shelby, he isn't sure.

Nicole is holding a pack of bar rags and a new mop. "Well, well," she says. "I can't go anywhere without bumping into someone." Right as she approaches, Jack finds the perfect nut and it threads onto the bolt seamlessly.

"Hey there."

Nicole wears a starched shirt, pale blue, that reminds Jack of a boat he fixed and painted once in the backyard and then ended up selling because he never took it out.

"Morning," she says.

"I'll be in later this afternoon." He sees a rack of yard sale signs and has a memory of his mother sticking small orange price tags on to everything and sitting in a picnic chair while crowds descended. *We made out like bandits*, she called to his dad.

"Whenever," Nicole says, and she hands the mop and bar rags to the AM, who leaves to go pay. "Use the right card," Nicole says. "Corporate, not restaurant specific." She pushes out a breath. "I'll have to remember the expense report because Shelby certainly won't." She rips off her glasses, looks at the shelves for something that isn't there, and puts them back on.

"I'm surprised to see you buy local. I thought DelDine only liked to support billionaires."

She shakes her head. "I am not the enemy, Jack Schmidt." She smirks. "Do you happen to know that all our produce is sourced from Delaware farms, and all our landscaping and snow removal, because of *me*, is via local crews whom we pay very nicely, not the big guns who exploit their workers? Even our Christmas trees this year were from Nuit's Farm." She looks at Jack's stuff. "Shelby," she shouts in a way that makes him blush for a second. "Tell them to ring up this A280 filter and a size seven nut on ours." She looks at him. "You need anything else?"

He winces. "I, uh, I can pay for this stuff."

She flicks her hand. "We got you."

A song by Chicago comes over the speakers, and it puts him in a good mood.

Shelby walks up to Nicole and hands her a printed page. "Here's the receipt," she says, and Nicole nods. Shelby looks at Jack. "Does he need a bag, they wanted to know?"

Nicole raises her eyebrows at him.

"Oh, no, I'm good," he says, and pats the filter in its plastic wrap. He slides the bolt and nut into his pocket.

"Perfect," Nicole says. She smiles at Shelby. "I'll see you at the restaurant."

"You don't need a ride back?" Shelby asks.

"Nope, I'm all set."

Jack stands there next to Nicole, the filter under his arm. "Why did she think you needed a ride?"

"Because we drove here together."

"Oh." He turns to her. "Are you walking?"

"Nice enough day."

As they head toward the door, he is reminded of a friend who slept over at his house in fourth grade and ended up staying for two days. "Doesn't he have anyone looking for him?" Jack's mom asked.

"I guess not," Jack had replied.

—

They walk past the museum, past Mini Mart, where Nicole stops for bags of Cracker Jack. She hands one to him. "May the odds be in your favor," she says.

He takes the bag. "Huh?"

"With the prize," she says, and winks. She tears hers open and digs inside. "Score." She peels the prize open, and it's a small tattoo. "Lovely," she says, and he is sure for a second she's going to spit on her arm and press it into place. Instead she slides it into her pocket.

He eats a few pieces of popcorn with a perfect glazed nut and finds his prize. She cranes her neck to watch him open it. "It's some kind of digital code for a game."

"Rattlesnakes," she says, and punches the air to show her disappointment.

He looks at her as they walk toward the circle, the sun over them, the occasional *squawk* of a seagull. Town is quiet in the last days of

May, and a few cars creep by. He has never met anyone like her. "You don't need to get back to the office?"

She rolls her eyes. "Jack, I'm smart. I can get done in two hours what some of those children can't do in a month. Maurice appreciates that, and he knows better than to get on my case." She pushes a handful of popcorn into her mouth and crunches.

"So what are you doing now?"

"Whatever you want," she says, and the sun shines on them.

—

They are walking by Grove Park, and he notices the white tents set up. He hears a guitarist playing Neil Young.

"Oh, it's the farmer's market," Nicole says, and slaps Jack's arm like he was keeping something from her. Before he knows it, he is following her through the front entrance where she is crouching down and petting someone's dog and making kissing noises at it.

When she stands up, she turns around to look for Jack, and he waves.

She heads to a stand with dried flower arrangements and sniffs one. She pinches a piece of eucalyptus. "You're too decent to work for those people," Jack says, but maybe she doesn't hear him.

The guitarist switches to Otis Redding. Nicole gets a look in her eyes that seems like sadness. When Jack looks up, he can see the sun between the branches of the trees. "Did you ever try the peach salsa here?" Nicole finally says.

"No, I've only been here once or twice." He shrugs.

"Ugh," she says. "Always working, right?" She clicks her tongue. "This is why you have to sneak out in the middle of the day. The whole world happens in the middle of the day." She looks up ahead, and Jack sees crowds of people, some holding bags with strawberries or red onions or focaccia in them. A little boy holds a big baguette and bites the end off it. His mom laughs. “When I was in high school,” Nicole says as they stroll, “I cut class all the time. I craved that middle of the day, just the mailman on the street, old ladies stooping down to pull weeds.” She smiles. “But pretty soon, Jack, you won’t have to sneak anywhere, right? All you’ll have is time.”

“Time and more time,” he says.

She buys him some iced tea that has herbs and flowers floating in it, and when he sips it, it tastes intensely wholesome. “Wow.”

She motions for him to follow, and they go to the stand with all types of homemade salsa. “One peach, and one tomato garlic,” she says, and hands over a ten, and they give her two little plaid french fry containers with tortilla chips and plastic cups of salsa. “You’ll love it,” she says.

Jack dips his chip and can sense the peach flavor as soon he tastes it, but it’s not overpowering. It is an unusual semi-spicy combination, and he wants more. “Oh boy,” he says. “I love the kick.”

She tries hers, and looks upward in pure joy. She points to Jack. “That’s what the iced tea is for,” she says. Jack drinks it, his filter slipping from under his arm.

“Here,” she says, and snatches the filter, resting it against a giant oak tree.

“But what if . . . ?”

“What if *what*?” she says. “What if someone takes it? Someone’s going to put down their lavender soap and churros so they can steal your air filter?” She shakes her head. “You’ve got to relax, bucko.”

Before he can say anything else, she is pointing to a crocheted crafts booth at the very end of the white tents and charging toward it. There are tall pine trees over them, and now the musician is playing Cat Stevens on the guitar with people gathered around him. Nicole sings the words, so loudly that some people glance her way, and then she squats down to pet a few more dogs, one of the merchants' chickens bobbing behind her and pecking the ground, and Jack just watches.

—

It is after 1:00 p.m. when they leave the farmer's market. "I should check in," Jack says as they walk toward his house.

"Check in for what?" she asks. "A flight to Cancún?" She laughs.

"At the restaurant." A landscaping truck rolls by, bales of pine needle mulch in the back, the shovels and rakes standing at perfect attention. "They don't even know where I am." He slides his phone out of his pocket, and there are no missed calls.

"The difference between us," she says, "is I realize the world can get by without me. You don't, do you?"

"Ha. I guess not," he says. "And I feel guilty when I'm not there." As they walk, he is suddenly so relaxed. "My son got by without me just fine," he blurts out.

She turns sharply to him, a guy in a reflective yellow vest going by on his moped. "Did you say your son?"

"Yeah." Jack looks straight ahead, wishing he'd brought sunglasses. "I didn't mean to. You loosened me up with the salsa, I guess."

Birds chirp in the trees, and they walk the road toward Beech Avenue. A long way ahead, he can see the end of the street where the ocean is. They are two blocks from his house, but for some reason he wants to get there as slowly as possible. He thinks of the term *slower lower Delaware*, and while he's never embodied that more southern take on life here, now, for a second, he wants it. He wants time to be easy and forgiving. He starts talking about Alexis and then Patrick. When they get to his house, he sits on the porch steps as Nicole leans against his Jeep and sips the rest of her iced tea. She crunches the ice cubes when she finishes.

She doesn't interrupt, she doesn't dispute any of his worries or interpretations. She just nods and listens, the sun reflected in her sunglasses. "I had no idea, Jack," she finally says.

The weather is so pleasant—warm without a trace of humidity. An occasional bee but no mosquitoes. They talk about a million things, and he doesn't even know when they switch subjects.

She tells him about her mother cheating on her father and leaving them when Nicole was in high school, and how she had to go into foster care when she was sixteen because her dad was working and fell off a roof and they couldn't track down her mother so there was no one at home to care for her while he was recovering in the hospital.

She tells him about the day she met her husband, Billy, at Skippers after that 5K, and how she knew immediately that she loved him because he made her laugh. She talks about the day he left for Iraq and how a part of her sensed he was never coming back but she told herself she was being silly, that people came back from combat all the time. She keeps her sunglasses on, and once in a while she flicks her fingers under them and turns her head to the side.

They go into his house because she has to use the bathroom, and he opens a bottle of white wine, putting on one of his dad's old records. She sits on the piano bench, and asks him for a coaster, laughing when he says he doesn't care if it leaves a mark.

The record comes to an end. At the piano, she plays "Chopsticks," then "Heart and Soul," and then a slow version of "Moon River" that almost makes Jack fall apart. The record spins and makes a static, quiet sound. She retrieves her wine.

"You know, when Billy was away, getting bad news was always

in the back of my mind. You get used to it being nothing, though—answering the phone every time a weird number comes up, or checking the phone first thing in the morning, knowing he's a couple time zones ahead, and when it keeps being nothing, you get used to that."

She hits a few more keys as if she's tuning the piano, and she listens to their notes. She takes a deep breath. "But nothing prepares you for the day it comes." She twists her mouth, and looks at the wall beyond his staircase. "I always imagined, if it happened, I'd be in my bathrobe or something. I'd be doing the dishes, and I'd see them pull up. I didn't think I'd be at work, filling in for the bartender." Her eyes widen, like some dam has broken behind them. Her voice cracks. "I was shaking a goddamn martini like an idiot." She swallows. "I think I was even singing a song."

"Oh, Nicole," he says.

He grabs a box of tissues. He walks over to her and sits on the piano bench beside her. He's not sure if she'd like a hand on her shoulder, so he just sits beside her and listens as she talks.

"In every way, Billy was a decent man. You know that thing people do when someone says something ridiculous. You know how everyone rolls their eyes or they exchange glances. Billy *never* did that. He was just pure, Jack. Like a version of us that's extinct or something.

"Wherever we went, he'd play peekaboo with a kid over the restaurant booth, or listen to an old man tell him at the grocery store what type of hot dogs were the best." She looks up at the ceiling. "I feel like he and I were just getting started."

Jack nods. He looks at her hands on the piano keys, and he thinks about her finger that used to wear a ring. "Nicole," he finally says. "You're decent, too."

She looks over at him and rolls her eyes. "Yeah, right."

“I’m not kidding.” He puts his hands next to hers, and he realizes he hasn’t played this piano once since the moving company brought it here from his dad’s house. He finds the places where his hands should go, and he plays a few notes, fingers thrumming on the keys.

“Is that . . . ‘Chariots of Fire’?” She laughs.

“I think so,” he says. “I can’t believe it’s still there.”

“We’re like time capsules, aren’t we? All that information stored somewhere.” She wipes her face on her shirt sleeve. “Once in a while, I wake up, and there’s that cut grass smell, the coastal air, and maybe someone’s frying bacon or something a few houses down, and I get this excited feeling, like I can’t wait for Billy to come downstairs. I want to say, ‘Let’s meet up tonight after work.’ And all day, I’d look forward to that evening. He’d yawn at the end of dinner, and I’d say, ‘Oh, Billy, not yet. Not just yet,’ and he was such a good sport, so we’d walk the boardwalk afterward, holding hands like we were seventeen or something.” She breathes in. “And it makes me sad, Jack, devastated sometimes, but I’m grateful for that time capsule memory, and the way it still shows itself for a second and my brain doesn’t immediately discount it.”

“That’s beautiful, Nicole.” Jack stares at the piano, and something about how easy and free she is, about the way she’s letting it all out, has made him more open than he’s been in years, maybe ever. He opens his mouth and knows he’s going to tell her.

FORTY-FOUR

"My mom killed herself." He lets the words hang there, so vulnerable out on their own. He wants to slide his finger across the piano keys so there is noise, but the words expand in the silence. He swallows.

No one ever talked about it. Jack's dad, his grandmother, Deacon, Deacon's parents—they all knew, and they all lived with it together, but he never even told Kitty. He assumed Deacon or Andie had filled her in, but it was strange she never asked him about it, even in their most quiet and intimate moments, and he never shared it with her. He often prepared himself for how he'd approach it once she asked him, what the right words would be, but she never asked.

Nicole is looking at him carefully. Harry has come out of wherever he was hiding. He lies by Nicole's feet.

"When I was twelve," he says, and his voice sounds hoarse, like he just woke up. "They sent her away to a hospital in Utah, and they told me she'd get better, but she never came back." He puts his head down and doesn't look at her.

"Here," she says finally, and hands him her wineglass. He sips it, and hers seems colder and better than his did. She pats his hand. "Oh, Jack. I'm so, so sorry." She is looking at him, and he feels naked—her eyes are like an uncomfortable spotlight he can't escape from. "You keep it all together so well, but the pain. I see it right at the front of your eyes now." He looks at her, and her eyes are red, too. He nods, and she touches his cheek for just a second and then looks away.

"Thanks for letting me talk about her. She was a great mom."

She smiles. "I'm sure she's largely responsible for who you are today."

"Definitely. I have thought about her thousands of times. I still wonder what she'd say, what she'd think of seeing me older. Feels like she should still be around—she'd just be turning eighty."

Nicole nods. "It's not fair sometimes." She sighs. "We have some heavy shit we carry," she says. "Don't we?"

"Yeah," he says. He stretches. He doesn't look at her. It's easier to say it if he doesn't. "I think sometimes I'm pissed at my dad. I never said that to him, but sometimes I felt like he was happy to have her out of the way or something, and maybe that's why I don't mind selling the restaurant. Like to get even. Maybe I wouldn't have wanted to otherwise."

"Hmm," she says. "I don't know how your dad felt. But maybe it's just that you worked there for several decades, and you're tired, and that's why you're ready to sell."

"Could be." He feels like he's been emptied out. But he also feels some sense of relief he hasn't felt in forty years.

"Restaurant tired is a whole other level of tired," she says. Harry jumps up in her lap now, something he hardly ever does with strangers, and Nicole doesn't flinch. She pets his head and chest and smiles at him.

"Yeah, but it's not doctor tired. It's not humanitarian-rescue-worker tired."

She shakes her head. "It's tired enough."

"What about you, though?"

"What about me?" Harry jumps off her. She stands and brings her wineglass to the kitchen sink. Jack stays on the piano bench, and his back hurts. The icemaker drops ice cubes, and the air conditioner clicks on.

"Aren't you tired, too? You're around my age."

"No," she says, and smiles. "I'm at least five years younger, and I still have a few chapters to write."

"Restaurant chapters?"

She shrugs. "Who even knows?" she says, looking at her watch. "Holy heck! It's almost four. We need to get to work!"

Jack smiles. He feels like they cut class. Like he went to the baseball field when he should've been doing something else. But now that the frog is boiled, he doesn't really care about getting to the restaurant before the dinner shift. His crew, the DelDine assistant managers—they can handle a weeknight.

"I wouldn't worry about Patrick," Nicole says. "As long as we're under the same stars, my dad used to say, there's still a chance." She reaches to the side and stretches like she's just run a marathon. "I'd better bolt."

"I should drive you," Jack says. "That's a hike to Schmidt's."

She shrugs. "Nah. I told you I'm young. It's a perfect day. I can walk across town."

Jack folds his arms and watches her leave. She bends down and kisses Harry on the head.

"Nicole," he says, the screen door creaking as she steps out into the light. "This was nice."

She looks back at him and shakes her head. "Why do you seem surprised?"

FORTY-FIVE

Early June. Two weeks until he turns the restaurant over to DelDine.

Andie and Deacon's law firm owns a few beach condos and they've been using one this week at the north end of the boardwalk, having a staycation. They've been going there every day, spending a few hours on the beach, Evie sitting under the umbrella and playing contentedly with sand toys while Deacon heads back and forth between his daughter and the ocean, bringing up buckets of water that she loves to splash her hands in.

They don't stay overnight because their house is only a few minutes away, and it's too much hassle, they say, to pack up all Evie's stuff. They invite Jack to the condo for lunch today, two weeks before Schmidt's is no longer Schmidt's. "The restaurant will close for three days," Nicole said. "That's when the magic fairies come with the new name and a few new features." She arched her wrist, miming an imaginary magic wand. "It will be officially *rebrannnnded.*" Jack's stomach flipped, but that's part of the deal. He's already gotten two of their installment checks that were laid out in the contract, which he deposited into his account and hasn't thought about. When he asked her what the new restaurant name would be, she cackled. "If I told you, I'd have to kill you."

Jack isn't ready for these next weeks. Things are getting busy, but early June is still semi-quiet and bearable. He is relieved to think he doesn't have to be sweating over Fourth of July, sitting in traffic and trying to smooth over customer complaints. Part of him wants to just get into the car and drive to Maine for a week or two. He imagines some cabin on a lake, chilly at night, a firepit maybe, a lot of cold beer, but he can't bring himself to look online for a rental. He's not programmed for this other life.

Andie cuts him a piece of quiche Deacon made and pours him some champagne and a cup of coffee. "So good to see you here, Mr. Soon-to-be-Retiree."

He gives her half a smile, looking at Evie, who is sleeping in her Pack 'n Play, and Deacon, who is slicing tomatoes for their salad. "How is that even possible?" He takes a deep breath.

Andie grips his shoulder. "You've earned it," she says. "It feels weird, but you put in your time."

He shrugs. "I don't know. I feel like I'm calling in sick when I'm not really sick."

"That's Stockholm syndrome," she says, and smiles.

He shakes his head. "But my dad was my age when he *started* taking over the restaurant. My grandmother was on her feet for sixteen-hour days in her seventies! What am I doing?"

Deacon puts the salad next to him on the table. Jack can smell the oil and spices in the dressing, the fresh tomatoes and cucumbers and red onion. "Oh no, has the whining started?" He rolls his eyes. "Wah, I'm a bazillionaire now. Whatever will I do?"

Sleeping Evie moves for a second, and they all freeze. "Voice down," Andie whispers to him, and sips her champagne.

"This looks delicious," Jack says, and stabs a piece of the quiche. "And I'm not whining . . . I'm reflecting." He gulps down some of the good coffee. "It's just the end of an era. That place has been standing for almost seventy years." He realizes he's biting his thumbnail now like Kitty did when she told him about Patrick. "Was it even my right to give it up?" He starts to feel like he's getting chest pain, and he takes a deep breath and sips champagne and hopes they don't notice. "It's the last thing left of our name, you know?"

"I get it," Andie says. "But your name will mean other things."

Deacon sits beside him now and puts his arm around Jack's shoulders. "You'll be okay, my man. You'll take us to Saint-Tropez and the Hamptons and we'll torch those sad Crocs, and all will be well." He looks to make sure Jack's smiling. "Seriously, change is always like this. Change is never the natural thing. We'd rather keep doing the shit that wears us out than move on to something new."

Jack lets him keep his arm there. He looks out their sliding door and can see the ocean: a meadow of waves, a blue postcard.

FORTY-SIX

A little while later, Jack has to head back to the restaurant. He walks slowly as he descends the steps of the condo, the wide swath of white sand and the crumbling jetty in front of him. The condo is on the northernmost part of the boardwalk, and there is a row of cars parked next to it at a spot overlooking the beach.

He hears a dad telling his kids not to go down to the beach empty-handed as he unloads their SUV.

"Where do you live?" someone says as Jack looks at the ocean for a moment. The sun is on him, and the day is pleasant, the beach bar a few doors down playing Caribbean steel drum music.

He turns back, and a woman is hunched over by one of the white benches, a cat beside her on a leash. "Me?" he says.

She smiles, and she is missing some teeth, but her voice is pleasant and reminds him of Janet's. "Of course *you*." She turns to the cat. "Sit, Craig," she says, and miraculously the cat sits. A family walks by holding an Igloo cooler and boogie boards, and the little girl asks to pet the cat. "Craig would love that," the lady says, and Craig closes his eyes as the girl cradles his skull and rubs each of his ears.

"Thank you," the girl says, and her parents smile as they walk down the ramp onto the beach.

"I live in the Pines," Jack tells her. He's about to turn back after she doesn't say anything for a second. Her hair is half pinned up and half falling down, and she wears a cardigan with a button missing and loose pants.

"You're going the wrong direction then, aren't you?"

"Huh, yeah." He clears his throat. "I'm not going home right now." The cat stays sitting like a statue. She squints in the sunlight.

"Park? Oak? Columbia?"

"Beech," he says.

"Ah, I grew up on Park. The road was still a dirt road then. We had a little sign hanging over the door: Content Cottage." Craig looks up at her when she's talking, and the sun halos him.

"Do you, um, still live around here?"

"You could say," she says. She winks, and Jack isn't sure what she means. But then he follows her gaze and sees a small hatchback among the other cars, crammed with things inside: groceries, blankets, paper towels.

He wonders how she pays for the parking meter. Summer parking is a fortune. He wonders if the cops bother her. He thinks of the moon and stars over the ocean, and her trying to sleep inside while Craig tiptoes through the clutter. He puts his hands into his pockets and doesn't know what to say. He thinks of the cold winter, the hot nights that are coming in July and August. He thinks of Rory, the woman who used to own his house, and how this town little by little became something bigger than it was: more expensive, more fast paced. There are so few things left of the old ways. He's not sure what to say, so he kneels down and pets Craig and asks the woman her name.

"Markie," she says. "Markie from Parkie they used to say." She looks at him. "You grew up here," she says. Not a question.

"I did." He stands up and rubs his hands together. He's surprised to see Craig doesn't shed.

"What was your mom's name?"

That question bowls him over for some reason. Maybe it's the champagne, maybe it's the restaurant being almost out of his hands, but he feels his eyes burn, his throat tighten. "Jane," he says. He hasn't said her name out loud in years. He says it like it's a secret. He hears her voice all those years ago. "Johnny, Janie, Jack! The three Js," and she comes back to him fully formed in the years before she went away. He remembers when she opened her bakery down by where the circle is now. How she stood on the porch and smiled, and they took her picture, the Brighton Bakery sign promising and immaculate.

"I knew a lot of Janes," Markie says, and she pulls off her cardigan and ties it around her waist. She gives Craig's leash a tug, and he follows her. "So long, Beech Avenue," she says.

Jack hears her singing something to Craig. "Miss Jane had a bag, and a mouse was in it," she says, and Jack hears his mother's voice again.

"She opened the bag, he was out in a minute," he whispers. A few seagulls squawk. He hears carts rumbling over the boardwalk, hauling beach equipment, and more of the island music from the bar.

He stands there in the bright day and doesn't even know himself.

FORTY-SEVEN

He is walking now, but not toward the restaurant.

He holds his shoes, barefoot and trudging through the sand. The boardwalk is behind him, and so is Andie and Deacon's condo.

He passes a playground and the lake on his left and keeps walking, his feet sinking into the warm sand, occasionally crunching a small shell or kicking a cigarette butt. He sees the waves lap back and forth, some boats out in the distance, a few rafts and beach balls. He walks past people renting umbrellas and a cart with hot dogs and shaved ice.

He doesn't know where he's going, but he feels determined, and he keeps heading north on the beach, the warm breeze against his face. He wonders if Nicole or Vivian or Sam will call him soon; he promised he'd only be gone an hour or two, but he doesn't care. His phone buzzes now in his pocket, but he keeps walking.

One day his mom told him she couldn't breathe in their house anymore. She might need to leave, she said.

"I'll come with you," he said, and he realized how ready he would be to say goodbye to his dad, his grandmother, the restaurant, everything they had, because of how much he needed his mom.

She shook her head, and he felt like a burglar came and took everything inside him.

"You can't," she said.

—

In the distance is a big barge with a few threads of white clouds over it.

He keeps walking and walking, and there are fewer lifeguards, and now he is on Olsen Beach, a permit-only area. Dogs are allowed here, and a couple of golden retrievers and labs are in the water, snatching Frisbees and balls their owners throw.

A big family sits in a circle of beach chairs around a small table set up with food and a grill. Jack looks at them and gives a half wave, and keeps walking. His feet are hot, so he walks along the tide line now, and the water is freezing but clear and honest, and it soothes him.

He imagines the sand rubbing away years of work. He looks toward the lighthouses in Lewes, still so far off in the distance, and all the big houses with balconies to his left. The sun warms him, and he thinks when he gets his moment, this is where he'll bring his beach chair, setting up here, not a far walk from his house. He would just close his eyes and sit back.

He keeps walking. He passes tennis courts and a few boats and people on paddleboards. Kids play tag, and more dogs frolic. He pets a small mutt whose feet are wet, and the owner waves. He walks and walks, and he goes back to the sand where his wet feet slowly dry, and the dry sand gets rid of the damp sand. He realizes where he's heading, and he can't stop.

After a while he's in the North Shores, and he sees the place where Alexis's Aunt Grace's house used to stand. He remembers the fire, years ago, after she'd died. He remembers how he drove by, and they had quickly demolished what was left: the charred wood, the stubborn chimney still standing, the pieces of railing from the porch that used to look out over the sea. Now a new house stands in its place, but he thinks about the dinners they ate in the old house,

Grace setting up Scrabble and putting out cheese cubes and fruit. Now every glass, every ashtray, every chair and footstool is dust.

But he stands on the sand, and he thinks of all those nights he and Alexis walked out here, nowhere else to be, just the moon and bright stars and suggestion of the ocean in the dark. Dune grass and no one anywhere, like they'd discovered something that was just theirs. Her hand in his, and again and again, they'd lie down here. Some of the same sand must be here, the same ocean in front of him.

How did their short time together lead to this life he's living now, these questions he has?

"Patrick," he whispers, alone in the middle of all this sand, his words a prayer of some type, a message that he hopes will bring them together.

February 18, 1982

Dear Mom,

I like the poem you sent me so much I taped it to my bookshelf in my room. Dad is okay, working a lot, but he's taking me to an Orioles game this weekend, and Grandma isn't coming. She says hi, by the way. That's cool that you're learning chess. Will you teach me?

Jack

March 3, 1982

Dear Jack,

You would love chess.

It's nice enough here, and I can see brown and golden hills outside the window. The weather is always pleasant, and they let us eat lunch outside under a canopy of aspen trees. I don't know if I'm learning anything.

I don't know if I'm getting better. I'm trying. How is school? Your dad? I hope you don't miss me.

Love,
Mom

FORTY-EIGHT

Two days later, Jack takes Deacon to see his mom. As he waits in his Jeep he watches a bumblebee crawl across his windshield. Two women in scrubs holding tumblers walk leisurely around the parking lot, and the willow branches above Pine Creek move in the slight breeze.

"She slept the whole time," Deacon says when he gets back into the car. He shakes his head and shrugs. He taps the dashboard in his usual nervous way. "Oh well, right? At least she wasn't scared of me."

"She's sleeping a lot lately?" Jack starts up the car, and the air conditioner blasts on.

"Yeah." He reaches down and picks up his leather workbag and balances it on his lap, meaning he's ready to go. Jack sees a familiar logo on the bag.

"Is that Pillar?"

"Yep," he says, and opens it. "Nothing but the best. Can't believe *you* know Pillar."

Jack picks up his phone. "Wait, hold still."

Deacon holds it and grins, used to having his photo taken. He keeps smiling, but says through his teeth, "What the hell are you doing?"

Jack looks at the photo and hits the send button. "There."

"Who did you just send that to?"

He looks up. "Oh. My, uh, Patrick's sister. She works for Pillar. I thought she'd like to see it. I was FaceTiming her yesterday because she was installing a new showerhead and didn't know how to handle the plumber's tape."

Deacon narrows his eyes. "That guy won't talk to you, but now you're cool with his sister?"

Jack nods. "She helped me pick out a suit for the awards dinner, so I sent her a box of tropical fruit. She even wrote last week to ask how I make mashed potatoes. Weird, right?"

"No, it just underscores what a good guy you are, and how her brother is a shithead for not giving you a chance." He shakes his head. "I mean, you are fully sister-endorsed."

Jack's text alert goes off. Lara with a celebration emoji. *#GoPillar* she writes. He quickly sends her back a smiley face. He looks up and sees Deacon watching.

Deacon rubs his hands together. "Anyway . . ." He looks through his bag. "Where you taking me today?"

"Oh, yeah." Jack puts his hand on the gearshift. "I was thinking Wawa. I could go for a red slushie."

Deacon exhales. "That shit will kill you, man. All that dye and sugar."

"And?"

"Let's make it happen," Deacon says, and Pine Creek is behind them.

December 1989

Dear Alexis,

I tried to call, but your dad, I guess it was, said you didn't live there anymore. I hope this letter forwards to you.

I know we lost something big, and I think about that something more often than you know, but I think it was the right thing we did, and I thought there was still a chance for us, wasn't there?

Deacon keeps trying to set me up with girls, but it feels wrong, like you and I aren't finished with each other. If you tell me we're done, I won't bother you anymore. School is killing me, and what do I have beyond that?

I don't know what the answer to anything is, but I wish you'd write back.

Jack

January 1990

Jack,

We're done. Okay? No hard feelings—it's just over. Please stop. Bigger things to worry about.

A.

FORTY-NINE

1982

Jack asked his dad if he could fly to Utah on his own so he could visit his mom. She had been there for six months. Jack imagined walking the grounds with her and seeing the things she had written him about: the bird's nest in the gazebo, the single wooden swing by the lake. He imagined sitting with her for lunch at a polished table with flowers on it.

His dad shook his head and looked at Jack with love and pity and told him she still wasn't ready. It was better this way, he said, but before Jack knew it, it was a rainy day in July, and her doctor called, the ringing of the phone sounding sinister in retrospect, and his dad wailed and kept saying, "No, no, no."

Johnny slumped down on the floor, and his hand shook as he held the phone. "How could you let this happen?" he shouted into the phone. "Why weren't you watching her?"

—

Although she had already been gone for what seemed like a long time, the house got even lonelier after she died. One day in the fall, Jack's dad came home from work and saw Jack sitting at the kitchen table. A box of cold Steelo's pizza he had barely touched was plopped next to his homework. Johnny's work shirt was stained with brown gravy and oil, and he pulled Jack to him and said, "Oh, Jackie, you look so sad." From that point on, he made Jack come to the restaurant every day after school.

All the bussers and dishwashers and waitstaff were nice to him, high-fiving him when they walked by, teasing him about girlfriends and his good grades. Jack's grandmother always smoothed his hair and gave him a bowl of rice pudding. Genevieve, who was young and new to Schmidt's then, told Jack knock-knock jokes. In this way, the restaurant became Jack's life, too, his family. It worked because it had to.

FIFTY

Jack pulls up to Genevieve's house the next day. The window is taped, and a whirligig spins by her front steps. An empty bird feeder swings from a pole, and the sun is warm. He knocks on her porch door, and he's reminded of the day in December with Ziggy. Even though he knows he's gone for now, Jack feels like Ziggy will be waiting for him.

Jack sees the curtain peel back, and then Genevieve opens the door. "Jack," she says, and barely smiles.

"Hey." He waits for her to unlock the door, but she doesn't. "I, uh, made this for you."

"You made a pie?" She looks down at it. It's a triple berry pie he's been experimenting with—blueberries, raspberries, and strawberries.

She opens the screen door and motions him inside.

He stands there and thinks of Ziggy slamming him against the wall, his awful words, what he said about Genevieve stealing. Jack's been angry with her for doing it; he would have given her anything if she'd asked. Maybe she didn't want to ask. He has wondered how much, how often. Was it just those promotions, or is there much more that he just missed? He looks at the living room, nicer since the last time he was there—neat and happy. It's as though all the bad energy has left. "Can I put this down here?" he says, looking at the dining room table, and she nods. "So how've you been?"

"I've been okay, Jack." She looks down at her feet. He and Genevieve used to have something together that felt natural and easy, but this feels rigid and difficult. He wipes his forehead.

"Are you working anywhere these days?"

She shakes her head. "No."

"Genevieve, I don't understand why you're mad at me. Your son tried to kill me. Shouldn't I be the one who's pissed?" She just shakes her head sadly, picks up the pie, and walks into the kitchen. He follows her, and she brings the kettle to the sink.

She sighs. "I'm having tea," she announces in an irritated voice. "I'll make you some?"

"Yeah. But—" She puts out her hand.

"Jack, please." She stands by as the kettle fills, and then snaps the lid back in place. She lights the flame on the burner, and the wet pot sizzles for a second as she settles it. She opens the cupboard and takes out a box. She removes two tea bags and hangs each one carefully over two blue mugs. Jack pulls out one of her kitchen chairs and watches her.

Jack looks down at the pie. On the top of it, he designed a lattice with a small dough strawberry in the middle. He can smell the sweet fruit. He watches her grip the counter, and now he hears her start to cry.

He stands up. "What? What's wrong?"

"You believed him," she says quietly, trembling.

He walks over to her. The water in the kettle makes a surging noise like it's heating up, and her hands shake as she crumples the tea bag wrappers.

She turns to him, and her whole face is hurt. Her frown stabs Jack. "You believed him when he said I stole from you."

"Not . . . exactly." He wants to tell her he never knew what to believe, that he of course had doubts, but he never felt sure. He touches her arm, but she jerks it away. "I kept waiting for you to tell me your side of the story. I kept waiting for you to come to me. *Someone* was stealing. I wasn't sure what to think. I just wanted to live."

She shakes her head. "I'm sorry about him. Now that he's away, I see how alone he was, how weak I was for not doing more to keep him safe and healthy, away from all the bad stuff." She rubs her eyes. "I see a hundred different ways I failed him. But me stealing? When he said it, you looked like he confirmed something for you."

Jack just remembers that knife so close to him, the way his stomach flipped and he felt like he would faint. He remembers feeling terrified, that there was no way out of what Ziggy was about to do. "How did you know?"

She wipes her eyes quickly. "It was in your eyes. I'm *used* to you, Jack. To your whole family. I could always tell what you were all thinking."

"Well, what about the night before Thanksgiving? I heard you close the safe."

"Are you fucking kidding me?" she says. Genevieve hardly ever curses, and Jack feels pressure building in his head. "I closed it because *you* left it open. Do you know how many times I've had to close it because of your absentmindedness . . . just like your dad."

"I didn't know that," Jack says, and feels foolish. He doesn't know what to believe. She had so much knowledge, access to everything. He's spent these months resigned to the fact that she was stealing and now doesn't know what to think.

She points at him again. "Ziggy never used to lie when he was little. He was like a Boy Scout. But the drugs made him cruel. Like a different part of his brain took over. He told Rose she had a different father a few years ago and told her he had found adoption papers. She was devastated." She clears her throat. "He knows how to read people, and he managed to say exactly what you feared. He's good at that." She rolls her eyes. "He should have gone into sales or something. But all those years! All those damn years at the restaurant. I should have at least earned your trust. I gave Schmidt's *everything*. I took time away from my family to give to the restaurant. That's the only stealing I've done!"

Jack nods. He glances down at that pie, and he wants to hurl it at the wall. He's so pissed at everyone. And he's pissed at himself. For letting the restaurant slip away—and for not doing more for all his loyal employees. Especially Genevieve. He should have gone to her with his suspicions. "I would have listened to anything you told me, Genevieve."

"I shouldn't have had to explain."

"Then tell me that."

Her nostrils flare. "That's not my job. You should have known better. *Forty years*, Jack! Forty"—she pauses—"fucking years."

He almost smiles for a second. He's heard her swear more times today than he ever has in his life. He's thought for so many months that she has let him down, like everyone else has, that he almost can't stop seeing her as guilty. He can't separate her from it, but he doesn't tell her this. "I'm sorry, Genevieve. I don't know what I'm doing," he says. He shakes his head, and the tea kettle whistles. "It doesn't matter anyway. I have to go." He blows out air. "But who did it then? Who stole? Where did the money go?"

She shakes her head. "I have my guesses, but I would never accuse anyone if I wasn't sure."

"Well, anyway," he says. "I'm sorry."

"I'm sorry, too, for putting you in danger." She crosses her arms and stares at the stove. "I'm grateful you came here that day. I knew you would."

He nods. "Oh well," he says. "None of it matters anymore, Genevieve." He looks at her calendar and sees that her granddaughter circled her birthday in June and wrote her name there with drawings of balloons and smiley faces. "The restaurant's not even mine anymore. In six days, it's all theirs."

"You sold it?" she asks. He can't believe she hasn't heard this from anyone: Vivian, general town gossip.

He nods. "They made a good offer. And my heart wasn't in it anymore."

"That's too bad. You're still young."

"Ha." He reaches into his pocket and thinks he's grabbed his car keys, but he realizes he's holding the keys to the restaurant, a big mess of them like a jailer's ring, some of them to cash register drawers they don't have anymore, a filing cabinet he got rid of, a safe deposit box that he's not even sure if he still has. He feels like he made the biggest mistake. He takes a deep breath. "I have a kid—that's some more news for you."

She furrows her eyebrows. "You've had a busy winter," she finally says, and then she gestures for him to sit at the table. She is pouring tea and taking out forks and plates for the pie. Jack thought he was leaving, but finds he's sitting where she tells him to and putting his hands on the warm mug.

FIFTY-ONE

A strange number flashes on his phone the next day. He's on the way to the restaurant, though driving there these last few days really fills him with dread. Who will he even be after this?

"Hello," he says, and there is a pause. He's not sure if he hit the speaker phone button properly.

He expects it will be Vincent or Paulette or one of the kitchen people calling out or telling him they're stuck in summer traffic, or maybe one of the river cruises he was checking out as a way to celebrate his freedom, but it's a guy's voice.

"Is this, um, Jack Schmidt?"

"Yes," Jack says quickly, and then he blurts out, "Is this Patrick?" He thinks how stupid he'll sound if it's anyone else. His heart races now. A lump blocks his throat, and he's not sure if he's even stopping at stop signs.

A long pause. "Yeah," he says.

"Oh shit," Jack says. He takes a deep breath, and his head goes blank. All those things he's rehearsed for months now have evaporated. He feels like he's out of his body. He's reaching for the right words.

"This is only going to be like a thirty-second call," Patrick says.

Jack swallows. "Okay, got it." He doesn't say anything. "I, uh, I know this is all really—"

"No, I don't want to get into the past. I talked to my sister Lara, who I guess keeps in touch with you or whatever."

"Yeah, she's great." Jack thinks of him as a little boy, and he doesn't really have a clear vision of what he looks like now. He used to try to picture Alexis after she left, and Jack couldn't remember her face exactly. He thought he'd always be able to see her with his eyes closed, but she was just a blur.

He imagines Patrick as a toddler, a teenager, and how something was robbed from him. Jack can hear it now in his voice: the loss he's always lived with. Jack knows what that's like. He lives with a wound that's never been able to heal. Not having a parent dents you. Look at Ziggy. There's an emptiness, no matter what you do to fill it. It's not Jack's fault, but it's not Patrick's fault, either. Jack wants to say all that to him. He wants to tell him they can take this slow, but to please give him a chance.

"Well, Lara shouldn't have done that," he says now. "She should *not* have visited you in the first place."

"Patrick, I hope—"

"Listen, we're not doing this!" he shouts.

Jack's eyes burn. He didn't know what he expected, but getting yelled at was not on the top of the list. "Doing what?"

"We're not like connecting."

"Why are you calling then?" Jack's sure he can hear his own heart banging away.

"I'm telling you it's never going to be anything. That's all." The sound of wind blows into the phone and Jack wonders if he's pacing outside his office or if he's on a walk or standing on his back porch. "I don't have a father, and that's okay." He snorts. "My mom's dead, and so is the man that raised me. I'm an orphan." His voice sounds terrible, and it worries Jack. "I'm an orphan, Jack Schmidt."

"I didn't know about you!" Jack shouts. "I didn't *know*!" He hasn't yelled like this in a long time, and he wonders what Patrick's face looks like as he hears Jack's roar. Jack is at the stoplight at Second Street and Rehoboth Avenue, and he feels adrenaline rushing through him. He watches two kids on bikes glide over the crosswalk in front of him. A grandfather follows them holding a new kite in its package. "If I'd known, Patrick, I would have been on the first plane out there. The first letter you got from me is exactly when I found out." There is just silence. "Please believe me."

"Who knows what to believe?" Patrick says, and his voice is hurt.

Jack resolves to stay calm. "I don't want to speak ill of your mom, Patrick—"

"Then *don't.*" He can see Patrick's face in his head now. It's so clear. His angry eyes. "Because I won't *let* you."

"I thought you were . . ." But Jack can't say it. He thinks of the relief he felt that day, how he thought Alexis would love him again.

Patrick laughs, a hurt laugh. He continues laughing for a beat too long. "All those years, no clue?"

"How would I know? She *lied* to me, and I guess I was stupid to believe her."

"Sorry she ruined your plans, *Jack.*" The way he says Jack's name. The disgust. It's more than Jack can take.

"They were *her* plans first," Jack says, and then he hangs up.

FIFTY-TWO

The day before Jack's last day, Sam pops his head in the office door. "Mr. Schmidt," he says. Jack looks up from clearing off his desk, and he's feeling overwhelmed. He should have told them he wants his furniture: the desk, the chair, the old chest of drawers the printer sits on. He left too much up to chance.

What will I be without this place? He doesn't want to walk away tomorrow and not have any of this, not see his crew anymore. He realizes after a few seconds he hasn't responded to Sam.

"Hey, bud," he says, and gives him half a smile.

Sam's face is pale, and he doesn't look Jack in the eyes. He has a big envelope in his hands, and he's holding it out to Jack as though he'll know what it's for. He shakes his head and starts fiddling with the button on his palm tree shirt with his other hand.

"What's this?"

"Mr. Schmidt," he says, and his face collapses. He starts crying.

"What?" Jack says, and he puts his hand on Sam's shoulder. "What's the problem?"

"I'm so sorry," he says, and he's hiccupping. Tears roll down his face. He puts the envelope in Jack's hand. Jack opens it, and there are twenties and fifties stuffed together.

"This is most of what I took," he says.

Jack steps back and looks down at the money again. "You?"

Sam nods, and he wipes his eyes. "I made a note anytime I swiped a twenty from the drawer, or I punched in refunds or discounts." He has a few zits around his mouth, and he is shivering now. "I'm so sorry. You've always been so nice to me."

"Sam," Jack says, and he leans back against his desk and crosses his arms. "I don't—"

"I never wanted to, honest to God, Mr. Schmidt."

"Then why did you?" Jack says quietly. He doesn't know how to feel. Maybe all those years ago, the counselor he saw as a teenager *was* right. He's so fucking sick of being disappointed by people. Maybe he does need to get in his car and drive far away. Maine, Canada even. He feels like he doesn't know anything, and soon he will know less.

He looks at Sam, his nails bitten down, his face so sad, and Jack thinks he really needs to tell Nicole about this, doesn't he? How can he know this and not? But their zero-tolerance policy. And what about the police? Does he need to involve them?

Sam looks terrible.

He opens his mouth, and his voice cracks. "Because they needed me," he says.

"Who?" Jack asks.

His eyes look so dark, and he starts crying more. "My boyfriend's family. They're so poor, Mr. Schmidt. They both worked nights together, but one evening, their car broke down and they couldn't get to work, so they got fired. No second chance, no warning. Without a car, they couldn't get back on their feet. The mom's inhaler prescription took everything out of their budget, and the dad was giving most of their food to her and to Cody, my boyfriend, and was practically *starving*. I'm so sorry, but it was terrible to watch.

"It was wrong to steal, Mr. Schmidt, but it felt good to give Cody money and have him bring it to them. He told them he mowed lawns and raked leaves and shoveled snow, and they were grateful, and it was like I had the power to make them better again. They were so . . . broken. You'd be surprised how even thirty dollars could turn their whole week around." He shakes his head. "I knew it was wrong, and I knew you could probably see it, but I kept telling myself I'd pay you back. I knew I would."

Jack looks at the sad envelope and wonders where Sam got all this from. He shakes his head. "Why didn't you *tell* me?" he asks. "They could have worked here."

"I asked you in September if you were hiring, and you said not at the moment because the summer rush was over." He blinks. "Which of course isn't any excuse."

Jack purses his lips. "That sounds like me." He rubs his chin and stares at Sam, who looks as defeated as Jack used to feel when he was young, lying in bed and missing his mom and wondering if things would ever be okay again. "How are they now?"

"Better, actually. I told my grandpa about them right after Thanksgiving—he has a lot of good connections. He got them jobs at Delaware State Parks." He wrinkles his face and takes a breath. "It took me a long time to talk to my grandpa about them, Mr. Schmidt." He looks down at the ground. "He didn't know I was, um . . . gay," he whispers. "So I couldn't tell him about them without saying I had a boyfriend, and I love Cody too much to have lied and said he was just a friend."

Jack nods. "How did it go with your grandfather?"

"He was really good about it." He fiddles with his button again. "He said he figured." He laughs for a second and wipes his face. "But I haven't taken anything since November, I swear, Mr. Schmidt. On my life." He stands straighter. He takes out a folded-up piece of paper.

"Here's a list of every dollar I took. Every paycheck since December, I've been putting it all back in this envelope." Jack takes the paper from him. He holds the envelope for a minute, and finally he puts it back into Sam's hands.

"Keep it."

"What?" he says. His eyes are puffy.

"You're as good as they come, Sam, and you'll find another good thing to do with it." Jack folds his hands and smiles. He thinks of his dad's eyes, how they would crease at the sides when he'd say something nice to one of the employees and how Jack always wanted to be like Johnny. "That took guts for you to come to me." He exhales. "I know you won't do it again."

"Never." Sam wipes his face. "This didn't go like I thought it would."

—

Jack rushed out of the restaurant minutes later and didn't say where he was going. He made one stop, and then he drove and drove, down Route 24, the sun peering behind clouds, and turned into Bay Manor.

He leaves the car door open now and holds a box out in front of him. Genevieve is sitting on the porch, braiding her granddaughter's hair, a new small fish pond in front of her porch with a trickling fountain. Jack looks down at the lily pads, at the two little fish flicking back and forth.

"Jack," Genevieve says.

Jack holds out the box of pizza from Steelo's, the same pizza she brought to his house the night his dad died. "I owed you this," he says.

—

"Lara Hammersmith," Sam says like a butler, popping his head in Jack's office door a couple of hours later.

Jack reflexively jumps to his feet. "Ah!" he says.

Lara smiles at Sam as he walks away, and then comes through the door, her big purse overflowing with various things, one of them a baguette. Her face looks flushed. "Sorry to bother you, but I had some stuff to do at the Pillar factory store, and I just thought I'd say hello," she says.

"It's nice to see you," he says. He realizes he's relieved. He imagined she'd be pissed about what he said to Patrick yesterday. He drums his hands on his desk.

"You heard about my call with your brother?"

"Bits and pieces," she says, and takes out the baguette and lays it on Jack's desk. "But we don't need to talk about Patrick. I, um, wanted to get *you* something."

"Get me something?" Jack can smell the bread. It looks like something from Paris.

"Yeah." She rummages through her purse, then lays a candle lighter on the desk, and then a white box, and then she pulls out two small bottles of champagne. "For your retirement," she says.

"Holy shit," Jack says. "Are you kidding?"

"Why would I?" She smiles. She opens the white box, and there's a perfect small cake inside, and now she's lighting the candle, her eyes reflecting the flame.

They sip from their champagne bottles and break off a few pieces of the delicious baguette and hunks of cheese she brought along. "This was, like, ridiculously kind of you," he says.

She shrugs and wipes her face. "I live alone, and sometimes I come home after work, and all the houses and apartments I walk by seem to be glowing with possibility and fun, and I know it's not always the case, but it seems like people have good things they're going to."

Jack sits back. "That's exactly what it feels like."

"And I feel like I just drive and drive and visit all the stores, and do my reports, and people are polite to me, but if it were my last day of work, I would hope someone would at least bring me a piece of cake."

Jack smiles. "If I'm around, Lara, I'll bring you the biggest piece of cake."

"Cool," she says. "Everyone likes to be thought about." She stands there, and her cheeks are less pink now, and her big purse looks deflated without all the groceries in it. He looks at her and is overcome. He reaches his hand out and she shakes it as if they're making a deal.

He wants to ask her what Alexis was like in her later years, why she decided to stop being a dentist. He wants to ask if she mentioned any good memories of him. But Lara standing here today feels somehow inevitable, and he's just grateful she's here.

—

"So what will you do after this?" She adjusts her purse on her shoulder as he walks out the back door with her. The cars are parked in every metered spot on the street, a sure sign that summer is in full swing, and in the distance he can see the sea dragon ride swinging back and forth. "My mom used to quote Mary Oliver: 'What is it you plan to do with your one wild and precious life?'" Her face changes then. "Sorry, I didn't mean to bring her up."

"Water under the bridge," he says. "It has to be, right?" He puts his hands into his pockets and stands there. He feels a little queasy from cake and cheese and bread and champagne in the afternoon, but he also feels better now than he did this morning. "I don't know what

I'll do. I think I might just get in my car and drive and be nothing for a while. I haven't not gotten up and thought about the restaurant in about thirty years, so maybe it will be a nice change of pace."

She nods. "I hope you're happy." She frowns slightly. "I don't know you that well, but you don't seem like a guy who wants to be nothing, even just for a while."

He shrugs, but feels a quick pain in his temple. "Who knows, right?"

"I definitely don't." She smiles and taps Jack's arm. "Thanks for letting me drop in here, and I'm sorry about . . . my brother."

"I am, too, but oh well, right?"

"His loss."

"Thanks for bringing this little party. You turned my day around, Lara."

"I'm always just across the bay," she says, and waves. He watches her for a few seconds, and the sunlight warms his face.

Back in the office, he looks down at their empty champagne bottles and the crumbs of cake, and he can't help but feel pleased. He thinks of Alexis then, who, no matter what else, raised this nice young woman. "I'm sorry you didn't get enough time," he whispers, as if she can hear him. He thinks about Patrick and how hurt he sounded, and he wishes he had the answers.

His dad used to say that the best thing about Monday morning was its possibility for the week. Maybe some Monday morning, Patrick will wake up and decide he wants to talk.

Jack puts the rest of his stuff into the box, and he still has one more day here, but he feels ready for it, thinking there might be some good things ahead.

FIFTY-THREE

Late at night, long after he's gone to bed, someone is banging at his door.

His heart pounds. He thinks about Ziggy. Could he be out, ready to finish what he started? Should Jack call the police? Or Deacon?

Harry runs into the room and scampers under the bed. Jack stands there, and the pounding resumes.

He trudges out, knees shaking, cell phone dialed to 911 and ready to hit the call button, and he flicks the porch light switch on and peers through the door's small window.

"Nicole!" he says, pulling the door open. Her eyes look wide, accentuated by the bright light, and her glasses are hooked over her sweatshirt.

"Hey," she says. "Is it late?"

"I think so, yeah. Come inside." He motions for her. His pajama pants are ripped, but he's too tired to care.

She wears stretch pants and flip-flops, and it looks like she attempted to paint her fingernails recently in mint green but only got halfway finished. She comes inside and looks around and seems to forget what she's doing here. Jack wonders for a second if she's sleepwalking.

"What's going on?" he finally says.

"Don't go through with it," she says, and now she's holding the ring on her necklace and twisting it in her hands, and Jack swears she's about to cry.

FIFTY-FOUR

"What?" He's never seen Nicole look like this, so frantic. Hell, he doesn't think her pulse would escalate if snipers crashed through her living room window. But now she is breathing hard and fiddling with that ring and looking nervous.

The house is dark except for the light coming from his bedroom, so he quickly switches on a lamp. "Sit down," he says, and he moves two of his boxes from the restaurant off his sofa.

Her eyes dart even more, and Jack wonders if she's been drinking or taken too many allergy pills or something. Or if she's having a breakdown. She can't seem to focus. She glances at the piano. "The wineglass never left a mark. Huh." She kicks off her flip-flops and folds her legs crisscrossed on his sofa, and Jack isn't sure how he should handle this. She puts her glasses on, and once they're in place, she seems more centered.

"What's wrong?"

She clears her throat. "I'm just going to say it." She takes her hands off her necklace and looks right at him. "In September, they're going to knock down your restaurant." She winces after the words are out; she lets the news hang there like the echo of a tree falling.

He takes a deep breath, and now he's sitting on the rocking chair he's hardly ever sat on in all the years he's lived here. It makes a creaking sound, so he anchors his bare feet against the floor. "Every other restaurant, you've kept the building pretty much the same, right? I *asked* about that. It was one of the first things we talked about, remember? Where the hell did this come from?"

She nods. "I just heard the new plans tonight. I got into a screaming match with Maurice." She tears up again, and quickly swipes her eyes. "The real estate's too valuable," she says. "They are going to run the restaurant through the summer, not do the name change as we originally thought, and keep everything the same. Then in September they are going to send out some press release that they've found all kinds of problems with the building and that it needs to be torn down. Maurice has guys that will do that. They're going to say they're taking time to make the best decision, and before long they'll raze it and subdivide the lot. They have tons of lawyers; they'll get a yes quickly.

"Maurice is already in talks with some guy who wants to build a huge hotel right there, even higher than the height ordinance. And then they're going to put some stupid beach shack restaurant on the remaining quarter that lets people order things online like wraps and smoothies." She holds her stomach. "I'm not supposed to tell you, Jack. Maurice expressly said I was forbidden and threatened me with legal crap, but I think about your grandmother in that photo, and I keep looking at the restaurant. It's one of the last. There's nothing like it left, and I keep thinking about what Billy would say, and I know the answer. I can't let them do it."

"Why bother running a restaurant when you can make tons more on a hotel?" Jack says flatly. All this information washes over him, and just like all bad news he's ever gotten, he can't feel it directly. It feels muted, far away. He imagines a wrecking ball, a bulldozer. He imagines the siding and roof shingles and the windows stacked in piles. He imagines the rubble of the restaurant, like what it looked like when his dad arrived after the storm in 1962 and told Hazel and Agnes it would all be okay.

He feels his dad and grandmother looking at him now, even his mom. *What have you done, Jack?* The same thing he thought when Alexis was pregnant. *I'm so sorry*, he thinks.

"I don't think I put anything about that in the contract," he says. He looks down at his lap and runs his hands over his face. "I should have said the building has to stay as is. I should have made them agree to that. I signed it, I took the money. It's their restaurant, Nicole. I signed it away."

She stands up. She doesn't look resigned. She looks electrified, ready for battle. "But there has to be some way," she says loudly. She taps her foot. Her eyes widen. "There is—it's PR. They hate bad PR. They want to always smell like a rose. They want the community to love them. They know if the locals turn on them, it's too long a winter to keep all the businesses afloat. Their model isn't sustained by tourists, it's from the returning customers. Community partnerships, too. We can hit them with bad press. You can threaten to turn Main Street against them, can't you? I'll help, Jack."

He listens and nods, and he's so tired he doesn't know what to do. DelDine takes over everything tomorrow. Well, today, since he's sure it's after midnight.

She walks to the door. Harry is standing by her feet, and she looks down at him. "I'm tired of it, Jack. I'm tired of how no one has a soul anymore. You're one of the only people I know who does."

"Thanks for thinking that." He runs his hand through his hair. "I'll do my best, Nicole." But he already feels defeated. The big guys like Maurice always win. She nods, and she looks so worried and lost in thought. The rocking chair is still rocking from him getting up, and they both just stand there for a few seconds, looking at each other.

FIFTY-FIVE

He never asked his dad the details.

For years he tried to guess. A scarf, the bathrobe sash. Maybe she even jumped from a window. She seemed to have a lot of freedom there. But he never knew.

He never knew that the woman who avoided the ocean all those years, barely ever putting her feet in the white foam, the woman afraid to grab a shell if the tide was coming back in, would walk miles down a Utah road to a bridge, the place she chose, the river below so muddy and ugly and final.

FIFTY-SIX

After Nicole leaves, Jack wanders around the house, but he can't focus on anything. He puts on a record, Billie Holiday singing "The Very Thought of You." He makes himself some coffee. He brushes Harry and works at a knot he has on his neck. It's 3 a.m., and he doesn't know what to think about anything.

He picks up the phone finally and dials Andie's number.

"What the hell?" Deacon says, his voice sleepy.

"Sorry," Jack says.

Deacon groans. "Are you bleeding?"

"No." He feels like a fool, standing in the house in his bare feet, all his lights on, the room a disaster, but he couldn't wait a second longer. "I need to talk to my attorney."

Deacon exhales. "Man, she might not be your attorney after this." Jack hears him adjust the phone. "It's our favorite former restaurant owner, honey."

"Thanks," she says, and she doesn't talk. Jack imagines her going into her office, or at least in the hallway away from Deacon. "What's wrong, Jack?" she finally says.

He tells her about Nicole. He tells her about the restaurant being torn down. He tells her they left all this out. "Isn't that a breach of contract?" he asks.

She clicks her tongue. "Fuck them." She sighs. "But I think it's within their rights to do whatever they want, Jack. I'm not sure we have a leg here."

He tells her about Nicole saying that they'll find someone to claim the building's in disrepair, that their plan is to say they're going to do what's best for the neighbors and knock it all down and wait until spring to start their master plan. Andie is typing on her computer and looking at the contract and reading paragraphs out loud. Jack doesn't understand most of what she's saying, but she seems to be on to something. "Those bastards," she says finally, and types a few more things.

"Right?"

"I have an idea," she says. She takes a deep breath, and the sleepiness is fully gone from her voice. Jack feels bad that her day is starting at this hour. She brainstorms some ideas with him, and they excite him and make his stomach flip. He wonders how she is programmed to think this quickly on her feet. He envies having such a logical, decisive mind. She has one final idea, and it's killer. "But is this what you *want*, Jack? The sale to fall through?"

He thinks about everything being reset. He thinks about sending the DelDine AMs away tomorrow—well, today, actually. He thinks about all the mornings after this, all summer, all fall, all holiday season, and Schmidt's being his again. Forever. It is easy to stay in that pattern. It's one he's worn a groove into. He can do it with his eyes closed. But he thinks of that beach chair, the way it sits hopefully in the back of his car now.

His dad's record gets to the end, and he keeps hearing the needle bob and play just static, the sound of nothing. "That's a good question," he finally replies.

FIFTY-SEVEN

There is a smell to Rehoboth in late spring or early summer that Jack can never get enough of. Like pine needles and wet air. It reminds him of being young, six or seven, and riding his bike behind his mom. She loved early morning bike rides, and they would head out from the house and ride the flat roads, him watching her straight back as she took in everything. They passed the park by his elementary school and they zigzagged along roads and headed toward Silver Lake, the geese and morning sun saluting them. Once in a while, she'd point to something—a heron, a turtle—and he never said anything because he seemed to sense then how fragile it all was, how the wrong word could ruin her mood.

Once, she jostled him awake early, and he remembers his dark bedroom, her smiling face over him, and she said, "Jackie, I have the best surprise for you." He knew it involved a bike ride. He got dressed right away, brushed his teeth, and she had set out toast with honey on a plate, which he gobbled quickly in the kitchen. "Let's go," she said, a quiet but excited squeal because his dad had such a hard time sleeping, always worrying about the restaurant. If they woke him, he'd be tired all day.

They took their bikes from the shed. They set off while the sky was barely light, and she took Jack to the beach block and pointed up to the telephone poles. There at the top sat what looked like a giant hive covered in pine needles and leaves. “Look,” she said.

Jack expected a baby alien to climb out from it. “What is it?”

“You won’t believe it when you see,” she said, and the sky got lighter, and they stood there, bike beside bike, and all of a sudden two green parrots poked their heads out and flew into the sky, their wings tipped with bold shades of red or orange.

“Parrots?” He looked at her, and he felt his whole face change. “Parrots!”

“They’re here by accident,” she said, whispering, and as they stood there, two more popped out. “They got mixed up in their flight, and we get to see parrots here. Little old us in little old Delaware.”

“I love them,” he said without thinking, and he thought right then that he would never forget that image. They heard the birds’ content chatter, a few pine needles falling from their giant nest as more flew out, and the sun, the new sun, made each one glow.

—

It is June 15, the day he’s supposed to turn the restaurant over. Harry is sleeping in his small bed by the window, the morning breeze and sound from the birds coming in through the screen.

He listens to another pot of coffee dripping slowly on the morning his restaurant will not be his anymore, his body so tired, and he wonders what it all meant.

What was the point of having his mother for just a few years; what was the point of never knowing about Patrick? What is he supposed to do with the restaurant now? He stands there and feels too young to be old and too old to be young, years and years of living ahead of him, if he’s lucky, nothing really certain. He drinks from his Green Awning Books mug, and he scratches his head.

He bends down to pet Harry's head, and he barely opens his eyes.

Jack drinks more coffee, and then it becomes clear.

He walks out to his shed and finds his bike. He pumps air into the tires, and he's just in shorts and a Pappy's Pizza T-shirt and flip-flops, and he's riding his Schwinn, the last thing his mom bought him.

"This is a grown-up bike," she told him. And over the years, even when Kitty or Deacon and Andie bought mountain bikes, he never had any desire to get anything else. It's faded green with a nice wide seat and foot brakes, and as he starts to pedal now, he realizes he's forgotten how much he likes riding.

He thinks of his mom, and hopes she enjoyed their mornings together. He thinks of Patrick and wonders, if things had been different, if he would have liked to follow him on a bike the way Jack followed his mom. As he rides toward the ocean, he feels something strange inside him. Something settled as he slowly moves, the air still a little cool, no one around except an occasional runner or person walking their dog.

It doesn't matter, he finally thinks. *It doesn't matter either way.*

He inhales the smell of early summer, of this town, and it feels right to be in this moment. He hears his mom's voice ahead of him, reminding him to keep his eyes open. He hears his dad in the car when they were stuck on the highway, squeezing Jack's shoulder and saying, *This will pass, and we'll have a story.* He hears Kitty saying she's sorry, she's sorry, and Patrick telling him to just stop. And then he hears his grandmother in one of the last conversations he had with her. They were setting up for Sunday brunch, and she said, "I need to take a seat." She motioned for Jack, and they sat by the wide window, her favorite place. Agnes was there helping out, and Jack's grandmother looked at her as she disappeared into the kitchen. Hazel put her hand over his. “It doesn’t matter, Jack,” she said. “Nothing matters, as long as you have love.”

—

When he gets to the beach block, he sees Markie sitting on the bench, Craig right beside her. Her eyes light up when she recognizes Jack. “Hello, Beech Avenue,” she says, and smiles, and Craig walks over her lap and lets Jack pet his head.

“Morning.” Jack stares out at the ocean, the sun like a patient Buddha watching them, the ocean water silky and rippled. A man drags the lifeguard stands down, one at a time.

“You look like you’ve figured out something,” she says.

He glances over at her and then back at the ocean. The same ocean all these years. The same sky and air. It’s astonishing, he thinks. Wondrous. All of it. “I think I may have.” He stands there for a little longer, and she sits and watches him contentedly. When he gets back on his bike, she waves to him.

“Go get ’em,” she calls.

August 1982

Dear Jack,

At the funeral, sitting next to you, I admired what a nice young man you're turning into. Someday you will have your own family and you will understand how complicated we all are. We are many, many things, each of us, and I wanted to say this today, but I couldn't find the words.

Your mother tried her hardest. Harder than that. She tried to get back but couldn't, and I think instead of feeling sad or disappointed, we should applaud the courage it took for her to get help. You will see what I mean one day when the answers aren't always easy. She and I didn't always agree, but I loved your mother from the first day your father introduced us. She was sunny and fun and whip-smart and vivacious.

She didn't mind the rain. I have always hated it, taking out my umbrella the minute it drizzles, but she basked in it, and she made your father bask in it, and she is much of the reason why you are such a fine boy. Remember that, please. Let's try to see her in her best possible light, in a way that can't be overshadowed by the last moments. I will try, and I will help you try.

Love,
Grandma

FIFTY-EIGHT

Jack has never met the president of DelDine, Maurice Engel, in person. He's seen him in commercials and at events, looking like a stereotypical mobster who would hold a tiny chewed-up cigar. When Jack gets to the restaurant on this last day after showering and changing, a black Maserati SUV is in his parking space behind the restaurant.

He pays for a meter, something he hasn't had to do in years, and walks inside.

It's wrong.

He knows it's wrong when he sees Maurice pointing at Sam and Vivian and Paulette and Saul and Vincent, Jack's crew he's known since most of them were kids, all of them looking uncomfortable.

Jack is not in his usual restaurant clothes. He wears linen pants Kitty bought him years ago for his birthday, and a polo shirt. Maurice stops when he sees him.

"Mr. Schmidt," he says, and he charges over toward him and shakes his hand. "Big day," he says, and keeps pumping Jack's arm. "Big day, eh?"

"Hello, Mr. Engel. I hear you have big plans."

Nicole, looking tired and subdued, comes out from the back

kitchen and stands beside him. "Jack," she says. "It's good to see you." He missed a call from her before. She looks at Jack, her eyes puzzled, and he just gives her half a nod.

"I'll be out of your hair shortly," Jack says. "I just wanted to say goodbye." Vivian is holding a pile of tablecloths Jack has never seen before, and she is watching him, and Sam is organizing cards with the specials on them that they never used. The regular laminated menus are gone, and a pile of pastel card stock stands in their place.

Maurice has a satisfied grin, almost to the point of giddiness. Jack thinks of him standing there, watching this place fall to the ground. He thinks of the garish hotel that will change the whole skyline, the look of this boardwalk. He thinks of the customers who have come back summer after summer, recognizing him and waving to him in the back, telling Jack they craved crab cakes and succotash all year. What will they think when they see a Coming Soon sign with an elaborate rendering of a new hotel and the overpriced organic grab-and-go? What happens to his staff after the restaurant is gone, the staff DelDine said they'd do their best to keep? Will they be funneled into the other restaurants like Marco's and The Pier?

"You stay as long as you like, Mr. Schmidt," Maurice says, and then the door opens, and he frowns.

FIFTY-NINE

Andie steps in, wearing a white suit. "Maurice," she says, and she holds a stack of folders, her hair pulled back. "Good morning."

His face seems to relax. "A beautiful morning," he says, and shakes her hand. His glee returns. Jack crosses his arms.

Maurice looks over at Jack. "Well, you played hardball and got yourself a great deal. Your family's place will be in good hands." He looks over at Nicole and beams. "Nikki here has created a wonderful partnership, and we would like to offer you a complimentary meal each time you come to a DelDine establishment." He licks his lips. "Max ten per year," he says softly. He smiles again. Jack imagines what his dad would say, his grandmother. All his training, all these years, was the opposite of this. Maurice is what they railed against. Jack feels like his family is standing behind him.

"How generous," Andie says, and smiles. She clears her throat. "But we're not ready to pack up just yet. We actually have a significant concern."

Nicole glances at Jack, and her eyes are a mix of fear and eagerness. "Oh?" she says, perfectly playing the part of Maurice's right-hand person. "I believe everything's in order. That's why we spent so much time on the transition."

"What? What?" Maurice says impatiently.

"Last night, Mr. Schmidt and I were informed of a very troubling rumor."

Maurice rocks back on his heels. He takes a swig from his water glass. His eyes dart to Nicole, and she raises her eyebrows. "Rumor?"

"You're not planning to tear this building down, are you?"

He looks at Nicole again, but she doesn't reveal anything. Jack sees Vivian take a few steps closer, looking over at Saul, whose eyes are saucers. Sam drops his cards and blushes. "Not at all," Maurice says, gritting his teeth. "Our plan for this moment is to follow the transition schedule and keep welcoming new and old customers at this location."

"Interesting," Andie says. She places her folders down and flips through one of them. "It was quite late when we got this information, but fortunately, you know Carl Williams, I'm guessing."

"Williams?" he says. He slips his finger into his shirt collar and flaps it. His forehead looks sweaty. He pulls his phone from his pocket. "I'd better contact my legal representation so I don't say anything incorrect while we, um, get this all settled."

"My partner is on the phone with your team right now," Andie says calmly. "I'm sure they won't mind my going over these concerns, and then they can follow up with you should you have any questions."

"Nikki, did you know about this?"

Nicole closes her mouth. Jack sees her wedding ring around her neck move as she shakes her head. "I'm as surprised as you, Maurice."

Andie slides a paper out. "The nice thing about having a father-in-law who's retired as president of the builder's association is that they never really retire, you know?" She looks down at the paper. "And all those guys—builders and inspectors—are up with the chickens, ready to help me out if I have an emergency, since they regard my father-in-law so highly."

"Builders? What are we talking about?" Maurice's expression has soured. He looks vicious now, and his cologne wafts in the air as he comes closer to Andie to retrieve the paper.

"Yes, why builders?" Nicole says, feigning concern.

"This is just one of many," Andie says.

Maurice takes the paper. "One of many *what*?"

"Certifications from builders that Mr. Schmidt's building is structurally sound."

He furls his eyebrows and bluffs. "Well, good. Good."

Andie crosses her two fingers and holds them up. "Those guys are like this," she says. "Tight. All they had to do was some asking around, all of them at the crack of dawn this morning in the Lowe's parking lot, and in ten minutes, they found out who you were asking to say this place would need to be torn down. And they all swarmed here in a caravan to give the building a full inspection. My husband was waiting for them before his run." She grins. "He's quite supportive," she whispers. "Needless to say, the guy who said he'd lie for you is no longer interested in that spurious task. I guess you'd call it peer pressure."

"I never asked anyone to do anything!" Maurice shouts. Sam is gripping Vivian's hand, and she pats his back like a big sister. Saul shakes his head. *Holy shit*, he mouths to Jack. Paulette stops wiping the blinds in the windows and takes a seat at a table.

"Douche," Vivian says under her breath.

"What is all this?" Maurice says. "We have an agreement, and we are executing it today." He starts to dial his phone, and a red rash creeps up his neck. He is breathing like a bull. "Get over here, Gavin," he says into the phone.

"I'm happy to talk with Gavin," Andie says, and puts her hand out. "But before we go too far down that avenue . . ." She glances at Jack, and Jack nods. "Mr. Schmidt would like to terminate this agreement, effective immediately—"

Sam gasps. Paulette squeals.

"Like hell," Maurice says, and laughs maniacally. "We are *proceeding*," he says, gesturing in the space between him and Nicole. Nicole covers her mouth and doesn't say anything.

"Should you go through with this, we've contacted Daisy Fargo at *Cape News*, who is more than ready to cover this story fully over the next day or two, outlining DelDine's plans." Andie shakes her head. "A trusted voice in Rehoboth Beach. I'm told she has a few very reputable sources who are happy to provide detailed information about these plans. This might not be good for DelDine's strategic position in Southern Delaware."

He flares his nostrils and looks to see if his phone is still on a call. "Gavin, are you on your way?"

Andie pulls out another form. "We are ready to submit this to the ethics board as well as Rehoboth Main Street Association." She takes a patient breath and looks at him. "Walk away now, and we will agree not to share this experience more publicly." She coughs. "We'll even say DelDine supported and helped rehabilitate a favorite restaurant if you back out quickly."

Maurice looks at his phone and hangs up. He glances around at all of them: Vivian, Sam, Vincent, Saul, Paulette. Jack. Andie. He looks at the stack of Andie's folders as if he's just woken from a fever dream. He opens his mouth but doesn't say anything. "I . . ."

Andie takes the paper that he's holding. "I think you should leave now," she says, and winks. "I'd hate for these employees to start talking about what they heard here. It might be awful for DelDine's, um, public perception."

Nicole's face. She is exuberant. She shakes her head in disbelief.

"Are the ten complimentary meals still on the table?" Jack asks.

Maurice looks like he's ready to spit. He points his finger in Andie's face and is about to say something when Andie says, "I'd advise you to extinguish that pronto." She smiles calmly. "And drop this whole thing, or I will be happy to flood the community with news of your less-than-admirable practices. Rehoboth has a very long memory, and people here love a good cause."

He starts to storm out. The assistant managers follow him, and he motions for Nicole. "We need to reconvene, Nikki," he says. "Did you have any inkling this was coming down the pike?"

She looks at Jack, and they lock eyes. "Not a clue, Maurice," she says, and sighs.

The AMs are holding boxes now, and their lead server, Martha, follows them with a stack of something. "That's nothing of ours, I hope," Vivian says, half blocking the door.

"Nothing," the first AM says.

"We'll probably see you in court, Schmidt," Maurice says, looking at Jack with red eyes.

Jack shakes his head. "Probably not," he says, and waves.

"Let's go, Nikki," Maurice says, and Nicole looks at Jack. He stands by the net with the lobsters hanging from it, the two old clam rakes his grandmother used to use when she was a kid fastened to the wood paneling. Andie taps her polished nails on the binder.

"I'm good here, Maurice," Nicole says. "And I hate being called Nikki."

"What?" His white shirt shows sweat on his chest and stomach.

"I'm good," she repeats. "The world needs less DelDine." She looks around. "I want to use my skills to save endangered species . . . like this place."

Maurice snorts. "You're under contract," he says.

"I know a good lawyer."

He takes a deep breath. "What is this?"

Nicole looks at all of the assistant managers and shrugs. She keeps a straight face. "I'll be in later, to get things settled," she tells them, and Jack can't believe this doesn't make her the least bit nervous.

Vivian is cheering and swearing, and Sam is clapping. Vincent puts his fingers in his mouth and whistles loudly. The rest of the crew comes out from the kitchen, Ernie and Smokes, and some of them are laughing, some are crying.

"Does this mean . . . ?" Saul says.

Jack shakes his head. "I'm still retiring," he says. "But the restaurant will be in good hands."

And as if it's a movie, as if life could ever be timed this perfectly, the door opens, and Genevieve is standing there.

Jack called her on his way in today and asked her if she had any interest in being in charge for a couple of months. *But if anyone has earned a retirement, it's you*, he told her. She had let out an exasperated sigh. "Retire? Not working these last few months has been way too dull. I'm ready, Jack." She's wearing an old Schmidt's shirt now. It's red and in perfect condition. It's the same one all the employees were wearing the first day his dad brought him here to work, when everyone was trying to show him all was not lost—that he had a new family.

SIXTY

That night, Jack pulls up to his house after working with Genevieve and Nicole to get things somewhat straightened out, and he's stunned to see the cars in his driveway.

The lights are all on, and music plays from his sound system in the living room. He steps onto the porch, and Deacon is there with a Hawaiian lei around his neck. He looks at Jack's linen pants, at his polo shirt. "You almost got the memo," he says, and he's slipping a lei around Jack's neck. Lit white lanterns are strung across the porch, and there's a bar by the front door, fully stocked with a grass skirt around it.

"What the hell's all this?"

Deacon hugs Jack. "Well, my friend, it's your kind-of-retired, kind-of-lost-out-on-a-lot-of-money party." He shrugs. "We couldn't just cancel it after your overnight epiphany."

Jack steps inside, and Andie and Evie are in the kitchen with Carl. Jack takes Deacon's cup of punch from him and has a big gulp. "Holy shit, that's strong."

"Yeah, probably don't hold the baby," he says, and laughs.

Andie comes over then with Evie. "What do you think, Jack?" she says.

"I think I owe you everything." He gives her a big hug, and Evie grips his shirt collar while he pulls away. "Your wife tore Maurice Engel to shreds," Jack says to Deacon.

Deacon kisses her cheek. "Someone had to."

Andie does a fake bow. "I do my best work in the very early morning."

"I think Carl and I might have to babysit again to repay you."

"Speak of the devil," Deacon says. Carl appears beside him and winks at Jack.

"Jackie, why didn't you just call me earlier? I could have shut that crap down pronto."

"You saved our asses."

"Happy to," he says, and he reaches over and pulls Jack to him with his strong grip and kisses his head the way Deacon did in the hospital. Jack is stunned, but it feels nice. He looks around and sees Sylvie and Daisy in the kitchen having a long talk with some other local restaurant owners. He sees Vivian and Sam come in the door now, waving shyly. Sam looks like he has the weight of the world off him, and Jack had already decided that they wouldn't ever talk about the money again.

He sees Genevieve walking in, holding her granddaughter's hand, and the sight of her calms Jack. "It doesn't seem fair that I'm kicking back while you'll be working," Jack said to Genevieve when they were at the restaurant earlier. "You sure you don't want to retire? You are owed a pension, and the restaurant will be okay."

She smiled. "This feels like my moment, Jack, and people my age often aren't offered moments." She patted his chest. "I'm honored you'd put me in charge. I'll give it a little time, and then we'll see." She reached up and hugged him. "Now shoo," she said, and waved him out. "You didn't clear out this office for nothing."

Often he thinks of Ziggy. He wonders if this time away will help him or make him worse. He plans to ask Andie if there is a way to negotiate with the judge and get him moved to a treatment center. He wants to be more like Johnny Schmidt, believing there are always chances for good. Or his mother, who squeezed his hand whenever an ambulance drove past and said, "Let's keep thinking the best." He wonders what's possible for Ziggy, what he can still be. He's young. Maybe this was his worst year, his rock bottom. He wants to help that boy in Ziggy who loved the dog. He is still in there.

After saying hi to a few more guests and getting a new drink, he scans the backyard where some people are playing horseshoes by the picnic table. He notices Saul and Vivian standing together. Saul reaches down and holds her hand for a second, and she smiles but slaps his arm. Then she reaches for his hand and kisses it quickly and drops it.

That's when Jack sees Nicole, holding a beer bottle, laughing with Paulette, tossing a horseshoe in the air when it's her turn, her mouth open, her eyes delighted as it lands on the metal pin. She jumps up and down because she scored, and from inside the house, Jack smiles.

SIXTY-ONE

Jack has soup on the stove, even though it's late June, and dessert in the oven. Lara asked if she could come by today, and he opens the front door to see her holding a big African violet in a pot.

"Hey there. What's this?" he asks.

She smiles, and he notices this is the first time he's seen her without her giant purse. "I brought this on the plane with me all the way from Nevada. Does it look familiar?"

"Not really," Jack says, and then he looks at it again, his eyes opening wider. "I brought your mom a violet once," he says.

"The very same." She holds it out to him. "It's yours, Jack."

He takes it reluctantly, and looks at the green fleshy leaves, the faded purple flowers. "It's gotten so big. They can live that long?"

"Apparently," she says. "My mom had a lot of different violets, they were her favorite, but this was the biggest, and the oldest she said. She was so fussy about taking care of them, and when we moved from California, she insisted that the house in Nevada have a big window for her violets.

"When I was home, cleaning out some stuff before we sell the house, I saw all the violets, still thriving on the windowsill, and I remembered she called this her Delaware violet." She reaches into her pocket. "She also regularly wrote in a journal, and though it's too private for me to read all her thoughts, I found this page was dog-eared," she says, handing Jack a folded-up piece of paper.

He turns his back to Lara and looks down at the words. He remembers Alexis's handwriting: it had an almost calligraphic or European style to it, her *F*'s and *R*'s more curved, and she pressed so lightly on the pen.

I didn't mean for it to go on this long. I wish they could all know that, especially J. and P. Flying home, the secret seemed too big to talk about, and I didn't know what to do.

It felt enormous and horrifying and wonderful to have options. I didn't make a decision on the plane, just like I didn't make a decision when Courtney said are you sure, are you sure, and we drove away, and I went to bed, where I saw J. for the last time. He stood over me, and I remember the violet he brought, so small then, and the smell of the soup. I wanted to talk to him, but fear had paralyzed me. At the end of the day, I felt like it was only me, and I would be alone with the weight of this decision forever. I had to live this question, as Rilke says.

I didn't mean to hurt anyone, and it's probably easier if no one finds out. I love P. in a way that I can't put into words, a different and separate love than I have for my other children. I was living this question, and finally one day I discovered I had found the answer—that I was going to be a mother, that I had made that choice. My life could have gone in two distinct ways, and I couldn't share the question with anyone.

I'm sorry for J. Too much time went by, and it always seemed too late to tell him. But it's haunted me, and I will forever see his face, the sun and beach behind him. I guess at some point, I decided he was better off not knowing. Todd has been a good father to P., but as P. grew up, I saw that he has his own question to live, and now I think it's too late for me to answer it.

Jack finishes reading and turns back to Lara. "Huh," he says.

"Does it help?"

Jack shakes his head. He glances at the paper and sees the creases where it can fold back to a square again. "Not much, but at least I have a violet now."

"There is that," she says. She picks up the plant and sets it in his window. She presses the soil. "You won't need to water it for another week, I think."

"Cool," he says. "Thanks for bringing it back to its home state."

"It's only right," she says. She stands there and looks around. "This place is so *you*," she says. She picks up a giant conch shell and holds it up to her ear.

"Hear anything?" he asks. She shakes her head. "The journal does help a little," he says. He looks down at Alexis's words again and folds the page back to what it was. "I mean, part of it is bullshit."

"I kind of thought so, too," Lara says and shrugs. "But the violet, though."

"But the violet." He looks toward the kitchen. "You hungry?" he says. "Dinner's almost ready."

"I could eat," she replies, and she makes herself comfortable, opening up the newspaper on his coffee table, plopping down on his sofa, Harry purring beside her, and he is stirring the soup, looking down at the onions and carrots and celery and the one bay leaf he added because his grandmother always did, and next to the sink he stacks his dad's bowls that he took when he cleaned out his house.

Jack opens the oven and tests the orange-cranberry muffins he made with the coarse sugar on top, from his mom's recipe box from when she had Brighton Bakery. Today was the first time he ever looked in there, her handwriting and smudges of oil on some of the cards.

He steps out back, and he shakes a tablecloth over the old picnic table. He puts out napkins for Lara and himself, and he opens a bottle of white wine and fills up a jug with water. "Need help?" Lara calls as he slices bread.

"Nope," he says. "You just relax. We are going to have a feast," he says, and he imagines for a moment that she will come regularly like this. That if she is dating someone, they will come, too. He is standing there filling the breadbasket, stirring the soup and adding a little more seasoning. He feels an odd glee, like he's going on an adventure.

SIXTY-TWO

In mid-July, Jack is at Carl's house after Evelyn's funeral. He finds Carl on the back porch and sits next to him on the rocking chair after a lot of the guests have left. Andie and Deacon are cleaning up, Evie at home with a sitter.

"We lost a good one," Carl says, staring straight ahead. He folds his arms across his belly and sighs.

"One of the best," Jack says.

He shakes his head. "She was just so, how do I say it . . . *content.* She wanted nothing. Just to be happy." He clicks his tongue. "It was beautiful."

"Easy happiness," Jack says, "is like a gift. I admire that." Carl doesn't speak for a second, and Jack sees a squirrel scurry up his birch tree. "I envy what you and Evelyn had."

Carl takes a breath, and his folded hands move as his stomach rises. "I tried everything, Jackie: jewelry, a new car for her. I tried to surprise her with flowers, and she would always smile and be thrilled, but I could tell she never really cared. I'd say, *What do you want for your birthday?* and she'd say, *A walk together.* I'd tell her you can't just get a walk for your birthday, and she'd say, *But that's what I like.* So when we turned sixty, I started listening to her. I started giving her a walk. Another day, maybe Valentine's or something, she asked to go to an ice cream place, and after that, something clicked between us. We got what we wanted that way. We were happier, and it all meant more. My birthday came, and I told her I wanted to go fishing. And we did." He looks at Jack. "I swear, it was one of the nicest days of my life. It was early summer, and she wore this vest and a fisherman's hat, and we left the house at 5 a.m. and packed sandwiches and drinks and cookies, and we drove to the bay, and got in the boat we'd rented, and it was like we had a secret, her and me. Like this whole world was that secret, you know? I can't even describe the sun coming up, the perfect half-lit sky, our bait hitting the water. It was just magnificent." He takes another deep breath and frowns.

"That's a splendid scene," Jack finally says, wiping his eye.

Jack looks back toward the house, and Andie has her hand on Deacon's shoulder, and he looks like he's upset. Jack thinks about going to him, but he's in good hands, and listening to Carl feels right. "It was so bad, Jackie, when I had to put her in that place. The day I drove her there, she panicked. She said, *Where are they taking me?* And I cried when I drove away. I felt like I'd failed her. And she said *they*, not even realizing it was me, just *me*, who made the decision." He covers his face the same way Deacon does sometimes. "But as long as she was there, I felt like there was a chance the phone would ring one day, and I'd hear her old voice—she wouldn't sound confused. Like she'd wake up and it would all come back." He groans. "I wanted that so bad. To have it all come back. I wanted another moment on a fishing boat. Holding her hand, watching the birds swoop toward the water. I felt like we were in a painting." He shakes his head, and Jack quickly swipes his eyes with the side of his palm. "And now it all feels bleak, but then I say, *Carl, Carl, man. Look what you got. Look what you got to have.* There was never a good time for it to end. There was never a way of being done with it, but you got to *have* it. It was yours for a while. And that means something, you know?" He looks over at Jack, and his eyes are wet with tears, and Jack's are, too, but he doesn't care.

"It was yours," Jack says, and they sit there, and Jack puts his hands on his stomach, too, and occasionally one of them rocks as the sky starts to lose its light.

—

When he leaves Carl's house, Jack doesn't realize where he's driving at first. He could just be going home. But he keeps seeing Carl in his mind. He keeps alternating between a sinking feeling and something uplifting inside him, like there's a concert about to happen, or he's about to get a letter in the mail he's been looking forward to.

The sky is dark now, and there are so many stars. Jack takes the exit to Rehoboth, and drives down the avenue, past Marco's and the police department and town hall, past the library, past Coffee Daze, its lights still on, people walking the streets. He drives until he sees St. Matthew's cemetery. He hasn't been here since his dad's funeral. It takes him a minute to find them among the rows, but finally, his cell phone flashlight illuminates *Schmidt*. He sees Jonathan and Jane.

The other graves have flowers on them, fake and real, planted and in pots, and theirs is empty, and he feels ashamed. He kneels down and puts his hand on the ground in front of the polished stone. He traces his mom's name, and then his dad's. He thinks of who he is, who they made him.

He remembers calling his mom in Utah. "I've been doing my

best to get back," she told him, as if she'd gotten caught in traffic, as if her flight was delayed.

"You will," Jack said.

"Oh, of course," she said, and her voice was sunny.

He sits there now, crouching in the dark, a few fireflies blinking in the distance, and thinks of who he is because of her. How she softened what his dad and grandmother would have made, how she had this laugh that he's noticed lets him laugh with the crew at the restaurant, lets him go easy when things get rough. He's sorry she couldn't see her way out. He's so sorry she was alone. He's sorry they missed the signs for too long, until it was too late.

He thinks of looking up at the parrots in their big pine needle nest, the wonder and sparkle on her face. And he wants to make her proud.

He thinks of his dad and how he brought Jack to the restaurant to save him, so he wouldn't be alone; how he used to just walk over to Jack, right in front of everyone—the bussers, the dishwashers—and hug him, and no one looked surprised. Jack would sit in Johnny's office, and Johnny would smoke a cigarette, and Jack could tell him anything. Once they were closing up, and he put his hand on the back of Jack's neck and said, "Don't think I don't miss her, buddy. I miss her more than I can tell you," and Jack nodded. He thinks of being trapped on 95 with his dad and how he didn't panic because he knew his dad could get them both home.

Jack looks at their gravestone, and he thinks, *You were loved.* Maybe the *you* is them, maybe Jack means himself. But it's true either way. He thinks of planting something here that will come up every year, something tough and hardy that will continue to grow even when Jack is gone. He'll look for it. He'll find the right thing.

"Rest in peace," he says out loud to his parents, to Janet, to Evelyn, and to his grandmother and Agnes, too. He hears the sounds of cars driving by, the illuminated rides and music from the boardwalk in the distance, and for just a second, he feels like they can all hear him.

SIXTY-THREE

The next day, the sun starting to set, one light is on in the little house Nicole shared with her husband. Jack walks up the path, and he imagines those notification officers, years ago, coming here first, not finding her, and then showing up at the restaurant where she was making drinks. He looks at the mailbox, one of her house number stickers missing from the faded bronze, and there are two pots of geraniums, some that need deadheading.

He knocks on the door, and she doesn't answer at first. Finally, the porch light clicks on. She is standing there in front of Jack, her glasses crooked, her hair in a messy bun. "I'm not drinking coffee this late," she says, "unless it's decaf."

Jack stands there on her doorstep, and he just smiles up at her. He tries to find the words, but he has no idea. "You make me happy," he finally says. "Nicole, every time I see you, I feel good. It's because you're good. I like how genuine you are, how smart. I like your boldness, your laugh. The way you couldn't care less about what people think. Oh, and your glasses, too. I love your goddamn glasses."

She shakes her head. Her faded T-shirt says California Sunshine. She wears cotton pajama pants with seahorses on them. She crosses her arms. "Is this a new discovery?"

"I guess, in a way," Jack says. "But that day at the farmer's market was one of the best afternoons of my life. I want more of that . . . if you do."

He points his thumb at his Jeep, where his beach chair sits in the back with a new red one he bought today. There is a small pouch hanging from the armrest where he imagines she could stow her glasses. "There's a killer sunset about to happen, and we don't have time to waste. Want to go for a ride?'

She looks down at herself. She shrugs. "Guess I'm good to go." She closes her door and steps toward him, holding on to the railing, smiling, squinting at the cotton candy sky. He feels a lump in his throat seeing her, as if she and this lit sky are too good to be true, some pocket of happiness that could never last for him.

"I knew you'd fall under my spell eventually, Jack Schmidt," she says, her eyes sparkling, and on the last step, she jumps into his arms. He holds her and pulls her tightly against himself. For a second, the air feels different and better, as if all this time, he's been in the wrong altitude, and now his lungs finally work. She kisses him, and he kisses her back.

—

You haven't seen anything like October in Southern Delaware. The crowds, which persist throughout September, consist of the delayed-gratification people who worked all summer finally kicking back, swimming in the still-warm ocean, eating dinner at Steelo's or Marco's, renting a boat with friends and riding over the wide water.

October is like May or June without the anticipation of summer coming. October is a last chance and a first chance. People are eating outside, and the town is getting ready for sidewalk sales and art shows and film festivals, and Boo-Hoo Halloween weekend, which fills up the town.

In mid-October, there are dog weekends, greyhounds everywhere one Saturday, golden retrievers another. Always on colorful leashes, and sometimes in autumn bandanas. People stop when they walk by and they ask about the dog's story. We all have stories. Autumn in Rehoboth Beach is so peaceful we call it second summer. We hold our candy apples and watch the pumpkin-launching event and stare out at all the people still in beach chairs, and it's easy to pretend winter isn't a thing. In Rehoboth, it really isn't.

—That's Rehoboth Beach: A Guidebook

SIXTY-FOUR

Jack has taken to wandering around town. Because he can. He hasn't driven his old Jeep anywhere in a while, and most mornings he just sets out on a leisurely walk, the big pine trees over him, the occasional jingle of a bike bell. He goes to the library and checks out books he may or may not read.

He sometimes buys an ice cream cone and sits on a park bench. He meets Nicole for dinner or for a drink, or for coffee, her favorite.

This morning, he filled out paperwork to be a vendor at the farmer's market, where once a week he'll make and sell the muffins his mom used to make, her cookies and sandwiches, too. And maybe even an occasional pie. He hasn't told Nicole about it because he wants to surprise her. He can just imagine the delight on her face as she heads toward the salsa stand and comes across a new stand she doesn't recognize: Beech Avenue Baked Goods.

Today he finds himself in First State Arcade, a covered collection of small shops off Rehoboth Avenue with a cobblestone walkway and an arched opening on either entrance. He passes the lemon ice stand (now closed), the crepe and pastry place, the toy shop on his right, and the café tables and chairs. The sun comes through the glass tiled ceiling, and one shop has flags in the window with beach messages: Life at the Beach, and Flip-Flops Only, and Happy Place.

Two women walk by him, their fingers locked. One taps the other and points to one of the beach flags and the funny message on it. "That's you," she says, and the other one laughs. He thinks of his grandmother and Agnes and wonders if they could have had that type of togetherness, not having to keep their relationship secret, if that's what they had. He sees someone putting new floral tablecloths on the tables at the cantina across the street.

The last shop before he leaves the arcade is a new stationery store. Over the years, he has seen places here come and go. He remembers a sticker shop when he was in school, and his mom would buy stickers there and put them in his lunch box. He remembers jewelry stores, a small furniture store, a doll shop. So many businesses come and go here, and years from now, Schmidt's will be a place only a handful of people remember. Maybe they'll find an old matchbook or a menu; maybe the museum will have one of their plates or old order receipts, or the ship's wheel that his dad used to have hanging on the wall.

Yesterday evening, after his weekly run with Deacon (before Jack gives up and begs to walk the rest of the way), he stood outside the restaurant, and looked at the new Schmidt's sign Lara helped them pick out: white with crisp navy-blue writing. Though Jack is still the owner, he hasn't been inside for a while. He hears bits and pieces from Nicole, but often they don't talk about work.

One day he will go inside again, but he wants them to get used to it without him.

He could see Genevieve, the general manager, inside, holding the new laminated menus and smiling at the customers, and Vivian, who is half server and half assistant manager, balancing the biggest tray on her shoulder.

Nicole was up on a ladder fixing a pumpkin garland that drooped from the lobster nets, and as Jack watched her—the restaurant's chief consultant, who has taken on other independent restaurant projects up and down the coast—he thought about the first day Nicole came to him a year ago and asked if he'd ever consider a DelDine partnership. "Probably not," was the first thing he said, and he remembers now that she didn't flinch. "We'll work on that," she just said, and started showing up at Schmidt's.

Now someone opens the stationery store door and flips the sign to Open, and turns all the lights on. The man nods at Jack, and Jack follows him inside. There are racks of expensive cards with gold- and silver-lined envelopes for all occasions: weddings, anniversaries, birthdays, funerals. There are seasonal autumn ones, pumpkins and black cats, and already stacks and stacks of Christmas boxes. It smells like citrus and fresh paper in the store. "Perfect day out there," the guy says, and he turns his key in the register and opens two boxes of deliveries on the counter.

"Sure is," Jack says. He wanders to the back wall where there are expensive pens, and the man turns on music, light jazz playing through the shop. Jack doesn't know what he's doing here, but he's enjoying his new life of taking things minute by minute.

The guy asks him something about rain tomorrow, but Jack hasn't looked at the forecast. "We need it, I guess," Jack says, and now he's starting to feel like he should buy something. What if he's the only customer all day?

He picks up the nicest pack of writing paper he's ever seen. It has a kelly-green border, and matching envelopes, and he knows what he'll do.

He steps outside and notices a few fallen leaves on the sidewalk. The air is clean, and Jack stands there and just inhales. He thinks of the package he will send Patrick and wonders if he'll understand what he's saying.

He won't tell Patrick he's bought a matching box for himself in case Patrick writes, or that he doesn't know what he'll do if this doesn't work.

He wants to tell him there is always still a chance between them. That each person has a hundred different possible versions of who they can be. He wants to say he's learned so much since he found out about Patrick, that he will wait as long as it takes. He wants to tell him about the parrots he saw that day that changed him, and that pain is the cost of living well and caring deeply.

He can help him through his pain, he wants to say. He's lived it, but like the parrots emerging, like the cars in the traffic jam moving again, like the seasons and weather in this glorious little beach town, there is always a new something waiting.

He holds his bag, and it bounces against him as he gets to the next block. Cars go by, and he sees a piece of hay in the street that tumbles for a minute. He wonders if it fell off a parade float or blew from a store's scarecrow display. He watches the hay, and it glows in the sun for just a second and lifts in the breeze. The stoplight changes, and Jack sees what looks like a younger version of himself walking right toward him.

ACKNOWLEDGMENTS

This book would have been more challenging to research and write were it not for the help of Scott Mumford of Warren's Station in Fenwick Island, Delaware. Scott helped me understand a bigger picture of restaurant life and running a family-owned business. Thank you, Scott, for letting me call you and text you repeatedly and telling me about pies and turkey portions and restaurant capacity and payroll and order forms. Thank you for letting me visit your restaurant in the off-season. You helped make Schmidt's a more authentic place.

To Madeleine Milburn, the most brilliant and kindhearted agent I could ask for. Thank you for plucking me from years of querying and letting me continue to have my dream job. To everyone at the MM Agency: you are a splendid bunch of people, and it was a joy to be in London to celebrate with tea and champagne right after I finished this book.

To all the "cardinals" at Scribner, the place my novels are lucky to call home. To Kara Watson, my skilled and trusted editor. Thanks for making every publication feel enjoyable. To Mia O'Neill and Ashley Gilliam Rose, savvy and thoughtful publicist and marketing expert. To the wonderful Sabrina Pyun, who has made every novel better with her insights. To Jaya Miceli and Elizabeth Yaffe for another perfect cover. To Wendy Sheanin, Tim Hepp, and all the rest of the wonderful S&S sales team for all you do to get my books out to readers. To Stu Smith for all your support and good instincts. To Nan Graham, legend of legends, who is always so generous. And everyone else: art department, sales, copyeditor, and proofreaders. I am grateful.

To Browseabout Books, you are Rehoboth Beach's beating heart. To Susan and Matt and all the amazing staff who welcome us over and over. Thank you from my very core.

To so many other lovely booksellers at bookstores I've visited along the way and met online: THANK YOU.

To the Rehoboth Beach Writers' Guild: always, always.

To all my students who teach me over and over.

To the book clubs that've let me visit—it's always a pleasure.

To the staff of Dr. Jeannine Wyke's office, for their support of my books. You make coming to the dentist a joy!

To the readers and bloggers who care about my words and continue to support writers in all forums. Thank you for everything! Thanks especially to the Bookstagram community.

To my whole Joella-Gallagher-Racciato-Romano family: much love. Especially my parents, who took four kids, no matter how chaotic, out to nice restaurants at the beach. There is a piece of each of those places, each of those meals, in Schmidt's. Also, for bringing me to Rehoboth Beach for the first time when I was two weeks old. As you can tell, I never wanted to leave.

To all the indie businesses that are doing their best not to be swallowed by giants: we see you!

To all our found family in Delaware: you know who you are.

To Gia and Frankie, the best daughters I could ask for. I couldn't be prouder, I couldn't be more in awe. Watching you grow up into such kind and intelligent and fun and loving people is the honor of my life.

And to Rebecca, the person whose beach chair I want to always sit beside.

ABOUT THE AUTHOR

ETHAN JOELLA teaches English and psychology at the University of Delaware. He is the author of *A Little Hope*, which was a Read with Jenna Bonus Pick, and *A Quiet Life*. He lives in Rehoboth Beach, Delaware, with his wife and two daughters.